JACOB'S JOURNEY

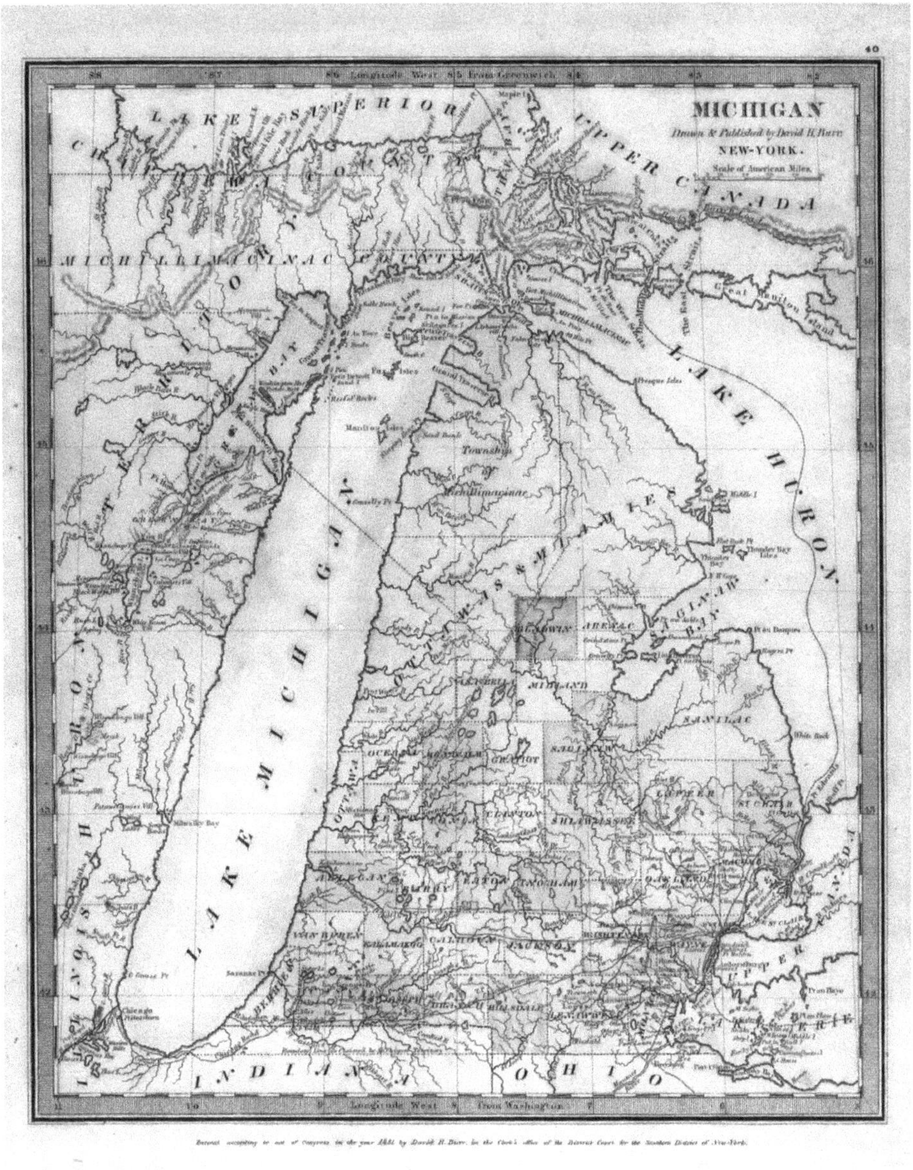

Published by Mission Point Press
2554 Chandler Rd.
Traverse City, MI 49696
(231) 421-9513
www.MissionPointPress.com

Design by Sarah Meiers

Softcover ISBN: 978-1-965278-14-7
Hardcover ISBN: 978-1-965278-15-4
Library of Congress Control Number: 2024921191

Printed in the United States of America

MISSION POINT PRESS

Jacob's Journey is dedicated to the concept of abandoning unchallenging routines that bring false comforts in life, and to pursue the life journeys that expand our horizons. Writing is also a journey that often leads to unexpected places. It's nice to have fellow travelers on this trek. I was blessed with a supportive community of family and friends during the writing process, especially my wife, Susan, with her unwavering "you can do this" attitude.

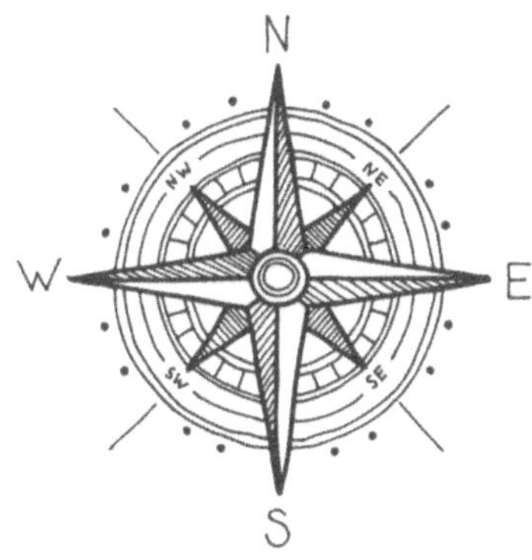

Chapter 1

JACOB AND ROBERT HAD SPENT a better part of the day baking in the merciless sun, hauling rocks from adjacent fields to fix a stone fence bordering their joint property line. After hours of backbreaking labor, they had finally earned a break under the shade of a large oak tree. But while hauling stones had drained Jacob physically, there was another weight he carried that preoccupied him, a burden that he desired—needed, really—to share with someone.

And Robert was the only person who'd proven himself trustworthy enough for such an honor.

"So, my friend, can you keep a secret?" Jacob said.

"You mean the so-called secret about you and Sally Baldwin getting married some day?" Robert said, giving him a cheeky grin before taking a long drink from the bucket of cool water taken from the nearby creek.

"No, you Highlands bloke. It's something serious. And you'd

damn well better not tell anyone, or I'll kick your ass all the way back to Scotland!"

As he said this, Robert poured the rest of the water over his head to cool off. He looked at Jacob as thoughtfully as he could, which was difficult given the mop of wet hair hanging across his face.

"That *is* serious! But I never thought of you as the ass-kicking kind. I just might call your bluff." He shook his hair like a wet dog. "It might as well be me that has to talk you out of doing something stupid. Again."

Jacob couldn't help but laugh; he'd dreaded revealing his secret for what felt like forever, yet Robert had found a way to break the tension. He could always rely on Robert to make him smile.

Jacob and Robert had spent a lot of time together since Robert's family moved to a neighboring farm in Vermont's Green Mountains. Now best friends, the pair could often be found on Spruce Peak hunting for deer, trout fishing on the Mettawee River, or, just as likely, in the nearby village of Dorset wooing impressionable young ladies. Though it had been five years since the MacIntosh family left the Highlands for America, Robert's parents still spoke Scottish Gaelic at home. As a result, he was fluent in both languages and spoke with a brogue his admirers would describe as sensual. And he had many admirers. Jacob envied Robert's accent and the attention it brought him from the fairer sex. But it wasn't just the lilt in his voice that attracted the ladies; Robert's magnetism also stemmed from his good looks, his irresistibly charming personality, and his perfectly tousled light brown hair, now doused by creek water.

Jacob felt plain and boring in comparison, but that twinge of jealousy never got in the way of his friendship with the good-humored Scots American.

Looking at his drenched companion, Jacob realized how much he enjoyed Robert's company, which made what he was about to say even more painful. Because if his plan succeeded, he would be leaving Robert, and his entire life in Vermont, behind.

"I'm preparing to leave the farm, Robert. I'm headed west, to the frontier."

Robert cocked an eyebrow, the gravity of Jacob's secret finally sinking in.

"You're … leaving?" His friend was visibly lost for words. "But your family, your friends, Sally—they're all here!"

Jacob nodded knowingly. As the eldest son of the Hart family, leaving the land of his birth was a drastic decision. Roots ran deep on the eighty acres of rocky hillside in the secluded valley he called home. The small farm had sheltered three generations of Harts, and for all of Jacob's life, this land was the assumed place where, as the eldest boy, he would raise his own family and take over the farm.

"I know I should be grateful the farm will be handed down to me. It's been in the family since before the War of Independence." Jacob looked across the rolling fields of the familiar Vermont valley, lush in the hot and humid summer, the only land Jacob had ever known.

"But I'm not grateful. The world has changed, Robert. It's bigger now—bigger than our parents imagined it could be."

Robert nodded. With the end of the recent war with Britain, and treaties with Indian tribes, America was suddenly vastly larger. Land and new lives on the frontier were now available for those with ambition and boldness.

"My dreams lie in the West." Jacob turned back to Robert, the fires of determination burning fiercely in his eyes.

"By God, Jacob, you're serious about this. How long have you been planning this?"

"Two years."

Robert's eyes went wide. "You idiot!" Jacob winced, readying himself for Robert to tear into his dreams with a vengeance.

"You've been keeping this from me for two years? What, you didn't trust me?" Robert clapped him on the back, then pulled him into a hug.

"I won't pretend I'm not surprised, but your dream … I'm proud of you, Jacob," he stepped back and looked his friend in the eyes.

"You've got a good head on your shoulders. Whatever you're looking for on the frontier, I think you'll find it, friend." A warm smile lit up Robert's face.

Jacob was elated. He'd made the right choice sharing his dream with his friend, and he felt a weight suddenly lift off his shoulders.

"Don't take it too hard, Robert! I had to make sure my plan had a chance to succeed before letting anyone in on it. And I didn't want to take the chance of my father finding out.…"

Nicholas Hart, Jacob's father, would most certainly not support what he would consider a harebrained scheme at best. Jacob knew that telling his family about his dream before he was prepared would only tear his family apart. So instead, he'd planned, gathered valuable information, and saved every penny he could.

ROBERT SHOOK HIS HEAD, HIS hands on his hips, still taken aback from the revelations of the day, but proud of his friend's bravery.

"I can't blame you for wanting to pick up and leave, Jacob." Robert swept his arm across the farmland that lay all around them.

"Out west, there's fertile land just waiting for an enterprising lad like yourself to step up and seed the ground. Here …" Robert kicked a fieldstone that stuck out of the ground at the base of the oak tree they sheltered under, "just about the only crop we can rely on is another layer of rocks to haul out of the fields. Sometimes I worry we'll have to start eating rock soup if we're going to survive."

While Jacob loved the land and intended to be a farmer like his father and grandfather before him, he wanted a more fulfilling life than theirs. Robert's joke was more fact than fiction. After 75 years, all there was to show for the backbreaking labor of three generations were stone fences, ever-growing rock piles, and a few hungry cows and chickens. The Hart family farm could no longer support all of them, nor could it compete on the new larger national stage. They barely grew enough crops to support themselves and their few livestock, let alone have enough left to sell at a profit. Jacob knew that if he stayed, he would still be carrying stones when he was an old man. It was not the future he wanted. His younger brothers could run the farm when the time came. His sisters would marry and raise families on nearby farms owned by future in-laws. It is how things were done in the tight-knit community.

Robert moved a hand through his wet hair, shooting a mischievous grin at Jacob.

"To be honest, Jacob, I didn't think you had it in you! You've never left Vermont, and now you're going to be trekking across half the world to God-knows where. And I don't know if you're any good at farming anything other than rocks...."

Jacob gave him a playful punch in the shoulder, and they both laughed, enjoying themselves all the more now that they knew their time together was limited.

"We're going to miss you here, Jacob. It's going to be harder to cause trouble without you around! I have no idea where to start looking for a new drinking buddy ... or who's going to be my partner when I try to charm the lovely local lassies!"

A person couldn't get into serious trouble on a farm in the mountains. But Jacob and his friends earned a well-deserved reputation just the same. One that kept them under a cloud of suspicion, especially from the parents of local young ladies. Too many pranks, too much liquor, too many Sundays spent sleeping during sermons.

Despite youthful distractions, Jacob was sure of one thing: he wanted more out of life than his current situation could offer. The kind of fulfillment he desired was not going to be found in the valley and small villages that defined his world. Though he appreciated the rhythm of his life, its sense of order and predictability, he knew he had to leave it behind. It was exactly that comfortable familiarity that worried him. It was addictive—a tempting lure, a trap leading to a life he knew he would grow to regret after it was too late for regrets.

AFTER SEVERAL MORE HOURS OF heavy physical labor, the fence was fixed, and the two sweat-drenched young men said their goodbyes. Jacob's body was exhausted as he began following one of the stone fences home, but in the glow of the midsummer evening, he was more determined than ever that his fate was to follow the setting sun west.

Jacob had not started his plan on a whim. It arose out of necessity as he began to feel the pressures on his family farm from a rapidly changing America. A new agricultural economic reality was making itself felt across the New England countryside. Small farms in the northeast could not compete with the highly productive farms in the newly formed states of the American west. As vast prairie lands became settled, the situation would only become more dire for small farms carved out of New England's stony terrain. The Erie Canal opened the fertile interior of the young country to settlement, which made it possible to ship bountiful harvests of western beans, corn, and wheat to eastern cities and ports. Small New England farmers could not compete with this new source of produce.

The rapidly growing states of the new American Midwest held a powerful appeal. Reports of that region being without equal for farming were well known and oft repeated. Prosperity and a good life, it was said, were achievable to people who previously knew only hard work and poverty. Three new states had already been carved from the wilderness between the Ohio River and the Great Lakes. Just a few years before, that region had witnessed bloodshed between settlers and natives, but treaties with Indian tribes gave clear title for that land to the federal government. Land offices were established throughout the region and government surveyors crisscrossed the wilderness. Unexplored wildlands were soon converted to legally described parcels offered for sale by the government at prices designed to attract buyers. Land ownership was a possibility for those with the nerve to leave the known and head into the unknown.

Construction of the Erie Canal removed the final barrier to westward migration. No longer must a person spend days on muddy trails through the rugged New York or Pennsylvania countryside. Traveling west was much easier now, and the time and cost involved dramatically reduced. Completion of "Clinton's Folly" seemed like a heaven-sent opportunity for countless thousands of restless people looking for a better life. America was on the move like never before.

The future of farming, Jacob believed, was in that vast region of the country that lay to the west. The new frontier was a powerful magnet, uprooting and pulling people westward. Farmland measured in hundreds of acres available at prices almost anyone could afford: that was the future he envisioned and the legacy he wished to pass on to his own sons one day. However, if he was ever going achieve his dream of prosperity on the western American frontier, he knew he had to act now.

Time quickly passed the following weeks and months, as Jacob's belief that America's future, and his future, lay in the West continued to grow. To that end, he had a plan to make it happen. Gathering information was a critical part of his preparation. He took every opportunity to speak with people who traveled west for business or as part of the military. Local veterans of the War of 1812 provided valuable information and opinions about the region near Lake Erie. He read the local newspaper, such as it was, and gleaned information about the creation of new states and territories and of their prevailing landforms.

In addition, saving up money and learning new skills was of central importance if he was to realize his dreams. Along with many of their neighbors, Jacob and his father pursued other work to put food on the table and pay the bills. Like all farmers, their skills were broad-based. Jacob was learning trades as a carpenter, stonemason, and mechanic, as well as what it took to be a knowledgeable farmer. He toiled at a variety of other jobs as opportunities arose. Jacob did not begrudge the hard work. He knew he was learning valuable knowledge vital to his own future. Most importantly, he set aside part of his earnings toward his secret plan.

Backbreaking work in a nearby marble quarry fell into the unpleasant category, but it paid well. There was demand for marble in America's expanding urban areas. A man could count on working at the quarry for as long as he wished. The realities of hard rock mining were incapacitating injuries and a lifetime of back problems. Jacob already witnessed the gruesome sight of men injured from the use of explosives and by falling boulders. Marble shards had blinded a neighbor after swinging a sledge. Ever-present dust meant a persistent cough. After working part time for just two years, Jacob already felt the pains caused by splitting and moving blocks of stone. However, it paid well, so he accepted the discomfort and worked as much as possible.

Meeting immigrants who worked in the quarry opened his eyes to the possibility of living beyond one's birthplace. Stories about faraway places that were so different from the farming community where he grew up fascinated Jacob. He felt a kinship with these men who left their homes in Europe because they, too, felt at a dead end and dreamed of a better life. Their religion and politics might be different, but they were driven by the same fire within. Being young and gullible, Jacob was impressed by the stories of adventure, danger, and intrigues the immigrants told in their thick brogue while enjoying a drink after a hard day's work. He absorbed all of it, and his desire for escape from his current situation grew stronger with each story. He wanted to create and live his own life, not inherit an existence that he did not want.

When he would arrive back home after a long day's work, there was one thing he looked forward to more than anything: learning to play a violin handed down from his grandfather, who lived with them. His taciturn father had no interest in the instrument, or in similar "distractions" for that matter. Jacob's father avoided everything that he viewed as a waste of time or that interfered with his work. Grandfather Hart was also named

Nicholas but referred to as "Senior" by his family and friends. He gave the valuable instrument to Jacob with the provisos that he learn to play it and protect it, emphasizing its worth as an old-world heirloom. At one time, Grandfather Hart was an expert violinist, but years of hard work and the infirmities of old age made it nearly impossible for him to play any longer. He taught Jacob the basics and enthusiastically observed as he practiced.

Mateo was a young Italian immigrant and skilled musician who also worked at the quarry. He often played his own violin at a local tavern when socializing after a day's work. He agreed to teach Jacob one-on-one so that he could accompany him with his own instrument. Jacob was a gifted student and progressed surprisingly fast. His grandfather and Sophie Hart, his mother, were pleased that he showed an interest in playing and preserving traditional old-world tunes. Though truth be told, he preferred the contemporary music styles becoming popular in the States. Senior frowned whenever Jacob referred to the violin as a fiddle, but it seemed to Jacob that an Italian violin did not fit into the social structure of the Green Mountains. A fiddle, on the other hand, fit in perfectly well.

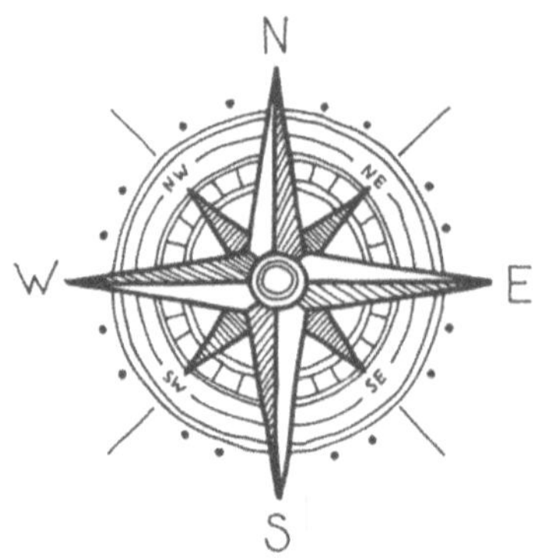

Chapter 2

ON A COOL EARLY APRIL day in 1832, the snow was melting, and spring, with its promise of new life, hovered close by. Jacob decided that the time to put his plan into action was nigh. He would head west on May 10th, his twentieth birthday. He understood the gravity of his decision: the emotional and practical consequences of leaving guaranteed this would be life-altering, not just for himself, but for his family. His leaving would upset them deeply. Especially his father. The melting snow meant that fieldwork loomed.

Once gone, returning to visit family and friends was highly unlikely. Distances were great, and even with the new canal, travel remained difficult. The demands of clearing new land, building a home, and getting a farming operation underway would severely limit his ability to leave for any extended period.

Having made up his mind, the next decision involved determining a destination. Land prices were rising significantly in rapidly developing places such as Ohio or Illinois. Patents for much of the best farmland were already in the hands of home-steaders or land speculators, leaving only marginal lands for latecomers. After considering all the information he was able to gather, Jacob chose to go north. The Michigan Territory was wilderness, but he knew that recent treaties opened lands in the southern portion of the territory. The best land was still available for those who acted quickly.

Though his plans were clear in his own mind, Jacob began learning an important lesson: the world was larger than his mountain valley. Faraway events were to affect him in unimaginable ways. His plan encountered an unexpected obstacle with news of an Indian uprising in Illinois. It was a topic of discussion at the quarry and among neighbors, though no one believed that it would affect them in Vermont. Relations with Indians in New England were peaceful, and questions of land ownership acknowledged, so the news of troubles elsewhere came as a shock. Jacob worried about the violence spreading, possibly even halting the sale of land.

Not all developing issues were as visible and obvious as an Indian uprising on the far away frontier. Even more consequential was the arrival of the *Constantia* at Grosse-Ile near Quebec on April 28th. When the vessel left Limerick, Ireland, she had 170 passengers on board. Twenty-nine died on the voyage from fever. The ship Master, W. Moyes, had been warned by health officials in London about a cholera outbreak among immigrants. Moyes worried that he had had the misfortune of carrying infected passengers and was relieved at the successful completion of this particularly unpleasant journey across the

North Atlantic. *"The sooner they're off my ship the better, now they're someone else's problem."*

THE UNCERTAINTIES AND IMPLICATIONS OF his plans would not cause Jacob to change them. Yes, it would be hard leaving the comfortable community of extended family and friends he knew since birth. Disappointing his family was going to be a difficult hurdle to get over. But that was not the worst of it. The thought of leaving Sally Baldwin, his hopeful future wife, created a uniquely awkward issue. She represented everything Jacob dared dream of in a wife; a delightful young lady who loved life in the Vermont mountains as much as he did. As a child, Jacob had given her the nickname Lilac because of her love for the smell of the blooming lilac bush in her yard. The name stuck and became a term of endearment as the years passed and their relationship strengthened.

They spent many pleasant afternoons walking together in the nearby hills. Without being specific, he occasionally talked to her about what she thought of the concept of moving, to see if she was flexible about the idea. He desperately wanted her to share his outlook about the future. She made it clear, however, that she was never leaving Vermont or her extended family and friends for any reason.

People who knew the pair would have given Sally the edge

in the arena of common sense, so her lack of support for the idea gave Jacob pause, but not enough to cancel his plans. Since the gentle approach failed, and as the time for leaving inched closer, Jacob tried convincing Sally of what he viewed as the facts of the matter; why some people they knew, of their age, were leaving. Ms. Baldwin was having none of it.

On a sunny late April afternoon, while sitting on a hillside overlooking her family farm, Jacob came right out with it.

"Lilac, I have something very important to ask you."

Sally smiled. *Here it is. He's finally going to ask me about getting married.*

"You have been a dear friend since we were children. You are a dream come true in my eyes. I have told you before that I want to live my life with you. I love you and I love our time together. I have something very important to tell you that I need to get out in the open."

Sally frowned. "What is it, Jacob? Something seems to be bothering you."

"Sally, I'm just going to say it. I should have plainly talked to you about this months ago. I plan to leave Vermont."

Sally gasped.

"I am going to move west to start a new farm and a new life of my own. I desperately want you to be part of it. I hope that you will join me, and we can be married there after I have built a home. I intend to leave in a few weeks."

"No! Jacob, stop!" Wiping tears from her eyes with the sleeve of her dress, she stood and looked Jacob in the eyes.

"I told you that I would never leave Vermont! My family and friends are all here. This is where my own children will be born and live. Why are you insisting on doing this? You have everything you could ever want or need right here! If you leave, it will be without me, and we will never see each other again!"

It was a difficult talk, and Jacob almost caved into Sally's pleas for him to reconsider. But he held firm. Sally's stunned reaction and tears greatly pained Jacob. He felt shame and guilt for having hurt a person he cared for so deeply. Tearful and heartbroken, Sally was unyielding. She would not move far away, leaving her family behind forever. If Jacob insisted on going, he would have to marry someone else.

Neither one wanting to part, they lingered on the familiar hillside, staring at the forested mountains. Little more was said. The sun slowly slipped behind the highlands on the opposite side of the dale, casting a dark shadow on the fields below them. A cool fog settled in the valley. The once bright and warm afternoon had turned cool and somber. Both knew there was nothing more to say. After a tearful, extended goodbye hug and exchanging wishes for a happy future, they parted ways, each heading in opposite directions toward their homes. Neither looked back. It was a gloomy walk for both, trudging through the mud in the evening chill, knowing their long relationship was over.

For his part, Jacob knew that although he would never marry Sally, he would always love her. Their time together had been a special chapter in his life that was ending, but the memories they'd created in the Vermont woods would never be forgotten. Her smile and voice were ingrained in his heart, memorized like verses of a favorite poem to be frequently recalled.

As Jacob walked home, a clearer picture of his future crystallized in his mind. He was doing more than simply moving away.

He was chasing a dream. One that always seemed to have been part of who he was. It was *his* dream and commitment; he could not expect others to share it, or more importantly, participate in it. Expecting Sally to be an unwilling partner in his quest was unfair to her. It would also likely cause the dream to fail. *Sally is doing the right thing,* thought Jacob. *She knows that coming with me would ruin both her life and mine. This is my journey, and I must do it myself, come what will.*

JACOB NOW FACED A NEW hurdle: how and when to tell his family. He knew his father was counting on his help during the upcoming planting season. Jacob felt that his younger brothers were old enough to assume that duty. After the emotionally tough conversation with Sally, he decided to put off telling his family for a day—he'd had enough anguish for one evening.

Walking home from the quarry the next day along the trail he strode so often, Jacob resolved to break the news at the dinner table. He would inform them that he was leaving and that they would have to get by forevermore without his help. He rehearsed what he would say, improving the message and practicing his tone of voice as he walked.

Jacob had never been so nervous. He was about to disappoint his mother and father, his grandfather, and his siblings all at the same time. His habit of cracking his knuckles at such times made it obvious to anyone who knew him that there was something on his mind. Clearing his throat, he tried his best to sound mature and confident.

"I have something very important to say. I am leaving. I intend to move west to start a farm of my own. The government is selling farmland in the west at a very low price. The land they're selling is more fertile than here. This farm will no longer support all of us; there isn't enough fertile land left in this valley."

The table, often boisterous at dinner, was stunned into silence. Jacob gulped, scanned his gaze to each of them in turn, then continued.

"I've had enough of poor soil and rocks. I intend to control my own destiny and build a life that is right for me. The west offers opportunities for young people starting their own lives. I intend to take advantage of it, now, while I can. If I stay here any longer, I will never leave. I am leaving on my birthday."

It didn't come out as polished as he had rehearsed, but it got the point across.

Jacob's father's face was flushed with anger and disbelief.

"Leaving! What do you mean you're leaving? Your life is here! I need you to help plant this year's crops!"

He swatted the air with his hand, as if dispelling his eldest son's childish fantasies.

"I hope you're not believing all the stories about how good life is out west, because I guarantee you it ain't! You need to put these foolish thoughts out of your head and put some sense back in it! And what about the Indian problems they're having right now out there? You don't have no idea of what the hell you're getting into!"

Jacob's mother likewise pleaded with him to forget his foolish ideas. Like her husband, she remembered all too well the not long-ago days when the frontier was a place of war and bloodshed. She told a never-before-heard story of a newly married couple, friends she'd grown up with, who moved to the Indiana Territory to begin their life there. Less than a year later, they and other families were brutally killed at a place called Pigeon Roost. Brutalities that had occurred during the recent war were still fresh in the minds of older folks. She finished her speech by mentioning the reports of new fighting by the Sauk chief Black Hawk and the possible dangers that it could represent in the frontier area. Ever the practical New Englander, she also noted:

"You will have no family or friends out there; what will you do in the wilderness if you're hurt or sick? What will you do for money once you spend what little you've saved?"

Jacob assured his mother that he had indeed considered all those issues and felt confident he possessed the skills needed to get by.

Jacob's two brothers lost their appetite. As one, they pleaded with him to change his mind, assuring him that danger and hardship would be the only fruits of his flawed decision. The small kitchen filled with shouting and pleading as everyone spoke at once, yelling to be heard.

Jacob knew he must take control of the situation before it spiraled out of control, or he might lose his resolve.

"Stop! Listen to me. You need to get it in your heads that I am leaving. I will be twenty in a few weeks, and it's time I moved out on my own. You didn't really think I was going to spend my whole life farming this land and working at the quarry until I died, did you? The future of this country is in the west. This land is all taken and will not support any more families. Why do you think we keep hearing about young people from this area leaving? I have been saving money for two years, and I plan to buy land in the Michigan Territory, which hasn't been settled yet, and where good farmland is still plentiful and cheap."

Jacob's father still wasn't convinced. Though he'd spent a lifetime toiling in rocky soil, he was sure that land on the frontier, especially territories that were still poorly explored, wouldn't be any better. His voice shook as he desperately pleaded with his son.

"You will be overcome with sickness by the end of the year, and then what the hell will you do? There won't be anyone there to help you. There is nothing but bears, wolves, and outlaws in that wilderness! A swamp is not a fit place to live."

Jacob stood his ground.

"I think you're wrong, Father, and I'm willing to bet my life on it. I believe those stories are exaggerated. A person can make a go of it if they are smart and work hard. My mind is made up. I will leave on the morning of May 10th."

Jacob did not want to appear disrespectful to his father. He admired him despite his gruff no-nonsense attitude. He had to make it clear, however, that there was no convincing him.

In the coming days, Jacob began finalizing his plans in earnest. He used part of his savings to purchase a new gun, a tin of DuPont black powder, and ball and shot ammunition. His fiddle was his most treasured possession for sentimental reasons, but the percussion cap muzzleloader would be the most important item that he carried. He had worked hard to be able to afford this latest technology. He knew the time would come when it might save his life. On a more practical level, the gun assured meat to eat until his own farm became a reality. He bought extra clothes, good boots, and other necessities such as camping gear and cookware. Next to his gun, boots were the most carefully selected purchase; he knew he would be doing a lot of walking! An oiled canvas tote bag and a rucksack to carry his belongings completed his list of supplies.

Jacob spent as much free time with friends as possible. Their feelings were mixed, ranging from awe at Jacob's apparent craziness to envy of his gutsy venture. Despite any reservations about the wisdom of his plans, there was little doubt that he would succeed. Those who knew him best understood that Jacob's abundant optimism was backed up by firm determination. He had many long conversations with Robert, who expressed similar thoughts of making a new home in the west.

Upon announcing his final decision to leave, Jacob decided to grow a beard. It seemed appropriate. He was a man now, not a kid.

His mother spent as much time as she could spare darning his trousers, shirts, and coat. Disappointed as she was at his decision, she still gathered food for Jacob to take with him.

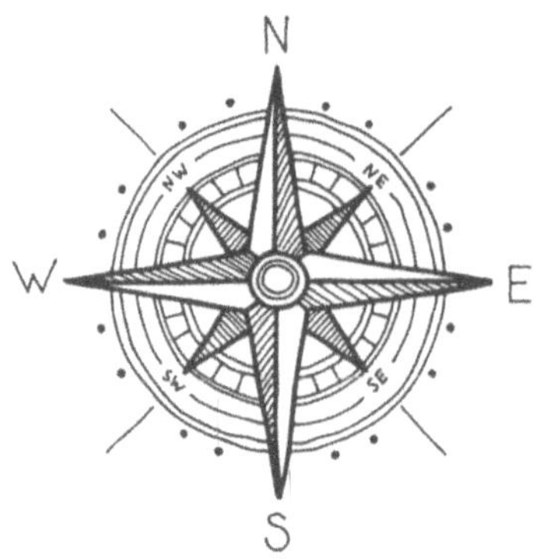

Chapter 3

ON THE EVE OF THE big day, Jacob packed his belongings. He wrapped his fiddle securely in oil cloth and placed it in the canvas tote bag. He packed clothes around it to provide maximum protection for the rough journey that lay ahead. He safely secured his money in a pouch to be carried in a reinforced inner pocket of his shirt. Sleep came in fitful episodes, and the crowing of the rooster found him already awake. Succumbing to pressure from his mother, Jacob ate a hearty breakfast. Robert arrived as he was finishing, much to his surprise and delight.

It was an emotionally difficult few minutes for everyone as Jacob gathered his gear and prepared to leave. His father was the first to speak. Looking squarely into his eyes, Jacob's father shook his hand—a firm handshake that lasted a bit too long.

"You are a man now. Remember all that you have learned and live your life in a manner that will make people proud to know you. You will face many troubles. Face them head on and do what you know is right. I pray that your dreams all come true."

After a brief hug, his father left to begin the day's work, though not before Jacob saw the dampness in his eyes.

The rest of his family saw him off with tears and admonitions to be careful. His sisters sobbed uncontrollably. He gave his mother a long hug and promised that he would be careful, and that he would write often.

His grandfather, the patriarch of the family and a veteran of the War of Independence, was the last to say goodbye. In the privacy of the kitchen, he gave Jacob a rare hug. As he did, he whispered in Jacob's ear that he was proud of him and certain he would prevail in his dreams. Jacob felt that he had never heard more valuable words from a more impeccable source.

A damp chill greeted Jacob as he walked out of the house that had been his home for twenty years. The sun, filtered through the early morning haze, had not had time to warm the air yet. He dressed in an extra layer that he knew would be removed by midmorning. Robert and Jacob's brothers promised to walk with him on the trail through the valley for an hour before turning back.

The wildflowers, with their Vermont beauty, seemed to beckon him to stay. Trout lilies near the end of their flowering period and trilliums at the early stage of blooming covered the forest floor with hues of orange and white. The profusion of wildflowers poignantly reminded Jacob of all the previous springs when he'd seen similar beauty, reinforcing just how much he loved this land. It took all his resolve to not be swayed by the powerful emotional forces at work in his mind and to continue walking with his thoughts focused on the future. With emotional parting embraces, and through tears that couldn't be suppressed, Jacob bid his friend and brothers farewell.

The four-day walk through the forested hills was easy. Years of hard work had given Jacob a wiry, muscular body that effortlessly managed the terrain. He was taller than average, with long, lanky legs made for walking in the forest or fields. That is where he felt most comfortable.

Years of living close to the land allowed him to take advantage of the landscape as he journeyed. Trout supplied a delicious supper and small game provided meat. He felt comfortable in the forest, feeling none of the fear that people less familiar with the wild might experience when darkness settled over the land and strange noises filled the night. A fire kept bears and wolves from encroaching too closely. Jacob knew there was nothing to fear from the other noises beyond the light of the fire: the rustling of leaves, the loud haunting call of great horned owls, and the growls of smaller predators as they fought for territory and food. Those sounds only served to remind Jacob how familiar and at ease he felt in his native land. He hoped that his new home would bring him equal measures of enchantment and fulfillment.

Jacob deeply considered his future while walking to Albany. His destination was Detroit, the new gateway to the great northwestern wilderness. Once there, he would decide where in that vast new land he would finally call home. He met few other people until he got near the Hudson River.

Using the first part of his money, he took a ferry across the river, beginning the final part of his trip to the Erie Canal. The sight of the bustling locale and jostling crowds near the canal came as a shock. He had never imagined a city as large as Albany, or seen so many people crowded into one place. He was taken aback when he saw the number of other like-minded people—single young men in rough homespun clothes obviously right off the farm like him, immigrants who spoke languages he didn't understand, entire families, Indians, well-dressed men who apparently owned businesses along the canal, rough-looking men he would be sure to avoid—all waiting to board the brightly painted and festooned packet boats custom made for the canal.

The largest of the passenger packets could carry up to 120 passengers during the day and had room to house 40 in special berths below deck at night. Space was tight, but conditions were surprisingly comfortable. Teams of horses pulled the packet boats along at four miles per hour. Shade and shelter from rain were available in the lower level, and meals were served on board for long-distance travelers. The only real unpleasantness occurred for those riding on top who had to "hit the deck" when the boat passed under low bridges. Compared to the heat, dust, cold, or muddy conditions that travelers endured on rough trails in the nearly four hundred miles between the Hudson River and Lake Erie, travel on the canal was pleasant.

Jacob did not want to pay the higher cost of riding on the passenger packets. He bought passage on a line boat, which was primarily used to haul freight and had fewer amenities for travelers. Only two horses or mules pulled line boats, so the pace was slow, but since it cost only about a penny per mile to ride the freight boats—about half of the packet's rate—Jacob happily accepted a bit less speed and comfort. Unfortunately, not only were amenities fewer on the cargo boats, the company of fellow low-cost travelers was also sometimes less appealing, as he soon found out.

Jacob made his way on board, weaving between workers loading cargo and small farm animals. He squeezed through the stacked crates and caged chickens to a vacant spot in the stern, then claimed as much space as possible by stretching out his legs. It came as no surprise that there were only a few other passengers. A half hour later, they were underway at the pace of plodding mules. The warm sun and the gentle rocking of the cargo boat soon had Jacob yawning, despite the presence of other travelers uncomfortably close by. Feeling content and pleased that his journey was going according to plans, he decided on a well-earned nap as the appropriate next step. He stretched out as much as possible, put an arm around his gun and pack, and peacefully slipped into darkness.

OVER THE NINE-DAY TRIP TO Buffalo, passengers regularly boarded and disembarked the boat. For the most part, they were men traveling alone. With a destination and rough plan formed in his mind, Jacob talked to other passengers to learn what he could about the world beyond Vermont. He was disappointed to find that many of the comments were rumors or assumptions based on little or no firsthand knowledge. One stranger, whose rugged yet well-kempt appearance and bombastic manner suggested he was knowledgeable, caught Jacob's interest but also put him on guard.

"Where you heading to?" he asked Jacob.

"Michigan Territory, looking for farmland to buy," said Jacob, not wanting to reveal too much to this man, whom he knew nothing about and didn't trust. The man scoffed and rolled his eyes.

"There is a hell of a lot of easier ways to make a living than farming."

"Like what?" asked Jacob. There was no way to escape this stranger, and it was obvious his unsought advice would continue regardless. Jacob decided he might as well see if he could gain useful information from him.

"You look like a country boy who knows his way around the woods; you might find surveying a good money maker. I don't mean busting your ass as a real surveyor—I'm talking about being a landman and getting paid by the likes of that rich man over there," gesturing toward a well-dressed man, "who'll pay guys like you to walk property they want to buy to see if it's worthwhile. Believe me, it's easy to spend a few days in the woods taking a look-see at some of the property land speculators are interested in, then telling them what they wanna hear. By the time they find out that it ain't exactly like you told them, you'll be long gone."

"It sounds like you have personal experience."

"Beats the hell outta walking behind a stinking mule all day, plowing fields under the hot sun. By the way, my name is Nathaniel."

Jacob introduced himself, first name only. He couldn't help but notice that Nathaniel also kept his longarm close at hand.

"So, where are you heading?"asked Jacob, continuing the conversation.

"Ever hear of Fort Dearborn or Chicago?"

"I've heard them mentioned but know nothing about them."

"Well, now that a treaty with the Indians has allowed settlement of all that land near Lake Michigan, the new town of Chicago is being built. Believe me, boy, it won't be long before that swampland will be a big important city. There's money to be made there by buying up land now and selling it in a few years to the developers and bankers. I already convinced one of those prissy city slickers to invest in land there. I'm going to stake the land and file a claim for him; he's paying me good money to manage his investments. And he is the first of many who need someone like me to do this for them while they sit in their fancy offices in New York. You might want to consider it as an easy way to make some extra money for yourself."

The idea of land speculation did not sit well with Jacob, though he wasn't sure why. *If someone wants to take a chance and buy land hoping that it will gain value, who's to blame them,* he thought. *I shouldn't be hasty in my judgment. Maybe being a landman would be a much easier way to earn a living instead of working my tail off as a farmer. At least there ain't any rocks to carry.*

More than one man told Jacob to beware of the Michigan Territory. One such person was a well-dressed gentleman who claimed to represent a land-buying syndicate. He said he was on his way west to buy newly opened land in Illinois for resale to investors and farmers. The businessman seemed knowledgeable about government lands issues, so Jacob asked him about land in the Michigan Territory.

"If you're thinking of moving there, then you should know about Mr. Edward Tiffin."

"Never heard of him."

"You never heard of the Surveyor General for the United States government?" declared the stranger. "He was assigned to survey the Michigan Territory to see if it were suitable for military bounty land—in other words, if it would make good farmland. Because back then the government wanted good land to give to soldiers who fought in the War of 1812. But Mr. Tiffin reported that most of the land was worthless and could never be productive farmland.

"In fact, Tiffin's report was so negative that Congress passed a law making the Missouri Territory, rather than the Michigan Territory, the region where soldiers could receive land grants as a military bounty for their service."

Jacob was speechless when the man finished. He thanked him for the advice, though the comments caused him great concern.

Another man told stories about clouds of mosquitoes, fevers, vicious wild animals, unfriendly Indians, and various other hardships and dangers a person encountered if he ventured north of Ohio. These shortcomings, along with reports of poor soil for farming, were enough to cause Jacob to consider changing his mind and heading toward Illinois instead. Maybe there were good reasons that the Michigan Territory remained mostly wilderness and lands to the south had already been developed and admitted as states.

Jacob also made the acquaintance of several families and single men like himself who were moving west, each expressing varying opinions and hopes of what lay ahead. One theme was ubiquitous: virtually all of them were heading into the unknown. Many were making the move foolishly ill-prepared. They had hopes about what opportunities the new land held and what their future lives would be like, but much of that hope was grounded in hearsay and blind optimism. Witnessing this gave Jacob pause. Was he guilty of the same sort of behavior? Was his family right when they told him that he was doing something dangerously foolish? He felt that he was different. He, after all, had thought out his plan for two years. He was certain that he knew more about what to expect than these other immigrants.

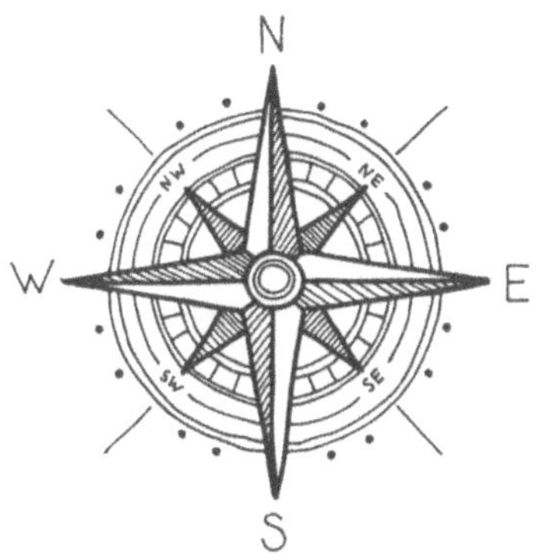

Chapter 4

JUST TWO WEEKS AFTER LEAVING his Vermont home, Jacob arrived in Buffalo. The trip down the Erie Canal had been a fascinating experience. He learned a lot about life outside of Vermont from the people he met along the way.

As evening approached, he walked the muddy streets with much on his mind. The scene he encountered was overwhelming in its strangeness and scope. Construction was taking place everywhere he looked. The completion of the western terminus of the canal had turned the sleepy village into a bustling boom town, with people living in hastily erected shacks and tents. Everywhere he looked he saw pandemonium.

Families on foot hurried across the road, dodging horses and mule-pulled carts filled with lumber and bricks to satisfy the demand for new stores and houses. Other carts, pushed by hand or pulled by animals, carried cargo and possessions from the canal to docks on Lake Erie.

The roads and alleys were a muddy quagmire, worsened by horse manure, making traversing the city an unpleasant as well as difficult undertaking. Workers hired to cart away the daily accumulation of manure could not keep up. Piles of animal waste on vacant parcels of land were covered with disease-bearing flies.

As in Albany, he was once again taken aback by the crowds of hundreds of people who, like him, were heading west. He had viewed his journey as a personal adventure and as an important part of *his* life. It came as a shock to see that many other people shared the same idea. Realizing that he was just one of thousands of people making a similar journey tarnished the experience for him.

Jacob made his way to the docks to figure out what to do next. The scope of the operation was much larger and more complicated than what he experienced at Albany. When he finally found the correct office, the sheer number of options only added to his confusion. The agent pointed to a sailing vessel tied up at the dock, with the name *Aurora* painted on the side.

"You can take that sailing ship all the way to Detroit, or, if you can afford it, you can take the steamship *Superior*. It is faster and a more enjoyable way to travel."

He pointed out the steamship anchored offshore. Jacob had never seen anything like it before.

The agent continued. "The cheapest choice is to take a ship to Cleveland and disembark. From Cleveland, you can continue your trip by land on what is called The Great Trail. The trail cuts through a huge swamp and goes all the way to Indiana. A branch of the trail goes north to Detroit. In fact, twice-weekly mail runs between Detroit and Cleveland are now made using that trail."

Jacob was dumbfounded by the choices, his head filling with questions. He learned that traveling the trail on foot was a risky venture. There were individuals who would carry freight or passengers for a fee, but their services were unreliable. The ticket agent also mentioned that while the official name of the route was the Maumee and Western Reserve Road, the most common name for the route through the swampy wilderness was The Mud Pike. It was rough, muddy, insect-plagued, and the availability of transport was uncertain at best. Walking the whole way was out of the question. It did not take Jacob long to decide to take a boat to wherever he ended up going; it seemed faster and more convenient. Of the two boat options, he only considered the sailing vessel. The thought of a boat that somehow used fire instead of wind seemed crazy.

Damn, am I even still going to Detroit? he pondered, *or should I change my plans now and go somewhere where I know there is good farmland and not just a bunch of swamps?* He knew he would have to decide before buying the ticket if he was to change his destination.

CARRYING HIS LIFE'S POSSESSIONS WITH him, he made his way through town and sat on the bank of a lake larger than he had ever dared to imagine. Jacob absentmindedly stared westward across the vastness of Lake Erie toward the spectacular sunset, pondering weighty choices that would shape his future. Deep in thought, he didn't notice a young man walk up beside him. The stranger was also carrying a bundle of possessions.

"'Tis a beautiful sight, isn't it?" said a strongly accented but friendly voice next to him.

"Robert! What are you doing here?" Jacob yelled, jumping up in surprise at the familiar Gaelic accent.

Upon seeing the voice had come from a stranger, he felt foolish.

"Sorry, I thought you were someone else—a friend from home."

"I'm sorry to disappoint you. Of course, it would have been a wonderful surprise to see a friend instead of a stranger. But, if I might ask, why the look of worry on such a fine day as this?"

"I'm not worried about anything," Jacob said, lying. "Just deep in thought about what I'm going to do."

The stranger put out his hand. "Michael O'Toole, though friends just call me Mick."

"Jacob Hart," replied Jacob in turn, shaking O'Toole's hand. The strength of his grip and the roughness of his calloused skin made it obvious that he was a young man who had spent his life working hard. Jacob attempted a too-firm handshake in response, meant to relay an unspoken message of strength and maturity, but felt a little foolish afterward. Though a bit shorter than Jacob, the stranger outweighed him by twenty pounds. It was also obvious that the difference in weight was all muscle. *If I was ever in a fight*, thought Jacob, *I'd want this guy on my side!* Despite his imposing appearance, Mike's quick smile and friendly manner made an immediate impression.

"You look like a man with something on his mind, Jacob. Perhaps a little companionship will help you settle things in your head. I just happen to have two days with nothing to do whilst I wait for the ship that's carrying me to Detroit."

"What boat are you taking, Michael?"

"The *Aurora*. It leaves Wednesday morning at daybreak."

"I saw the *Aurora* at the docks. My original plans were to take that ship to Detroit also, but now I am not so sure." The look on Jacob's face told the whole story.

"Homesick? Thinking about heading back to wherever it was you came from?"

"Hell no, I'm not homesick!" said Jacob defensively. It made him uncomfortable to have given the impression that he might be scared or longing for the security of home.

"It's just that when I left home, I had a clear plan in my head of my destination and what I would do when I got there. Now those dreams have mostly turned to doubts."

Jacob explained his newfound concerns about his destination and of how the affordable promised land of Michigan Territory now looked like a bum deal.

"Until yesterday, I worked at Black Rock, making bricks and sawing lumber. I've got a spare shilling or two in my pockets. What do ya say about lettin' me buy you a brew? It always helps to have a beer in hand when talking about life and all its problems. And by the way, call me Mick."

"Sure, Mick," Jacob said, relieved to have an outlet for his troubles.

"That might be just what I need."

They went to a nearby, rudimentary inn to talk. The tavern was packed, and the only remaining seats were at a table tucked into the far corner. The young man at the table waved them over to sit down. He introduced himself as Jim from New York City. After introductions and sharing summaries of their life stories, the conversation turned to each man's future plans. Though Jim's background was vastly different, he turned out to be like them—a young man seeking his future. He was making this happen by temporarily working as a sailor on the Great Lakes. Jim's hometown tales bore no semblance to Jacob's and Mick's lives. His time in the slums of New York formed dissimilar strengths and resulted in different dreams. Jim wanted nothing to do with the life of a farmer. He was saving to move to a new city and a better life away from the tenements.

Though Jim's stories were unrecognizable to the others, they left them in awe of his courage and cheerful outlook, and with an aching gut from laughing at the youthful predicaments of city life. Jim said that his time working as a sailor was going to be just long enough to save money and make plans for settlement in one of the new cities that were developing on Lake Erie. He felt he had the gifts to be a successful salesman and thought that the future looked promising for those with such skills. This year, he said, would be his last working on sailing ships. It was his second year as a sailor, and the job was too dangerous and the work too difficult for his taste.

When the topic of Jacob and Mick's intentions to sail to Detroit came up, Jim asked which ship they were sailing on. When Mick said he had paid for passage on the cargo schooner

Aurora, Jim smiled broadly. "That's the boat that I work on," Jim proudly declared. He then inadvertently poured some cold water on their plans by telling them that sailing on Lake Erie was more dangerous than sailing across the North Atlantic. That was not what Mick wanted to hear, though it meant little to Jacob.

Jacob and Mick, it turned out, could have been brothers separated at birth. Their childhoods were spent in separate places, but their personalities were eerily similar. Mick was a year older, but the difference ended there. They had both spent their youth on hardscrabble farms that grew rocks better than crops—Jacob from Vermont and Mick from Ireland. Because of that shared experience, they shared similar dreams.

O'Toole talked wistfully about his life. He left his home at eighteen, taking a leaky ship to Canada. British overseers made passage to Canada easier than to New York, his intended destination. A year later he crossed the border, spending the past year in the Buffalo area working odd jobs.

"My Mom and Pop were surely disappointed in my leaving," Mick explained. "As the eldest son they figured I would take over the farm and continue raising sheep in the O'Toole tradition. But as much as I loved my family, I wanted something more than living in the cold winds of Donegal, digging peat and herding sheep."

"A neighbor girl by the name of Colleen almost convinced me to stay. Everyone assumed we would marry someday; it was almost expected of me. And believe me, her charms were powerful enough to make any man do whatever she wanted. Truth is, I could have enjoyed a nice life married to her, raising a family, and living in a warm stone cottage full of kids. She is a lovely lass who I really liked, and amazingly, she actually liked me, if you can imagine that! But America was calling to me. I wanted to see what life in the promised land offered, so I handed over three pounds and ten shillings—all the money I had in the world—and sailed a disease-ridden leaking old scow to Quebec.

"I have learned a lot in the last two years, working a variety of jobs and gaining important skills, but now it's time to settle down and look for that farm I've been dreaming about. And I want a farm that doesn't have any rocks on it. That is why I'm heading west too. I have saved some money and I plan to earn more once I get to Detroit. Then I will look for land and live my life there. To be honest, I hope Colleen doesn't marry someone else, and next year I might surprise her with a letter asking her to come to America, to our own farm."

Hearing Mick's story about first loves left Jacob feeling pensive for a few minutes, but he put thoughts of Sally out of his mind as best he could.

The newfound friends discovered many similarities in their attitudes and plans for the future. Spending an evening in a tavern talking with others about life made Jacob feel less like a boy on the family farm and more like a man on his own. The two young strangers impressed him. Here are people like me, he thought. Not afraid of demanding work and having the strength of character to tackle the world on their own. Seeing the quality of his newfound friends' characters, Jacob felt free to talk about the uncertainties of his own plans. Jim, with no knowledge or experience about the realities of farming, made it clear he had no advice to offer. Mick listened but said little.

As the warm beer flowed, topics of conversation moved from serious to fun. Mick suggested that it was time his new friends learned some old Irish drinking songs. To the delight of some patrons and the chagrin of others, he loudly regaled the tavern with traditional tunes from Donegal and bawdy refrains he learned during his passage across the Atlantic. Jacob unpacked his fiddle and began playing along with the melody, the crowd responding with lively cheers. The old drinking song "The Wild Rover" was a particularly big hit because many men in the tavern were familiar with it. They sang along with gusto, if not on key or in rhythm. After Mick's Irish drinking tunes, Jacob played dance tunes popular in the east. "Durang's Hornpipe" set the stage, followed by "Fisher's Hornpipe." By the end of the second song, everyone was clapping and stamping their feet. A few couples were dancing. The newfound friends were disappointed that there were not any single young ladies present to share a dance, a drink, or perhaps the night with. Then again, this tavern was not the sort of place that young single women would frequent.

Jacob wrapped up the evening with a tune called the "Constitution March." It was a resounding hit. He viewed the enthusiasm of the crowd as a mixed blessing, however, because the music resulted in more drinks bought on their behalf. Overall, it was great fun and a wonderful evening, perhaps the most enjoyable of his life.

Completely drained and feeling the effects of too much alcohol, the trio decided to call it a night well after midnight. Mick raised his mug to make a toast. "*Slainte agus Tainte*," he said with cheerful gusto, wishing Jacob and Jim health and wealth. Mick emptied the last of the ale in his tankard, let out a powerful burp, and said that it had been a mighty fine evening. Jacob packed up his gear and followed him out the door. After saying good night to Jim, who headed back to the ship, Mick turned to Jacob.

"Jacob, my friend, I've got somethin' to say to you, but you have to promise you won't get angry with me."

Jacob nodded, too drunk and mellow to disagree.

"Your life in the backwoods of Vermont has made you a strong man, Jacob, but also a man that is just a little gullible. Do you think those men who criticized your plans and said wonderful things about other places or other ways to make a living were doing it to help you? That's a lot of sheep shite, friend. And I know a thing or two about sheep and about ne'er-do-well bastards who try to convince you that the smell of manure is perfume.

"Those story tellers have other motives. Some of them are land speculators who don't want settlers staking out a hundred acres of prime land that they themselves hope to buy. Wheeler-dealers don't want to see men like you filing a claim until they own it—then you pay them *their* asking price instead of paying the government a whole lot less. Speculators are buying entire townships of land as quickly as they can. Forget about all those deceits you've been told and follow your original plan. That's what I intend to do. I'm not sure what the future holds for me, but I know it'll be what I make it, not what someone else tells me I should or shouldn't do. We have a term in Ireland that we use when things seem stacked against us: *misneach*. It is that inner strength a man must call on to keep going when things get tough. It's clear to me that you have it, so go chase your dreams on your terms and to hell with everyone else! Now, my friend, I think it's time to call it a night and go get some sleep."

Jacob assured Mick that he appreciated the advice, though he was not certain if it had been all that welcome. No Vermonter wants to believe he has been hornswoggled or fell short of resolve to do what they felt was right. The friends departed. Mick headed to a boarding house and Jacob to a nearby wooded area where he set up camp and quickly fell asleep.

IT MIGHT HAVE BEEN AN owl call or the sound of a branch snapping underfoot that brought Jacob partially awake. Then he felt the slight but unquestionable movement of his pack lying next to him. Awakening quickly, he saw a short, wiry man stooping over him. The man had his hand around Jacob's gun, gently pulling it toward himself. Jacob seized it firmly and yanked it out of the stranger's grip. With unexpected speed and strength, the thief grabbed ahold of Jacob, trying to wrench the gun away. Hardened muscles earned from years of demanding work, and his height advantage, gave Jacob the necessary edge. Fighting his way out of the man's grasp, he swung his fist with all his might and sent him tumbling. Pulling a large knife from a sheath on his belt, the thief attacked again. This time Jacob was ready. Swinging his gun like a club, he struck the man in the head, knocking him to the ground and causing him to drop his knife.

Before the man could recover, Jacob grabbed the assailant by the collar, raising him up to full height. The badly bleeding stranger was nearly knocked unconscious from the blow. He offered little resistance. Jacob pondered what to do. He assumed that there was some sort of law enforcement capability in the town but had no idea how to find them. He also had no intention of leaving his campsite, and all his possessions, unguarded. Giving the man his angriest look, Jacob told him that he was loading his gun and if he saw him anywhere near his camp, he would shoot him without hesitation.

Giving him a hard shove that sent the thief sprawling on the ground, he told him to leave and never come back. The outlaw begrudgingly complied. Holding his head, trying to stop the bleeding and clearly in pain, he headed toward town, tossing a few angry words Jacob's way. *Lesson learned*, thought Jacob. He realized that he needed to pay more attention to the cautionary advice he'd received from well-meaning friends before he left home. *I'm not in a quiet valley in the Green Mountains anymore. But at least I have a much better knife now, thanks to that incompetent burglar*, he thought to himself as he straightened his campsite and picked up the knife that the would-be thief dropped.

The remaining few hours of night passed quickly and peacefully. As usual, Jacob woke early on Tuesday morning, before the sun had fully risen. A heavy dew made everything wet and cold to the touch; he shivered in the morning fog. His head throbbed from too much beer and his fist was sore from the fight. Jacob felt that he handled himself well given the danger he confronted during the night. But he also realized that he lacked experience in what it takes to be a man on his own. Did he have the grit it would take to make it without the help of others? If he did not, he would have to get it quickly, he told himself as he walked through the wet weeds to a grove of trees to relieve himself.

He dug out a pan to boil water for coffee and ate jerky and old bread spread with bacon grease. He decided that he should consider O'Toole's advice. *Choosing one place over another was a huge decision that needed careful attention,* he thought to himself. He concluded that he ought to talk with other people to get more information. Walking into town after eating and breaking camp, he inquired about the location of the government land office. He assumed they would be a trustworthy source of information.

Jacob spent an hour talking with the land agent, who had been involved with land claims since 1815, when migration into Ohio increased sharply. Indian troubles and the war suppressed settlement prior to that time, but with victory and clear title over this vast area of land now firmly established, settlers poured in. The land agent first gave a basic explanation as to how government land is surveyed and parceled. He explained the concept of 640-acre sections, thirty-six sections to a township. He then explained that many homesteaders seek a quarter section—160 acres of land—as the best option. He gave valuable help to Jacob about the process of gaining ownership of homestead lands. One of the more helpful bits of information concerned paying for it.

"Land in the west," he explained, "used to sell for two dollars an acre, but the government allowed a person to pay for it in four payments. In 1820, Congress changed the law. Now the cost for each acre has been reduced to a dollar twenty-five cents, but a buyer must pay the total amount up front, and parcels must be at least 80 acres in size. Most purchasers buy 160- or 80-acre parcels. My advice is that if you don't have enough money on hand to buy the amount of land that you want outright, you should find work first to come up with the money you will need.

"If you buy the minimum amount first with the intention of buying more land later, it will be too late. Adjacent land will all be spoken for before you get a chance to buy more. I recommend that you buy as much as you can all at once. One more thing: when you get to wherever you are going, check out the banks. If you have at least half of the money you need, many local banks will loan you the rest on credit. They know that if you fail in your plans, they will have no trouble selling your land at a higher price to other buyers. The government is selling land cheaply, but once it is resold, the price goes up a lot."

Jacob thanked the agent for his advice. The overall procedure seemed straightforward, but it still required diligence, lest a lot of work be for naught. Jacob had no experience using credit, and therefore he assumed that he would have to pay up front in cash. But his plans were also based on buying a smaller parcel first, then adding to it a year or two later. Given the need to buy all the land he wanted at once, rather than in two or three small purchases over time, Jacob knew he did not have enough money. This meant that he would have to work for a year or more to come up with the needed money. *Damn,* he thought. *That changes things.*

PONDERING ALL THAT HE LEARNED and experienced since leaving home, Jacob felt overwhelmed. The realities of life on his own, and the process of buying a farm and running it successfully, were proving to be more complicated than he initially considered. In fact, life in general was going to be more demanding now that he alone was making decisions that required wisdom, knowledge, and no small amount of courage. For the first time in his life, Jacob felt gratitude for what schooling he'd received, and of his ability to read and write at a level that would see him through the process of filing a claim, buying land, and the many other tasks that depend on the ability to do basic math, reading, and writing. *If a person didn't have these abilities, they could be badly fooled and taken advantage of,* thought Jacob. He made a mental note to be on guard and make sure that nobody ever played him for a fool.

Walking down the muddy road that served as the main street of Buffalo, Jacob was beginning to feel better about things. Plans began to gel in his mind. He would not be dissuaded; the Michigan Territory was his destination. He made his way to the docks and bought passage to Detroit on the *Aurora,* as it was significantly less expensive, though slower, than a steamship. Jacob felt that fate must be confirming his decision when the agent told him that he just purchased the last available ticket on what was primarily a cargo-carrying vessel.

He crossed the busy road again, confident that he'd made the right decision. The strangers he passed by, stressed and hurried as they dodged heavily laden carts pulled by teams of oxen and horses, probably wondered about the smile on his face.

Jacob tried to avoid the flying mud, horse manure, and puddles of filthy water, mostly unsuccessfully. He saw beyond his immediate surroundings, knowing he would forever leave them behind the next morning. He stopped at local shops to buy more supplies for the journey and to replenish his store of food. At the last minute, he decided to buy a bottle of whiskey, thinking there would be an opportunity to open it for a celebratory drink once he arrived in Detroit. He also stopped at the government office again, this time to post a letter to his family. In the letter, he confirmed that his next stop would be Detroit and stated his intention to live the rest of his life on a prosperous farm in the Michigan Territory.

After mailing his letter, he began to think about what the words he just wrote really meant, imagining his life ten years hence. He momentarily fancied himself married, with children who would help on the farm. This notion caused him to stop suddenly in the middle of the road. After Sally's refusal to move, Jacob had not given thought to the likelihood of finding another woman who might agree to marry him. It abruptly occurred to him that this, too, was a part of a future that he must think about. Without giving it serious thought, he always assumed that his future would include a wife and family. But it dawned on him that it would not just happen—he would have to make it happen. He suddenly felt older and burdened with more responsibilities as he resumed his walk.

He sought a campsite near the dock, ultimately choosing a vacant area at the river's mouth on the north side of Buffalo. A foul odor at the first location he chose led him to a ditch filled with muddy water and sewage flowing into the lake. Accustomed to the pristine rivers he fished near his Vermont home, the sight shocked and disgusted him. Finding another secluded location as far from the open sewer as he could get, Jacob set up camp for the night. He found it hard to sleep with his mind whirling. Not only because of potential danger lurking nearby, but also because of the realization that in a few hours he would board a sailboat, and five days later get off at Detroit. It was going to happen! Though this had been his dream all along, after all the recent turmoil, it felt like a decision he had just made.

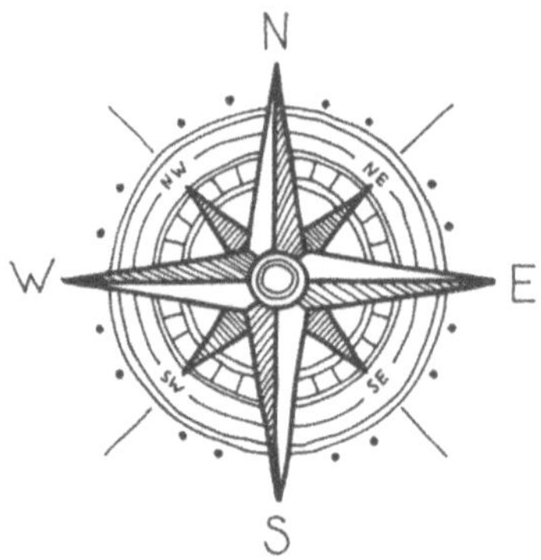

Chapter 5

JACOB ARRIVED AT THE DOCK as the vernal sunrise brightened the eastern sky with shades of pink and lavender. His fully loaded pack weighed heavy on his back, and his canvas bag, slung over his shoulder with a sling, was an additional cumbersome burden. The weight he carried caused him to walk with a forward stoop, but being used to carrying heavy loads, it did not bother him. He knew that he would have time to relax on the boat. He was also aware that once he arrived in Detroit and left for the wilderness, he would spend a great deal of time exploring on foot. Jacob mused about this rapidly approaching adventure and wondered how many weeks or months he would explore before he found the land he would want to claim. Remembering that he first had to find some manner of work to bolster his current cash holdings brought his daydream to an end. He momentarily pondered where he would even begin to look for work.

As he walked along the shoreline, softly lapping waves could be heard over the increasing clamor of the port city as it came to life. The raucous din of seagulls arguing over dead fish washed onto the shore competed with the sounds of workers at the busy docks. A distinctive smell drifted from the lakeshore, carrying a potent organic scent of mud, rotting seaweed, and fish. Jacob considered the vast difference between the early morning smells of Lake Erie and the aroma of dawn in the Vermont mountains.

Gentle waves caused his ship, the name *Aurora* proudly displayed on the bow, to tug at the ropes securing her to the dock. A gangplank spanned the open water between the dock and the boat, angling upward to the vessel's gangway. Draymen were already unloading supplies and cargo from their carts, cursing as they carried heavy boxes and barrels up the ramp. Once on board, other workers moved the cargo to its proper locations on or below the deck. Staring at the ship from a safe distance, fascinated by its symmetry and graceful form, Jacob thought it one of the most impressive things he had ever seen. With a length of sixty-eight feet and a seventeen-foot beam, it was small as sailing ships went, but Jacob did not know this. With its two tall masts and large, though sagging, canvas sails, it struck him as the kind of ship that could journey across an ocean.

A shout of "Hey, Jacob!" broke his reverie. In the gathering daylight, Jacob recognized Mick O'Toole heading his way. His intense blue eyes and no-holds-barred smile belied the early hour. They greeted each other warmly and sat down near the dock to await boarding the ship. Jacob told him all about the run-in with the would-be thief, but avoided mentioning that he had suffered the effects of a hangover the previous morning to save himself from the embarrassment. Unlike some passengers, they had no large chests and boxes of possessions to load, so they waited and talked while the few other passengers were busy overseeing loading their valuables. Jacob was pleased to be traveling together with Mick. O'Toole seemed savvier in the ways of the world, and Jacob already valued his opinion even though he barely knew him.

After all the cargo and supplies were loaded, the passengers boarded. Jacob estimated that there were a dozen passengers on the ship. Except for one family with two young children, all the passengers were men. Most were clearly farmers or settlers, while a few were better dressed and seemed to be traveling on business—land speculators, no doubt. Since their sailboat was one of the older styles of ships carrying passengers and cargo, with limited passenger accommodations, Jacob assumed that the businessmen had not yet enjoyed much success. He thought to himself that the ship would be crowded, and for the first time wondered what accommodations would be like on board. *But what the hell*, he thought. *It's only for five days.*

Captain Miles, skipper of the *Aurora*, personally greeted passengers as they boarded. He was a strong, weathered man in his forties who cut an impressive figure in his fashionable blue swallow tailcoat with brass buttons, nankeen pants, and low shoes with white stockings, all topped off with the latest style tall hat. A tanned, deeply lined face spoke of many years spent in the sun, and scars disclosed a battle with smallpox at some point in his life. Jacob and O'Toole were immediately impressed with his appearance and surprised by his friendly manner. They expected someone with a gruff and demanding demeanor, the kind of captain in charge of the ship that brought Mick across the Atlantic. The skipper was clearly a man confident in his role, commanding respect and obedience because of his character rather than his position.

They saw Jim and waved to him. He helped them get situated in the small cabin they were to share, where they stashed their possessions. They then hurried back to the deck to watch the fascinating hustle and bustle of the three-man crew and passengers. They looked on with amazement as Jim climbed the masts to adjust lines and trim sails. Captain Miles made his way to the helm in anticipation of sailing. The order and logic of the operation impressed Jacob.

When Jim had a chance, he came over to talk with his friends. He said that this was the second year that he sailed on the *Aurora.* He explained that it was a new vessel, built four years earlier at Erie, Pennsylvania, primarily for use on Lake Erie. Its small size and shallow draft made it an ideal vessel for the lake, enabling it to access poorly developed port cities along the shoreline and on connecting rivers. Last summer, Jim further explained, they ventured to several Lake Michigan destinations. Because of large waves, they sailed within view of the shore all the way, taking a dozen soldiers to Fort Howard and government surveyors and Indian agents to Fort Dearborn.

Responding to a call from the captain, Jim left. The two friends found a quiet area and observed the harbor come to life. Boats of every description and size were on the water. Fishing vessels headed west onto the open lake to cast their nets in the deeper waters far offshore, while large cargo-carrying canoes and skiffs made their way north on the river. Single-mast sloops carried payloads bound for Lake Erie ports on both sides of the border.

Thick black smoke began streaming from the two smokestacks on the *Superior,* still anchored out in the bay. It was larger than the *Aurora* and of an altogether different construction style. This was the first steamboat Jacob had ever seen, and the sight made him uncomfortable. It seemed so unnatural without sails filled with wind. His knowledge of watercraft was limited to those propelled by hand or by the wind, or by mules like on the Erie Canal. A ship gushing black smoke that came from a large fire on board just didn't fit his mental image of what ships were supposed to look like. *So that's the future?* he thought to himself. *What will it look like when every ship has a chimney belching black smoke?*

Mick, having spent much more time near large waters, witnessed many steamboats on Lake Ontario and at the Buffalo port in the past.

"Steamboats are faster than sailboats, and they don't need the wind," Mick noted. "Because of that, it only takes a steamboat three days to get to Detroit, instead of five for the *Aurora.* They burn firewood as fuel for their steam boilers, and there is plenty of wood around here to burn."

He opined that in a few years there would no longer be any sailing vessels left, only steamboats. Jacob was glad that he chose passage on a sailboat. If sailing vessels were going to disappear forever, he was grateful for the chance to ride on one of the last ones.

By 8:30, the ship was ready to sail. A bell rang to make known to all persons and nearby craft that the ship was weighing anchor. A dockworker untied the two hawsers from the bollards and tossed them on board. Two longboats with teams of rowers tied ropes to the bow of the ship and began the arduous task of swinging the bow toward the open water. The dockworker also helped push the bow lakeward with the aid of long poles.

In response to a rapid series of commands from the skipper, Jim and another crew member raised and adjusted additional sails to maximize the effect of the light breeze. With a fully spread canvas billowing in the breeze, the ship slowly began to respond. In less than an hour, it was able to proceed on its own. Mick explained, in the knowing manner of someone who had sailed before, that early morning winds are calm.

"A person must be patient and wait for the warming of the day to increase wind speeds," he said. Mick further reminded Jacob that they would be traveling into the prevailing winds, not with them, and that such sailing is slower and required special skill. The whole scene fascinated Jacob, and he wondered if a life at sea might be in his future.

Once the flurry of activity required to get underway lessened, Jim was able to join them for a few minutes and explain their route for the day. Jacob was disappointed to learn that there were scheduled stops to make, with their first at Erie, Pennsylvania. They would then sail west to stop at Cleveland, where some passengers would leave and a few new passengers would board. The next stop was the coastal village of Sandusky to off-load passengers who were going to travel on the new trail across the Black Swamp. The Sandusky stop was offshore, with a row-boat delivering passengers to the village due to lack of a safe port at which to dock. After Sandusky, the ship was to travel among the numerous islands on its way north to the mouth of the Detroit River.

Jacob's momentary disappointment about their travel schedule faded away as he gazed toward the open lake ahead of them. He had heard the Great Lakes described as the "Sweetwater seas," but it was not until he was in a clear position to peer westward across miles of fresh water that the true meaning of the description hit home. *It was truly a marvelous sight*, he thought, and just one of many new and fascinating things that he knew his future held. He decided to just relax and enjoy the sailing experience rather than be in too much of a rush to arrive at Detroit.

It was a calm and sunny day, so Jacob and Mick stayed on the deck enjoying the warm sunshine. They appreciated that there was nothing to do except relax. Sailing west into the flat vastness of the lake, they could see clouds on the horizon that looked like mountains rising out of the water. They walked the length of the ship, watching the bow cut cleanly through the water, and then peered from the stern as the ever-widening wake stretched behind them, leaving a clear trail of their passage. After lunch, progress remained slow but steady, and the gently rocking boat soon put both young men to sleep.

Jacob awoke in the midafternoon to find that Mick had gone below deck. He discovered him lying in his cot reading a book called *The Dairyman's Daughter*. Jacob was surprised at first, as he'd assumed that Mick could not read, or at least would not be one who read books solely for enjoyment. Mick looked up and, suspecting Jacob's surprise, held up the book.

"Yes, Jacob, I can read," he said wryly. "I brought a few

books along to pass the time—hopefully I can get through two before we step back ashore. I might not be the fastest reader, but I try to read every chance I get!"

"I hope you don't mind my surprise. Reading isn't exactly common among farm boys with calloused hands like ours!" Jacob said.

Mick gave a knowing chuckle. "Our parish priest, old Father Mullalley, thought we would be better men if we learned to read and write, and to sing. So, he made us spend Sunday evenings at church where he taught us the finer arts of life. My father thought it was a waste of time, but I think my mother secretly convinced our priest to turn us into something other than sheep farmers.

"To be honest, I'm grateful for what I learned. Reading and writing have their own rewards in life, and I learned years ago that the ladies like a man who can carry a tune! My father taught me how to work, neighbor boys taught me how to fight, and Padre Lolly taught me how to be the sophisticated gentleman you see before you."

"Where? I don't see any sophisticated gentlemen in here," Jacob said with a laugh. "Just a couple farm boys who probably don't know what the hell they're doing!"

In truth, Jacob was once again surprised and impressed by his companion. Mick truly was a young man of substance. Jacob allowed that since he, too, would have many hours to fill on the trip, that perhaps he could borrow a book to hone his own reading skills.

After supper, the two travelers sat on the deck in the cooling breeze. There were some card games taking place nearby and

Mick joined in a game of whist. Jacob was unskilled at cards. He'd played occasionally at the quarry when men gathered at the end of the workday. His father's strict attitude about cards, music, and other unholy distractions meant he never played at home. He decided to wait and watch a bit to refresh his knowledge of the game before he risked his hard-earned, and desperately needed, money. He watched closely as the teams played hands, and after an hour, he thought he remembered the logic well enough to participate.

He filled in for one of the men that Mick and his partner were playing against. He soon realized that there was far more skill involved than he possessed. After losing two games, he decided he still had a lot to learn and excused himself. Mick proved himself to be a skillful player, even with a partner he'd never played with before this evening. He later told Jacob that many hours on the ship across the Atlantic were spent honing his card-playing skills. Once again, Jacob was impressed by the knowledge and experience of this young Irishman.

It soon became too dark to play, so the men strolled the deck, smoking, drinking, telling tales, and singing coarse songs. They watched the sun disappear into a bank of clouds, creating a beautiful display that covered the western sky. The westerly wind increased a bit in speed, keeping forward progress at around four or five knots. Jim was kept busy adjusting the sails to tack into the wind.

The friends enjoyed the splendor of the open lake and the sight of clouds moving rapidly overhead until chill winds and damp fog prompted them to seek warmth below. With only the light of a small lantern, Jacob broke out his bottle of whiskey and proposed a drink to celebrate being underway. Mick gladly agreed but suggested they should save enough for a nightcap at the end of each day of the trip until their arrival in Detroit.

"*Slainte!*" said O'Toole. "Cheers," Jacob responded, as they downed their downsized shots.

DURING THE NIGHT, THE CREW anchored off Erie as the passengers slept. At daybreak on Thursday, they proceeded slowly to the small dock. Most of the passengers, except two or three who'd seen it all before, stood on the deck and watched the bustle of activity associated with docking. After the process of securing lines was completed, three men got off and a family boarded. Three young kids, eyes wide with excitement, ran around the deck to check out the amazing scene that lay before them. Jacob overheard the father tell the oldest child, a boy about six years old, that he was responsible for the safety of his two little sisters.

Being an eldest son himself, Jacob smiled at the memory of his father having assigned him this same responsibility. Since the stop was meant to be very quick, passengers headed for further destinations stayed on board. The skipper said that the stop in Cleveland early the next morning would be a bit longer, allowing passengers to leave the ship. The journey west along the coast was uneventful, though a freshening cool wind from the northwest required a close watch on the wheel and sails. Jacob and Mick spent the day talking, firming up their plans, and reading old newspapers that other passengers had brought onto the boat. Jacob regretted reading two articles in one journal: one story reported that a storm in the Mediterranean Sea the prior year had sunk one hundred vessels, and another article was about a sloop called the *Acorn,* which sank off Nova Scotia during a storm, taking 115 with it.

While walking on the deck, Jacob encountered the father and his young son standing at the gunwale, gazing at the lake. Approaching, he introduced himself and began a conversation with them. He found that their story was like so many others he'd heard in the past week. The couple, John and Anne Carter, left John's parents' small farm in the Pennsylvania mountains, where conditions were similar to what Jacob had left behind in Vermont. Jacob and John alternately laughed and groaned as they compared stories of carrying stones, cutting large trees with an axe, and plowing fields of rock. The youngster, who introduced himself as James, listened in silence. He was old enough to understand that something of great significance was happening in his life, but too young to fully comprehend the consequences.

After a half hour, Jacob noticed that James was getting bored and asked him if he wanted to play at being a pirate, saying that he had a friend who knew all about pirates. James shouted his approval, and Jacob went to the cabin and brought world-famous Pirate O'Toole back with him. They soon took over the deck with pirate talk, imaginary sword fights, and forcing hapless pretend victims to walk the plank. Jacob and Mick got a kick out of acting like kids, and young James enjoyed himself immensely. Being on a real sailboat in the role of a pirate was a memory he would carry for years. After the excitement ended, Jacob followed up with a lively tune on the fiddle to the surprise and delight of everyone on board.

Order was restored to the deck at dusk, and James went with his family to eat supper. Jacob and Mick relaxed in the cool breeze, contentedly concluding that life was good. Well after dark, they ended the day with another nightcap on deck, watching high clouds come out of the west before scuttling across the nearly full moon. Both of them, familiar with weather patterns, knew that rain was heading their way.

Friday morning dawned cloudy and cool, with a moderate wind from the northwest. The ship arrived at the unimproved port in Cleveland, skillfully making its way to the dock. Captain Miles seemed ill at ease and stated that he wanted to be underway again as soon as the cargo was transferred and a new passenger had boarded. Shore leave was going to be kept short. Jacob and Mick made their way to a shop where they replenished their supplies of food. They walked the main street of the small town and went back to the shore area to watch the other boats on the bay. Like at Buffalo, the lake was bustling with watercraft in motion everywhere they looked. Waterways were the main highways for the growing nation. The movement of people, products, produce, and every manner of supplies depended on a fascinating variety of watercraft. The clamor of crowds and workers along the water's edge at small but rapidly growing port cities along inland waterways added an exotic aspect to the mostly empty American landscape.

After boarding, the process of pulling away from the dock was repeated, with the wind and waves making the job more difficult. To avoid the rocky shallow area near the shore, the boat sailed further out into the lake. Waves of steel-gray water broke against the starboard side as the ship sailed west, and travelers could see whitecaps breaking on the rocks just offshore about a mile away. As the day went on, the wind picked up speed in the gathering gloom, and the effect of the waves on the boat became more noticeable. The captain seldom left the deckhouse, and Jim and the other two crew members made frequent adjustments to the lines and sails.

The passengers stayed below for the most part because the rocking motion of the deck made it nearly impossible to walk about. Cool, windy conditions made lounging in the open air ill-advised. By midafternoon, significantly higher wind speeds brought bands of horizontal rain, making it unwise to remain on deck. The captain ordered passengers to remain in their cabins for their safety. Jacob and Mick fretted in their compartment, wishing that the trip, heretofore so enjoyable, would come to an end. Their stomachs were queasy, and neither man could even think about eating supper. They decided against a nightcap, because as O'Toole declared, there was little to celebrate about the day that was just ending. The unspoken truth was that neither man believed they could hold down a shot and did not want to risk getting sick in front of the other.

On Friday night, the storm raged, and there was little sleep or rest to be had.

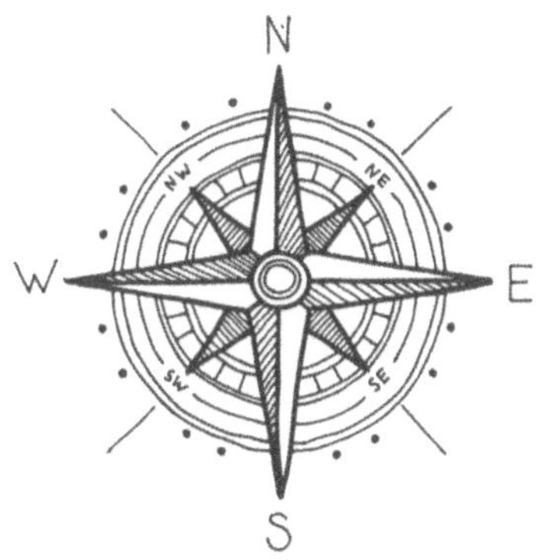

Chapter 6

WHEN DAWN FINALLY BROKE, THE scene that the passengers and crew witnessed was one of torrential rain, strong wind, and whitecaps breaking all around them. A veil of fog and rain limited visibility to a couple hundred yards at the most.

The travelers may not have fully grasped the danger they were in, but the captain was all too aware. He already decided against going to Sandusky as scheduled, because negotiating through the islands and rocky reefs off the Marblehead Peninsula was now too treacherous to attempt. Captain Miles pondered whether he should find a safe anchorage and wait out the storm or attempt to go north of the many islands that lay north of Sandusky Bay to get to open water. The northwesterly wind convinced him that anchoring in the shallow water near shore was not a safe option. He was all too familiar with the many ship carcasses littering Lake Erie after having been blown ashore, hitting hidden rocks, or running aground on treacherous, shifting sand bars hid under shallow water near the shore. Many more, he knew, were in the depths of the lake having been sunk by monster waves.

With what visibility he had, Captain Miles made the decision to head north northwest to skirt the islands. Sailing directly into the teeth of the wind tested the captain and crew's skills to the utmost. All through the day, the ship zigzagged its way into relentless waves and wind, the captain desperate to pass the islands before dark. Experience told him that a last-ditch attempt to ride out the storm by dropping anchor was their worst possible option. They must keep going. He was also aware that they would soon be sailing blind in perilous waters.

Hour after distressing hour, the ship fought against the forces of wind and water. Each wave lifted it high, only to drop it precariously into the inevitable trough that followed. The wind blew water across the ship in sheets of spray, keeping passengers below deck, protected from the rain and out of the way of the crew. By nightfall, the captain reckoned he had sailed far enough north to pass by the islands, and that he could turn to a westerly course. The light of a full moon was powerless against the thick clouds and rain, limiting visibility to a few yards. The small schooner groaned and creaked as 10-foot waves attacked from every angle.

By now, everyone on board was aware of the danger. They faced it in a variety of ways, ranging from prayer to liquor. Captain Miles hoped that daylight on Sunday would bring some relief, both from the intensity of the storm, and from his inability to determine their true location. With the waves pounding the ship and threatening to capsize it, the captain turned to a southwesterly direction, hoping to lessen the force of the waves on the ship. He concluded that he was left with only one option: "running" with the storm, heading south with the wind and waves at his stern. Miles knew that this maneuver would take them well off course, and that running with a storm had its own unique dangers, but he felt there was no option. The ship moved swiftly with the wind, reducing the risk to the bow, but shifting the danger to the stern. Waves washing over the rear of the boat increased the possibility of it being swamped, the most common consequence of this maneuver.

Jacob contemplated going onto the deck to escape the confines of the dreary compartment in steerage that smelled of years' worth of stale urine and vomit. In his cramped cabin, the sound of creaking wood beams made doom seem more imminent. The worrying sounds of the ship being tested to its limits were amplified in the enclosed space, and fear grew in the dark like an infection. Mick was stoic, claiming he experienced worse conditions sailing across the Atlantic. He said he would rather ride out the storm below deck, rather than face the wind and rain topside. Jacob was not fooled by his companion's false swagger. He assumed that the Gaelic phrases he heard Mick muttering were prayers.

In addition to needing fresh air, Jacob decided that if he was about to be sent to a watery grave, he wanted to face Neptune man-to-god to show he was not afraid. He was scared to death, of course, but it did not do for a 20-year-old mountain man, off to start a new life, to show fear. The Vermonter decided that fear of the unknown was more frightening than seeing the storm for himself, so he made his way onto the rain-lashed deck. For the sake of pride, he also wanted to be sick in private, knowing it was imminent.

After vomiting over the gunwale, Jacob crawled back to the center of the deck. With his arms wrapped tightly around the base of the forward mast, he stared at the waves ahead of them as wind and rain continued to push them from behind. While the force of the waves was frightening, it was the sudden feeling of falling into the watery depths that immediately followed, when the ship plunged into a trough, that was the worst. All that could be seen were walls of water on either side. As unpleasant as it was on the deck, he craved the fresh air. His stomach was in revolt, and his head ached in a manner he had never experienced. Any thoughts of pursuing the life of a sailor were extinguished.

Jim and another crew member, both accustomed to walking on a wet, bucking deck, hustled to secure sails on the masts before they were torn to shreds. Spotting Jacob on the deck, Jim shouted at him, trying to be heard above the wind.

"What the bloody hell are you doing, Jacob? Get below deck to your goddamned cabin! The captain said no one can be up here. You're in the way and are gonna be washed overboard!"

"I'll be okay, Jim. Don't worry about me. I will stay out of the way."

Jacob's muffled response held no conviction. He figured that Jim probably could not hear him anyway, and he didn't care. In fact, he cared about extraordinarily little at that moment, except how terrible he felt. No one had warned him about the reality of seasickness, and it wasn't something he thought about when preparing for his trip. His life in the rocky fields of Vermont did not prepare him for such wretchedness. As sick as he felt, he lacked the energy needed to be heard above the din of the wind and flapping sails, or to care anymore.

"If I fall overboard don't worry about me. At least this misery will end…" he said to only himself.

Being on the deck made the threat understandable, and Jacob at least felt some control over his destiny, even though it was clear what that fate was likely to be. He was certain his short, hard life would end that day in late May 1832, in the watery depths of Lake Erie during a spring storm. *What the hell did I get myself into*? he thought, wishing that he could get off the boat and walk back home.

Jacob did his best to maintain an appearance of composure as another massive wave broke over the bow. The ship lurched and wallowed in the void following the wave, almost capsizing as the wind relentlessly churned the water. He tried to reach the leeward side of the sailboat in search of a safer place to empty his stomach, but before he could get halfway to the gunwale, he fell to his hands and knees on the slippery deck. Abandoning all attempts at proving he was the equal to the storm's fury, he crawled on all fours to the rail and lost the last of what little food he had forced down an hour earlier. Never had he felt so helpless. Leaning against the rail, Jacob allowed breaking waves to wash over him—he was already soaked to the bone, so it hardly mattered. The chilly water swept away some of the nausea and helped clear his mind.

The wind caused the furled sails on the rear mast to pull loose and flap wildly. The captain, fearing that the sail would be ripped to shreds, ordered Jim to secure the sail. Jacob was shocked when he saw Jim begin to climb the mast on the rope ladder, which was also whipping in the wind. Near the top of the mast, Jim gained a foothold on the wet crosstree, holding onto the mast with one arm while untangling the rope and reaching for the canvas sail with the other. Jim's actions high above the deck were frightening to watch.

Jacob watched in amazement, captivated by his friend's skill and courage. *Not for a thousand dollars would I do that*! Jacob thought. His admiration turned to horror as he witnessed Jim slip and fall, screaming with flailing arms desperately trying to grasp anything within reach during his twenty-foot plummet. At the last moment he looked at Jacob with terror-filled eyes, as his body hit the wood deck with the gut-wrenching sound of breaking bones. Silence followed while the captain and Jacob stared in mute shock. Jacob arrived at the same time as the captain to Jim's lifeless body. After confirming that Jim was dead, the captain ordered the other crewmen to cover Jim's body. Jacob was shocked speechless. He'd never witnessed someone die before, and never imagined seeing someone die in such a horrible manner. Seeing the life of a young man like himself slip away so easily left him in a state of utter dismay. He knew that the look of terror in Jim's eyes would haunt him for years to come.

There was no time to grieve. The captain ordered another crew member to get some spare canvas, then asked Jacob to inform other passengers of the accident. When the crewman arrived back on deck with the material, the captain instructed him to wrap Jim's body in it and to secure it with ropes, preparing the body for a burial at sea. There was no option. While this was taking place, Jacob went below to tell Mick what happened.

"*Dia leat*," Mick whispered, tears in his eyes. Jacob then told other passengers about the incident and of Jim's planned burial at sea later that day.

The captain resumed his duties at the wheel to attempt to save the ship and passengers. As the storm slowly abated, the captain rejoiced inwardly as the gift of light spread across the water. Though the sun was still hidden behind storm clouds, enough daylight broke through the gloom to enable him to visually check for signs of islands or reefs. Soundings showed that they were in waters deep enough to safely navigate, so the captain continued the southerly course. Captain Miles knew that the western portion of Lake Erie was shallower than the central and eastern sections, rarely exceeding twenty-five feet, so the feeling of safety was tenuous at best. Reefs, rocks, and sand bars could appear at any time. It seemed to the captain that the wind had shifted and was now primarily from the north.

Jacob and Mick made their way back to the cabin where they sat in speechless grief over the sudden death of a young man who had quickly become a friend. Both knew that Jim's death was not an isolated occurrence; it reflected the dangerous situation that affected all of them. Mick's usual upbeat smile had disappeared, replaced by a worried look. He was all too aware of their precarious situation and did not hold out much faith that the small ship could stay afloat much longer. It would soon either be swamped by the waves, suffer structural damage, or hit a rock. He had little hope for any other outcome.

The physical misery of seasickness added an additional layer of grief to their plight, and once again water and bread, this time with a piece of salt pork, comprised their noon meal.

They spent the afternoon mostly in silence, or unsuccessfully trying to read. Jacob felt it was the longest afternoon of his life. When the appointed time arrived that evening, the remaining two crew members slipped Jim's wrapped body overboard while the captain and Jim's two friends stood as honor guards. The other adult passengers paid their respects to the brave young man.

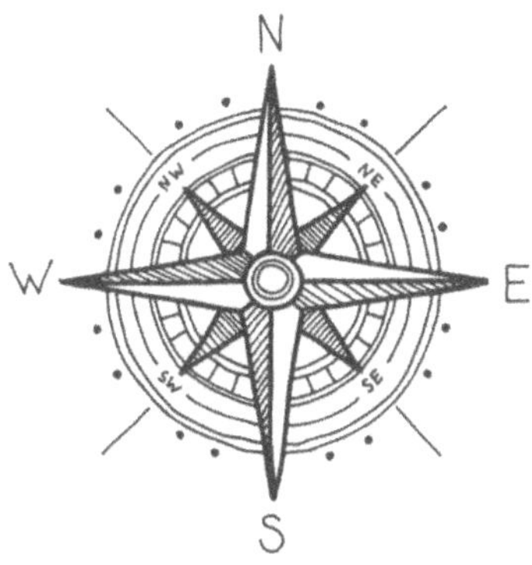

Chapter 7

DARKNESS ARRIVED, ADDING TO THE gloom. Dozing off for a few minutes was the best rest they could hope to get before a jolt or sudden turn of the ship brought reality into sharp focus. Sheer fatigue caused both men to finally slip into a deep sleep well after midnight.

The sensation of flying through the air awakened Jacob with a start, followed by a painful crash into the bulkhead. Stunned, Jacob began to crawl along the floor, unable to stand due to the tilted floor beneath him. Everything was strewn about, collected at the lower edge of the angled floor, making movement even more difficult. Jacob immediately knew that their worst nightmare had occurred. Shouts all around him confirmed that it was not just a bad dream. A child's screams could be heard nearby. Though Jacob could not see Mick in the darkness, he could hear him cursing. He crawled to the hatchway door and tried to open it but found it jammed shut. In the blackness, panic crept into his mind. He fought hard to control the terror of being trapped in a sinking ship. He called to Mick for help with the door, but even together they could not budge it. The sounds of yelling and pounding on doors echoed through the walls, filling them with dread. If other passengers and crew were also trapped—or worse—who would come to their rescue?

Jacob and Mick moved along the slanted floor in the dark, scrambling over their scattered belongings and using the inner bulkhead for support. After a minute of checking out their living space, they leaned against the wall to ponder their situation and devise a plan. They could tell that the ship was at a standstill, only moving with a slight rocking motion rather than wallowing in the waves. Since the floor of their compartment was dry, and there was no water leaking through the bulkhead, they concluded that they were not sinking; at least not yet. They agreed that they must have hit a rock or the shore, and if that was the case, they might be close to land. In the black gloom of the cabin, they dared to grasp onto a slim thread of hope. With hope came a plan for survival.

They dug through the debris on the floor until each found two critical items; their boots and the large knives they carried in their gear. With these, they splintered and pried the door ajar enough to grasp the edge. Pulling with all their might, they opened it wide enough to crawl through. In the cargo storage area, they found almost total demolition, with barrels broken open and boxes and crates in a jumble. Most of the contents were spread on the floor, making it difficult to crawl on all fours.

After moving just a few feet through the darkness, they heard pounding and yells from the adjacent cabin. Making their way to the door, they kicked as hard as they could until the door budged, and between their pushing and the occupants pulling, it finally gave way. They then went to the berth where they knew James's family was and could hear shouts and pounding. With a heavy bar Mick found on the floor, they pried and pounded on the door until the edge board cracked and finally gave way. Between the two friends and the father, they got the door open enough for the entire family to escape. Jacob found himself giving James a hug before moving on.

Moving cargo and debris out of their way in the dark was difficult and dangerous work. Eventually, the remaining trapped passengers were reached and freed. The young family that boarded with them at Buffalo was the last to be located, and the two small children cried in terror despite their mother's best effort to console them. Several passengers were injured, but everyone was alive.

A promising sunrise added a strong dose of irony as the last of the passengers below deck were located and freed. The injured were laid in an area cleared of debris and made as comfortable as possible. Jacob and Mick encouraged other passengers to locate essential items, such as boots, extra clothing, and water and food. A few men then made their way up top and observed a scene that made their hearts stop. One mast had snapped in two, the top half hanging precariously over their heads by a tangle of ropes. It swayed and creaked in the wind. The canvas sails were torn, waving in useless tatters.

After looking for crew members, they found Captain Miles and a crewman in the bow. The captain was bleeding badly from a severe injury to his head. One of his legs was badly broken, with bones visible through the skin. He was incoherent and moaning in pain as the crew member cradled his head in his lap. The young sailor was frightened and desperate. He asked them to find bandages for the captain and help set his leg. He also mentioned that the other sailor might have fallen overboard when the boat ran aground and pleaded with them to find the missing youth.

Jacob, Mick, and other passengers were confident they had not missed the lost crewman when they searched the hold earlier, so they quickly searched all portions of the deck. Finding nothing, the passengers frantically scanned the water around the boat. Even though the weather was less severe and visibility better than the day before, it was clear that no one who fell into the water in the blackness of night, with the wind and waves pushing everything in its path away from the boat, could have survived. They circled the boat multiple times searching the choppy waters for any sign of life. After a half hour, the searchers gave up hope of finding the young man alive.

The hunt for the lost sailor made the cause of the ship's sudden stop clear. The water around the boat was a murky brown and waves continued to stir up silt from the bottom. They had clearly run aground on a sand bar or mud flats. A passenger named Tom said he'd sailed Lake Erie before, and he declared to those standing nearby that it was fortunate to have hit bottom in the mud, as the boat would have been ripped open if they hit rocks. As it was, initial appearances suggested that while the boat was too damaged to ever leave its current location, at least it was not in immediate danger of capsizing. From the vantage point of the deck, however, it was also all too obvious that powerful waves continued to pound the ship. It was just a matter of time before the craft broke apart.

IN THE GROWING DAYLIGHT, A glimmer of hope became visible through the foggy haze. An unmistakable shadow on the southern horizon hinted at land two or three miles away. Under the current conditions, it might as well have been ten miles, but the survivors held onto the hope that if the boat didn't break up in the ebbing storm, they would be able to reach land once it subsided. The ship's rowboat was lashed to the deck, and inspection showed that it survived with only minor damage. The small boat could be launched in calmer conditions and used to transport everyone to safety in a series of relays. In the meantime, there were injured people to tend to, the captain chief among them.

Almost everyone on board suffered non-life-threatening cuts and bruises, but two men below deck complained of significant pain and were badly bleeding. The survivors decided to move everyone onto the deck so that a full inventory of passengers could be made and ensure that no one else was missing or required immediate medical attention. Despite the tilt, it was easier to treat injuries on deck in the light. A makeshift tent was erected with pieces of the ripped canvas sail to provide a relatively dry place to work. The improvised structure kept most of the wind and lightly falling rain off the passengers, adding a measure of comfort.

Captain Miles and the two most seriously injured men from below deck were carried to the shelter for attention. Since there was no one on board trained in medicine, teams of passengers did their best to bandage the worst cuts on the three men to stop the bleeding. One of the men had a broken arm, so the passengers with the most skill and courage undertook the painful task of setting both his arm and the captain's broken femur. The helpers experienced almost as much trauma as the victims as they carefully set the broken bones. There was nothing they could do to alleviate the pain of the injured men.

Years of independent living on rural farms or small villages meant that most of the passengers had gained basic medical skills from experience. They knew how to take care of cuts, bruises, and various maladies, but setting broken bones exceeded their abilities.

A person did not have to be a seasoned sailor to realize that the ship could soon begin breaking up below the water line. Everything below deck was in danger of being ruined by water. With the injured attended to, the remaining passengers gathered to discuss their next move. The captain was in no condition to continue command, and the young crewman did not attempt to assume control. A plan quickly evolved. It was agreed that food and water must be gathered from below and brought to a safe location. Other supplies necessary for survival such as clothing, blankets, tools, guns, and powder and shot needed to be located and brought topside near the rowboat.

Passengers whose injuries prevented them from rummaging

in the cramped darkness below stayed topside to protect the children and the injured from the many potential dangers on the slippery, tilted deck. The other men went below to begin gathering belongings and, hopefully, clean water from the scuttlebutt. Though Lake Erie is fresh water and could be drunk in an emergency, everyone was aware of the sickness that would almost certainly result. Jacob and Mick made their way back to their compartment.

As soon as they reached the lower level, their heart skipped a beat—two or three inches of water had already gathered in the lowest portion. In the darkness, they used their sense of touch to gather all their belongings and carry them topside. Jacob was thrilled to find his violin undamaged. They then went back down to help others and to search the storage area for food and other supplies. Finding a lantern that was not ruined in the accident allowed them to shine some light in the dark hold, making the gathering of food and supplies easier. The light also allowed them to finish the search for the missing sailor in the event he was below deck at the time of the accident. Unfortunately, the young man was not located.

Every time the boat shifted slightly due to the waves, passengers were reminded of the seriousness of their situation. Even small movements were amplified inside the hold, while on deck, the dangling mast swayed ominously overhead with each wave or gust of wind.

It was midafternoon by the time they had brought as many supplies and personal belongings as could be salvaged onto the deck. Pieces of spare canvas and burlap from below were used to cover the possessions from the light mist. Passengers gathered to distribute food and water and to make plans. The worst of the storm was over, but fog, light rain, and a moderate wind still plagued them. As evening twilight ended the long, difficult day, thoughts turned to how best to survive the upcoming darkness.

It was agreed that, for safety, everyone should sleep under the protection of makeshift canvas tents on the deck. There was a fear that if the wood structure of the ship suddenly gave way below the water line, the hold would quickly fill with water, trapping anyone sleeping there. Moving about on the slanted deck was difficult but manageable at its current angle. Everyone silently hoped that the boat would not lean further or break up until they could attempt their escape—which would be the next day if their plans, and the weather, held true.

Providence gave their escape plan a seal of approval as the morning dawned bright and clear. A slight wind out of the north on the back side of the storm system blew away the fog that had plagued them for so long. The waves were still higher than normal, but not dangerously so. The broad and high-walled rowboat, designed for use in near-shore areas where waves were a near constant presence, could manage them with little trouble. The shoreline that had looked so distant yesterday in the mist loomed closer in the bright sun. This increased the confidence of the passengers that they could make more than just one trip during the day, shuttling everyone and their portable possessions to safety.

Passengers decided that the two men most familiar with handling boats and with some knowledge of the lake would make the first trip. The two men chosen for this exploratory trip were Tom and Mick O'Toole. Basic survival supplies were to be the only other passenger on that first trip. The two-fold goal of the exploration was to try to determine their location, and to find a safe spot on shore to which they could eventually transport passengers and belongings.

They lowered the heavy boat with the use of ropes, being careful to ensure it did not take on water. The crewman secured the rope ladder used to scale the side of the ship in place. The attitude of the *Aurora* made it more difficult than normal to use the ladder and to load supplies in the rowboat, but eventually the workers were successful. Mick and Tom climbed down the precarious rope ladder and took their places at the oars. The passengers wished them good luck and a speedy return as they began the trip into the unknown.

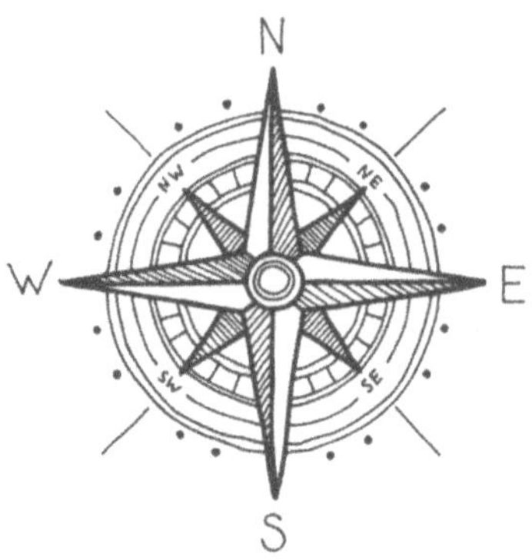

Chapter 8

TOM AND MICK ROWED IN silence for hours. The slight northerly wind and wave action made the journey south to the shoreline relatively easy. As they approached the shore, they were dismayed to see nothing but swamps as far as the eye could see. Tom turned to Mick, his expression grave.

"I've got some bad news," he said. "I did not want to say anything in front of everyone back on the ship, but I'm quite certain that we are at what is called the Great Black Swamp. It is nothing but dreadful swampland for many miles, with no high land or towns, and I don't know if we need to go east or west from here to find dry land."

They had a difficult choice to make—turn and row east or head to the west along the shoreline. There was no obvious correct answer, and yet it was critical that they choose wisely. There was no dry land in the immediate vicinity they could transport passengers to. They decided to take a short break to drink some water and eat some bread and jerky while they discussed their best course of action. As he was taking a drink, Mick made a sudden jerk and turned to face west. He thought he saw smoke rising in the distance. Pointing out the smudge to Tom, they agreed that it was worth inspection. Even if it were a campsite for an Indian hunting party or trappers, at least it would mean that there must be some higher land present, and someone who might be able to help in some manner.

The men rowed with increased effort to the west. After fifteen or twenty minutes, the dark smudge took on the more definite appearance of smoke, and they continued toward it as quickly as they could. With the wind and waves no longer at their back, the work of rowing the heavy wood boat through the pounding surf became more difficult, and rest was frequently required. The appearance of the swampy shoreline remained the same, with no change in sight after two hours of rowing, but the water took on a muddy tint, indicating that they were nearing the mouth of a river. The noon sun was high overhead when they rounded a small point of land. The mouth of a large river greeted them. The smoke, now quite clear, was inland about a mile up the river. Heartened, they pulled with their remaining strength, rowing against the powerful current to the source of the smoke. The presence of fallen trees all along the shoreline of the river required that they stay near the center of the rapidly flowing stream to avoid submerged branches and tree trunks.

By midafternoon, the men arrived at a cluster of log cabins and crude buildings. They secured their boat to a wood dock that extended ten feet into the river. They noticed a flat-bottomed boat, resembling a barge but with a two-foot-tall parapet around the edge and a sail in the center, tied up to shore along the same crude boardwalk. Two long dugout canoes were tied to trees just past the dock. There were about a dozen cabins in the settlement, along with one larger building the size of a barn. Chickens ranged freely in the clearing. Behind the buildings, livestock and horses could be seen barricaded by a split rail fence. The smoke they had followed rose from a building from which they could hear the telltale pounding of a blacksmith's hammer.

Their yells brought two men out of the barn, one about fifty and the other much younger. The older man introduced himself as Joseph Baldwin. The younger man said his name was Jack, his son. Tom and Mick quickly apprised the men of the situation on the *Aurora.* As they talked, three other men, including the blacksmith, appeared out of the cabins and sheds and joined the conversation. The family of one of the men, including two small kids hiding behind their mother, stood in a nearby door-way and watched. It was clear that Joseph was the unofficial leader of the group, and he spoke on their behalf. Tom and Mick explained that they were seeking help in bringing the stranded passengers to shore before the ship broke up in the waves. They implored the men to use their watercraft to follow them back to the *Aurora* immediately. After much discussion, the settlers convinced Tom and Mick that there was no way for them to get back to their stricken vessel before nightfall. They argued that it would be much too dangerous to be caught on the lake after dark in small and unseaworthy craft, and that there was no way to locate the *Aurora* after dark.

Joseph invited them to stay at his home, the largest of the cabins, which had multiple rooms. They reluctantly agreed to spend the night in the tiny settlement, aware that those they left behind on the *Aurora* would be worried when they didn't return.

Joseph's wife greeted them, providing water and jerky to bide them over following their strenuous journey. With the pair's immediate needs taken care of, she and her children began preparations for supper.

"Welcome to the Michigan Territory and the village of Port Lawrence," Joseph said as they took seats around the crude kitchen table.

"Michigan Territory!" exclaimed Mick. "I thought we were still a long way from the Michigan Territory—that's where I plan to live. But I'm headed to Detroit, how far away is that?"

"A good distance yet, either by water or by land. But yes, this area is within the Michigan Territory too, though the governor of Ohio doesn't agree with the boundary. He wants Port Lawrence and this river mouth to be part of his state."

"Maybe just as well," Mick said. "It's seems way too swampy around here for farming."

"I disagree," Joseph responded. "Someday, this river will be a main highway bringing products from the west for shipment to the east coast of America and beyond.

"In the meantime, our small community is self-sustaining with what crops and livestock we raise. The supply of fish and wildlife around here will provide food for residents forever, and fortunes can be made from trapping and selling the fur from beavers and muskrats.

"We are also beginning to serve the needs of an increasing number of travelers who came by boat on Lake Erie with the intention of heading upriver to western Ohio, Indiana, or Illinois.

Port Lawrence will soon become the preferred jumping off point for immigrants and settlers from the east coming west on the Erie Canal and Lake Erie. Mark my words, this small village you see today will someday be a very busy place!"

Joseph went on to explain that a series of rapids lay upstream near the abandoned Fort Meigs. A small settlement called Perrysburg had formed at the rapids in recent years. From that point, he explained, improved trails through the wilderness were cut north to Detroit and west all the way to Illinois.

Joseph said that his flatboat, along with canoes belonging to other families in the settlement, were capable of being poled to the whitewater. Beyond the fort, a trail allowed settlers to continue westward journeys. When Tom heard this explanation, he asked what the name of the river was, hardly daring to believe what he hoped to hear. Joseph said it was known as the River of the Miami, but more commonly called the Maumee River. Mick had no knowledge of the stream, but Tom did, and he was surprised that they had drifted that far west in the storm. Tom had intended to get off at Sandusky and follow the new trail through the Black Swamp to the Maumee, which he would follow west—it turned out that he had already reached his destination.

After supper, the group discussed the situation and agreed that at first light, if the weather held, they would take all four vessels and go back to the *Aurora* together. Joseph's flat-bottomed boat was not made for extended use on big water, but so long as the swells were not unusually large, it could navigate the required distance without too much trouble.

They hoped for a friendly breeze to help propel the ungainly craft, as it was normally poled in shallower water than they would find farther from the lake's shore. It was agreed that with the four boats available to them, they could bring all passengers and possessions to the settlement in one trip. The craft would be heavily loaded and the undertaking successful only if the calm weather continued for two more days—one day for them to get back to the *Aurora* and then the final day when the ship would be emptied of cargo and passengers. The plan of action brightened Tom's and Mick's spirits, even though they worried about what the stranded passengers must be thinking. When the scouting team did not return that day, stranded passengers would assume they had met with disaster. If so, the fearful travelers knew that help might not arrive before the *Aurora* broke up.

Good fortune continued to be on their side as the next morning dawned clear. It was a beautiful early summer day, and the parade of vessels departed as soon as enough light was available to provide safe passage downriver to the lake. They followed the shoreline east, with Tom and Mick watching for landmarks that they'd noticed in their first passage. Scattered clouds, seemingly low enough to touch, followed them on their easterly journey, moved by a moderate northwesterly breeze on the backside of the storm. The choppy shallow waters made paddling a challenge, but because the boats were empty, they still made satisfactory progress. Upon reaching the appropriate landmark, they turned north, the sun now burning directly overhead. Paddling into the wind made their work difficult in the scorching heat.

After hours of challenging work, they could see the hulk of the crippled *Aurora* outlined on the horizon. Another hour of desperate paddling brought them close enough to hear the enthusiastic cheers of those stranded on the deck. After securing their crafts to the disabled ship, the rescuers climbed aboard on the rope ladder and received an exuberant welcome. The rowers sated their need for food and water and found some shade in which to rest and recuperate. Everyone then gathered to discuss the plan for the next day's departure. Once a strategy was agreed upon, the loading of possessions soon began so that early next morning they could embark without delay. Some offered prayers of gratitude while others opened bottles of whiskey in celebration.

Their luck held; the day of departure dawned calm and clear. The three most seriously injured men were carefully lowered onto the raft for comfort, as were the children, since it was the safest of the vessels. By now, the captain was once again lucid, though unable to be of any help with the physical work involved in the rescue. With loading completed, the frail armada set off. The heavily loaded boats proved difficult to propel, and they sat so low in the water that great care was needed to keep them from swamping. Waves broke over the bow of the canoes and rowboat, requiring frequent bailing. It was late afternoon by the time the flotilla reached the settlement. Weary passengers with cramped and sore muscles clambered onto shore, paying no mind to the deep mud and rapidly flowing water. The residents warmly welcomed them. A hearty meal of venison, fish, preserves, and freshly baked bread awaited. After eating, the children played games outside. It was a rare treat for the kids who lived at the settlement to enjoy the company of other children, and they made the most of it.

The adults broke out tobacco and spirits and relaxed as they discussed their plans for the future. As it turned out, the only ones seriously inconvenienced were Jacob and Mick. The other passengers planned to proceed west from Sandusky. Finding themselves on the Maumee River was a godsend. They could use the services that the men at Port Lawrence offered for travel by river, and upon reaching the upstream limits at the rapids, they would continue overland on a well-traveled trail. Their doomed lake voyage saved them the trouble of walking on the nearly impassable military road through the Black Swamp from Sandusky to the Maumee rapids. The easily traversable trail west of the rapids was used for centuries by Native Americans traveling from the mouth of the Maumee River to the foot of Lake Michigan for the purpose of trade and migration. By the 1830s, this path was becoming well-trodden to the point it could be considered a road. Farms and villages were springing up along the trail.

Captain Miles and the surviving crewman accepted an offer for them to stay at the settlement so the captain could finish his recuperation. His broken thigh was bothering him greatly, and he was in no condition for travel. Joseph said that it was just a matter of time before another boat arrived at the settlement from eastern lake ports. The captain and sailor would have no trouble eventually finding passage back to Buffalo and their homes.

Jacob and Mick were faced with a more difficult problem. Their plan for boat passage all the way to Detroit was not to be. Rather, they must locate a company with a boat capable of carrying them up the west shore of Lake Erie and the Detroit River, or find a way to walk to Detroit. Unbeknownst to the young men, in 1829, soldiers from Fort Shelby in Detroit finished improving the old Hull's Trace, the former military trail connecting Detroit with the Maumee River and Fort Meigs. Once Joseph brought this fact to their attention, their choice became clearer. They decided that they would accompany the other passengers to the foot of the rapids. At that point, when everyone else continued west, they would part company and follow the new trail north through the forests and swamps to Detroit.

It was settled. The flotilla of small craft would depart upstream in two days. In the meantime, workers at the settlement had other tasks to see to, and the travelers would use the time to rest and recuperate and repair belongings they salvaged from the ship.

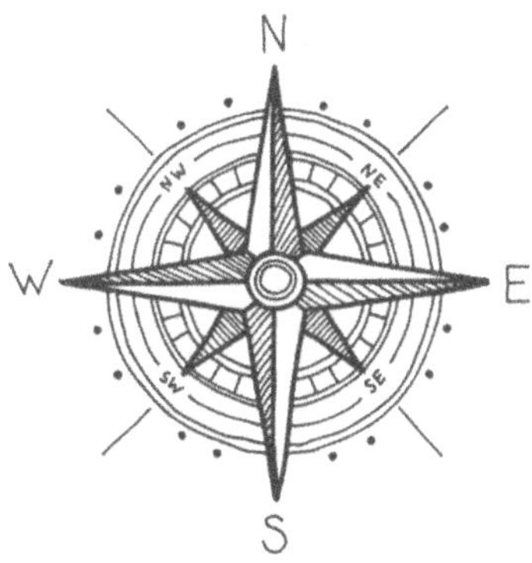

Chapter 9

IT WAS A TOUGH AND unpleasant trip upriver. Long poles were used to push the heavily laden craft against the strong current and around fallen trees and branches. After several tedious hours, the boats reached the upstream limit, pulling ashore on the north side of the river in a well-used clearing at the base of the unnavigable rapids. Across the wide river, a small blockhouse, all that remained of the fort that had played such a crucial role in the history of the region, could be seen.

The landing was a surprisingly busy location with several enterprises designed to accommodate the needs of travelers. On both shores of the rapids, livery stables with teams of horse-drawn wagons and men offering the use of flat-bottomed scows provided transport services. While westbound travelers sometimes portaged around the rapids and continued upriver, on this day, the *Aurora* passengers chose to continue their westward trek toward Illinois on the trail.

Since it was already midday, Joseph and the other river men wanted to begin the journey back to their homes as quickly as possible. The *Aurora* passengers gathered their belongings and paid the boatmen for their services. Within minutes, the flatboat and canoes were floating downstream, allowing the current to carry them back to their homes.

The two friends bade heartfelt farewells to their companions from the *Aurora,* hoisted their heavy packs, and walked into the small bustling waterside village. The remaining passengers made their way to the livery stables to arrange transport to the west.

In the settlement, a large house served double duty as a tavern and hotel, providing lodging if a person did not mind sharing a large bed or sleeping on the floor. The tavern also housed a postal station where letters could be dropped for the weekly mail service linking this portion of the country to points east. Once again, Jacob was surprised at the amount of development and bustle in a remote area. America was on the move, and he felt closer to his future than ever.

Both men had been under the assumption that the seventy-mile trek on the military plank road to Detroit would have to be on foot. They had no idea how many businesses were already in place to transport people and goods to the west or north. The tavern seemed an appropriate place to talk about plans while enjoying a beer and some food. While there, Jacob also posted another letter. The thought that a letter could be delivered from this remote location all the way to his former home in Vermont was difficult to imagine after his recent experience on Lake Erie.

The pair thought that it best to get to Detroit as quickly as possible. Once there, final plans would have to be made. For

Jacob's sake, he knew that he would have to find employment before venturing into the interior to locate farmland. It seemed logical that the busy port city of Detroit would be the place to find such work. Mick agreed. Having little knowledge of what the territorial capital had to offer in the way of short-term employment, both lacked clear ideas as to what form their immediate future would take.

They met various locals at the tavern who offered services for travelers. After much discussion and haggling, they finally agreed on a plan. They would ride along with a teamster named John who was hauling a load of cargo to Detroit in a buckboard wagon. It would be a bone-jarring ride on the plank road, the man warned them, and without shelter from the elements. The three nights on the road would be spent camping, not at a tavern. Furthermore, the two young men were expected to help however necessary should they get stuck in mud or have other difficulties. It was the most economical option, so they agreed, though they were not fully aware of what they were agreeing to. They were to meet early the next morning.

After John left, Jacob and Mick decided to stay at the tavern a while to relax. They struck up conversations with other young men and family groups who were also heading into the territory. They both awed the crowd with stories about their shipwreck adventures. Descriptions of their friend Jim's skills and bravery were highlighted to the amazement of all.

After a couple drinks, Mick declared that it was time to sing some songs in honor of Jim and the captain of the good ship *Aurora*. Jacob unpacked his fiddle and played while Mick sang with his distinctive tenor brogue. Once again, people in the tavern enjoyed the music, applauding and stamping their boots on the hardwood floor. After Mick finished singing all the songs he knew, Jacob continued playing. Mick took advantage of his celebrity status and approached a young lady who was part of a family group. Mick asked her if she would like to dance, not expecting the angry response of a well-dressed man who turned out to be her brother. He grabbed Mick by the shirt, pushing him away and nearly knocking him down.

"My sister ain't dancing with no goddamn Paddywhack!" he yelled, making a drunken ineffective swing to punctuate his point.

The drunkard quickly realized his mistake when Mick regained his footing and swung a hard fist at his jaw. It knocked him off his feet and he tumbled backward, falling over a table filled with patrons eating their supper. This got more people in the fray, yelling, pushing, and swinging at anyone they did not know. Mick found the culprit who had started it all and, lifting him off the floor, threw him hard against the wall. This was followed by two lightning-fast swings of the fist which laid the man out on the floor. Others, seeing his anger and fighting skills, opened a path as Mick made his way back to their table, giving a nod and sly smile to the young lady as he passed. Her knowing smile in return made him regret even more that her obnoxious brother ruined what could have been a memorable ending to an enjoyable evening. As it was, he and Jacob agreed that it was best if they left the tavern.

Shaking his head as they departed, Jacob asked, "What do you think that guy's problem was, strong drink or a weak mind?"

"A bit of both, no doubt. He surely wouldn't have said what

he did without the whiskey providing the courage. But he'll be talking with an accent now too, since one of his teeth is laying on the floor back there!"

They were still laughing about the turn of events as they found a place to camp on the edge of nearby woods, away from the bustle of the village. It turned out to be the best option anyway, given the warm early June night. They agreed that their facilities were much better than the smoky tavern, where they would have had to use valuable funds to spend the night lying on a hardwood floor amongst the loud talking, snoring, and farting of other guests.

"Well," said Jacob, "as we start off on this next portion of our journey, it's fitting that we begin it with a toast to our friend Jim. May he find happiness in his new home. And to our future lives, wherever they may lead."

He got the whiskey bottle from his pack. Holding it high, he said, "May fate be kind," and they shared what remained.

It was the first time in two weeks the friends were alone. The peace and quiet of the setting were powerful medicine to soothe damaged nerves. The sound of the wind in the trees, the haunting call of a whippoorwill, and the hum of insects provided a relaxing backdrop. The howl of a distant wolf reminded them that they were on the edge of the wilderness. The presence of wolves brought back a memory for Jacob. He recalled that years earlier, his father had killed a wolf and taken the dead animal somewhere to collect a twenty-dollar bounty—a substantial amount of money. He wondered if there was a similar bounty for wolves in the Michigan Territory. It would be another source of money to consider.

Just before sunset, they witnessed the fascinating breeding dance of the timberdoodle in a clearing near their camp. A peenting male bird flew high into the air, then plummeted straight down to within a few feet of the ground, at which point it flew upward again—all to impress a well-concealed but observant female bird. Though Jacob witnessed the mesmerizing ritual many times in Vermont, it was a first for Mick, who was spellbound.

LOUD NOISES AND SHOUTING MEN woke the friends at sunrise. There was much clamor as teamsters hitched their teams of horses and oxen to wagons and buggies. Jacob was amazed to see one large, heavily loaded wagon pulled by a team of four oxen heading west. They ate a quick breakfast and packed their gear in the dim light of a foggy dawn. Anxious to begin the final portion of their journey, they made their way to the agreed-on location to meet John. Sure enough, he was almost ready to leave. His wagon loaded, he was in the final stages of hitching up the team. They paid John the agreed-upon amount and threw their possessions onto the wagon.

The road north was an eye-opener for both men. It was clearly a road built with the future in mind. A hundred-foot swath of forest had been cut down. In swampy areas, tree trunks called stringers were laid along the roadway, with rough-cut planks nailed across them, making the route passable, if not smooth. Teams of horses or oxen could not have pulled wagons of freight through the mud and standing water without the tree trunk base and board surface. Even in its improved condition, it was a rough ride at best. Jacob and Mick both would have preferred to walk rather than ride on the bone-jarring wagon, but the horses were traveling slightly faster than they could walk. Frequent problems also kept them busy and worn out.

Rotten or broken boards resulted in traps in which wagon wheels would slip into, requiring much effort to lift, pry, and push to get rolling again. Wood spokes sometime broke when an uneven plank was encountered. They spent as much time prying, lifting, and pushing the cart, or fixing a broken wheel, as sitting on the wagon. The young travelers began to think that when they agreed to help to lower their cost, they seriously underestimated the amount of labor involved. Clouds of mosquitoes were a constant irritation. *At least there were not any bugs during the storm on the lake*, Jacob sourly thought to himself.

In areas of dry ground, the earthy surface was leveled and tree stumps were removed, making a relatively smooth roadway. Jacob could not help but wonder what the dirt stretches were like after a heavy rain. The occasional deep rut in the road provided evidence. Clearings along the road, with newly constructed cabins and barns, gave an indication of the amount of settlement already taking place in the territory. Both young men were pleased with the quality of the soil they saw along the road—it was dark and fertile.

In the quiet of the morning, with only the sound of the horses' hooves and abundant flocks of crows to distract them, they discussed many topics. The teamster explained that the road net-work was meant to ensure the future security of this remote area, which was only quite recently restored to American sovereignty following the war with Britain. The road clearly accomplished its purpose of allowing quick transport if needed for military purposes. It also brought settlers, businesses, and growth to the area. The number of people they encountered on the trail—on foot, on horseback, or families in wagons with a few precious belongings—astounded both of them. Jacob wondered if there would be any land left to purchase by the time he settled down.

Late on the second afternoon, they arrived at the village of Monroe on the western shore of Lake Erie. John said he would be there for two hours to unload some cargo and pick up addi-tional crates destined for Detroit. The friends took advantage of the time to cool off and clean up. They bathed and washed their dirty clothes in the River Raisin, finding a secluded area just west of the village, upstream of the tannery. They then walked around the small town of about a thousand residents. It was a day of surprises. The first was the sight of a steamship heading north about a mile offshore. The plume of black smoke from the ship's tall smokestack trailed behind the boat, visible for miles. The number of Monroe residents who spoke French also came as a shock. They learned that until 1817 the town was called Frenchtown because of its many French-Canadian settlers. It was another bustling settlement on the frontier, with two grist mills and three sawmills busily meeting the needs of a growing population.

They saw John's wagon parked at one of the sawmills where he was off-loading needed parts. He said that the process of unloading crates and picking up additional cargo from other sources was taking longer than expected. Jacob assumed that John would be frustrated at the interruption in his schedule, but he appeared in good spirits. John told them they would be on their own for the rest of the day and that night. When John said he was going to spend the night with a friend, the reason for his positive attitude became clear. They took their belongings back to the secluded location on the river and set up camp, then walked back into town.

Once again, they came across a home doing double duty as a tavern and crude inn. A faded sign on the front proclaimed it as the *Presidential Inn.* Going in for a beer and some stew, Jacob inquired about the name, thinking that such a bold name had to have a story behind it. The homeowner's wife assured them that President Monroe himself indeed stopped there when he visited his namesake village about fifteen years earlier.

Their surprises continued when they were offered muskrat for meat by the woman's husband. He explained that eating "marsh rabbits" saved many from starvation during the war and had become a standard fixture. Extensive swamps surrounding the village provided a bountiful supply of the animals. Their education continued when the host told them stories of a deadly battle that occurred near the town during the war. Strong feelings of resentment clearly still existed in the minds of many residents against the British and their Indian allies. Reports of the troubles in Illinois and west of Lake Michigan opened old emotional wounds from a massacre that had occurred here twenty years earlier.

At sunset, the friends made their way back to their campsite, where nature was fully on display. The river seemed alive as uncountable numbers of fish flies rose from the surface, attracting predators. The slurping sound of countless fish ingesting flies on the water's surface sounded eerily ghostly in the quiet dusk. Ducks and geese joined the feast. Occasional splashes spoke of beavers and otters, animals that were the original reason this area had been explored. The sounds of the wild, so close to a growing town, provided evidence of how superficial development still was on the frontier.

The haunting call of a nearby loon awakened the friends early, as the eastern sky was brightening. A morning fog enveloped them in its damp chill, requiring jackets to be dug out of their packs. Starting a fire and boiling water for coffee was their first priority. After they had drank their morning elixir they ate some jerky and broke camp.

Carrying their possessions, they again walked into town. Since few residents were up and about yet, they walked all the way to the lakeshore to wait for John. On the shore, they witnessed a magnificent sunrise over the waters of Lake Erie. The sun was almost blinding as it reflected off the slowly rolling waves. Seagulls noisily squabbled as they fought over small fish and bits of nourishment that had washed ashore overnight. A sailing vessel, sails fully deployed but hanging slack in the early morning calm, seemed stationary offshore. It was heading north, to Detroit, or perhaps to Sault Ste. Marie or the new village of Chicago on Lake Michigan.

They arrived at John's wagon just as he was getting his horses from a nearby stable. Familiar with the process, they helped hitch the team, and within a half hour they were underway again. As they traveled north, signs of settlement increased. Many new farmsteads appeared along the road, increasing in number closer to the territorial capital of Detroit. The sight of settlers cutting trees, building rough homes, clearing small fields, and burning piles of brush was common. The presence of a steady supply of horse-drawn wagons and other travelers made it clear that times were changing.

"We're none too soon," Jacob said. "The best land is being bought up."

The end of the war and apparent peace between the States and Great Britain meant that development of the Great Lakes region could move forward. Commerce and settlement were free to proceed at a rapid pace, and treaties were in place with most of the Native American tribes in the region. Government surveyors mapped the wilderness after native claims on the land were extinguished, a process that took years given the region's size and rugged nature. Progress was slow until completion of the Erie Canal. With the opening of that water highway, the resulting land rush was remarkable. As a result, Detroit quickly evolved into a bustling gateway into the upper Great Lakes region. Detroit's purpose shifted from military to business, especially commercial enterprises catering to the needs of travelers and settlers.

Upon arriving in Detroit, Jacob and Mick gathered their gear and bid John adieu. Jacob was quite surprised. He expected to find another hectic city like Buffalo, though perhaps not as large. Detroit no longer looked like the wilderness military outpost it had been for decades, but it also did not have the unruly appearance of a boom town. It was not only smaller than

Buffalo but was an overall more agreeable place. The presence of wood plank sidewalks along storefronts and the orderly layout of streets were a surprise. Despite its small size, the town was a beehive of activity. The roads and walkways were packed with people and businesses were thriving. The dirt streets were filled with horses and oxen pulling carts. Unfortunately, the presence of so many beasts of burden meant that the smell of manure, along with the resulting flies and vermin, were inescapable.

One of the new businesses that both Jacob and Mick noticed were storefronts with newly painted signs offering financial services. A sign for the government land office was prominently displayed on one of the newer buildings, with a boardwalk in front and anxious customers inside. Detroit's new primary role of serving the needs of settlers in the territory was clear, and by all appearances, the town's residents intended to capitalize on the phenomenon. Detroit in every way seemed to be a city on the brink of a grand future.

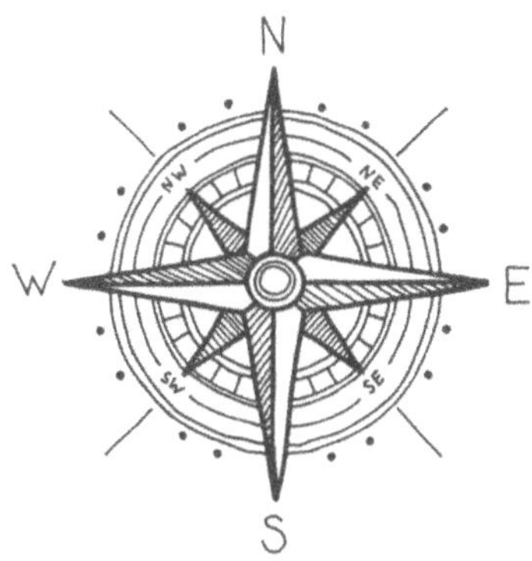

Chapter 10

WHILE RIDING ON THE WAGON from Monroe, the pair devised plans for the near term. Both knew that their actions in the coming days would affect them for years. Their immediate needs were to find work and arrange lodging. Jacob suggested finding the local newspaper office to talk to the owner about places where work might be found. He recalled that the newspaperman that printed the local flyer in Vermont seemed to know everyone and everything of importance.

They had no trouble locating the newspaper office. A new, prominently displayed sign informed the public of the existence of the paper, grandiosely called the *Democratic Free Press and Michigan Intelligencer*. It was only just established the year before. The pair entered and were surprised to find that the paper was owned by Joseph Campau and Campau's influential nephew John Williams. Teamster John mentioned Campau's name in conversation, claiming that he was one of the wealthiest and most powerful men in the territory. It seemed a fortuitous stroke of luck, as not only would these two luminaries be familiar with everything occurring in the city, but they also controlled several of the local businesses which could be potential work locations.

The businessmen viewed Jacob and Mick as just two more poor farmers seeking land in the wilds. As such, they didn't share any valuable information with them. Mick and Jacob understood that. What they were hoping to receive was information about jobs, and reliable room and board places. Their hopes were fulfilled, because Campau informed them that two large projects just got underway for which workers were needed.

"The first project," he explained, "involves excavating and installing underground sewer lines throughout the city. The rapid growth of the city and the influx of travelers makes eliminating the flow of sewage in surface trenches a high priority.

"The second project needing workers is the construction of roads approved by Congress or the Territorial Legislative Council. The road network will extend out like wagon wheel spokes from the riverfront port area. There are a number of roads in the system. They're often referred to as territorial roads, because the Territorial Legislature approved their construction and is paying for the construction. One trail already exists, heading southwest from Detroit and then west near the southern state line all the way to the growing city of Chicago. It is currently being upgraded to a more reliable roadway that can handle stagecoaches between the two cities.

"A new road, called the St. Joseph River Trail, is to go directly west, terminating at the mouth of the St. Joseph River on Lake

Michigan. The Saginaw Trail will be improved, and a road to Fort Gratiot on the lower end of Lake Huron is also in the works."

Mr. Campau explained that these government-funded priorities paid good wages, and contractors were currently hiring laborers. On the topic of government land sales, he shared that the land being made accessible by the new roads was surveyed. It would make valuable farmland and sell quickly. He advised not waiting too long to stake out the land they wanted. As a businessman knowledgeable in banking and finance matters, Campau confirmed that there was no reason to acquire all of the money needed to make a purchase from the land office. Credit, he explained, was easy and generous, even to young men with little in the way of wealth or possessions. The market for land, he told them, especially cleared land, was so strong that lenders knew they could recoup bad loans by selling defaulted parcels at a higher price.

With names of men to contact regarding a job and boarding house locations written down, the pair headed back onto the bustling streets. They were fascinated by what they saw. Detroit was a palette of change and contradiction. Mingled with well-dressed businessmen were rugged looking voyageurs and *coureurs de bois*—French Canadian traders—in from the wilds, Native Americans dressed in traditional garb, groups of immigrants recently arrived dressed in old-world styles of clothing and speaking unrecognizable languages, beggars down on their luck, and young families appearing perplexed as they hustled from one place to another. Soldiers were also present, representing a fascinating connection between the old and new. Remnants of the military presence resulting from continued distrust of British soldiers stationed across the river in Upper Canada were mixed with young soldiers brought in because of new troubles involving restive Indians on the frontier. Dust raised by horses and oxen pulling carts, and the smell of open sewers and farm animals, were inescapable. This otherworldly scene of lively frontier life fascinated Jacob.

A place to stay and safely store their belongings was the highest priority. When they stopped at the boarding houses on their list, a sense of desperation began creeping in; the first four were filled with young men chasing the same dreams as theirs. The fifth home, part of the Antoine Beaubien farmstead on the edge of town, proved successful. It was owned by a widow named Jeanne Du Bois. Unlike the newer homes being built in Detroit, this farmstead clearly had deep roots and a long history. A small, well-maintained orchard of plum, peach, and apple trees graced the property, as did a grape arbor covered with vines. It was obvious to anyone familiar with farming that this place required a lot of meticulous work to maintain. Both friends assumed that Mrs. Du Bois had a husband or hired hands to do the extensive work of operating the farm. They were shocked to learn that she ran the place by herself, her husband having died years earlier.

Two small rooms were available in her cottage. Both men felt that they were adequate for storing their belongings and for sleeping. Agreement about renting the rooms was not reached until the owner grilled the two about their intentions and their lifestyle. Mrs. Du Bois's English language skills were limited. Her lack of fluency was more than made up for by her strong opinions about many things. Inflexible attitudes and rules stood out. She clearly had disdain for newcomers she referred to as "Bostonians." These were east coast immigrants who were changing the nature of Detroit. She resented their transforming it from a village on the frontier with a lingering French influence into a busy town that was rapidly threatening her way of life. She longed for the Detroit of old. The sense of disorder that took over daily life bothered Mrs. Du Bois. The fact that she no longer knew everyone in the village like she had a decade ago made her unhappy. She was also angry about encroaching development that threatened the farm that was in her family for over fifty years.

Satisfied with the boys' agricultural background and intentions, she agreed to let them rent the rooms for an indefinite period. That hurdle having been cleared, the issue of rules came up. She listed strict rubrics that the men also had to agree to; one rule she stated in French to be sure she was clear. *"Pas de fêtes et pas de femmes dans les chambres!"* They both understood enough French to understand her rule that there were to be no parties or women in their rooms. In broken English, she also made it clear that they were responsible for their own meals.

Always the quick thinker, Mick made a suggestion that caught her off guard. What if, he proposed, they helped her take care of her farm animals, do upkeep and repair work on the small sheds and fences, and maintain the orchard and grape arbor in lieu of her providing breakfast and reducing rent by one-quarter? He knew that living alone on the small farm, performing the many difficult tasks that needed to be done every day, must have been a problem for the petite older woman, despite her strong character. He assumed she would find the task of preparing breakfast and the cost of a little income preferable to keeping up with the unending work of the farmstead. She clearly loved her small farm and keeping it operating was more important to her than accumulating wealth. She initially greeted Mick's proposal with a frown, which turned to an agreeable look reflecting cunning negotiating skills on her part as she agreed to the terms.

Jacob was elated at finding living arrangements. After a month during which he had to carry everything he owned, especially his violin, he couldn't have been happier to safely store his belongings and get started on his new routine. His feelings of thankfulness were enhanced when upon completely emptying his rucksack for the first time since leaving home, he found a handmade wool scarf tucked away in the bottom with a note attached which read: "Good Luck Chasing Your Dreams." Signed by Diana MacIntosh, Robert's mother.

With lodging arranged, a walk through town to locate key offices was the next priority. The government land office was an important stop in Jacob's mind, even if only to ensure that there were no significant changes since his meeting with an agent in Buffalo. It turned out that the land office and contractors hiring workers for road building projects were all in the vicinity of the new territorial capitol building, located near the old fort. Built just four years prior, the impressive structure signified the importance of this up-and-coming town.

Major John Biddle, the U.S. Land Office agent, confirmed that there were no noteworthy changes to the law whereby land patents were obtained, nor to the cost of the land. He did say, however, that demand for land in the Michigan Territory was growing rapidly. It was now one of the most sought-after locations on the western frontier for land purchases. A large map on the office wall depicted all available land in the surveyed southern portion of the territory. The map showed that, once away from established villages, most land was still unspoken for. Despite this, Biddle's parting words were to buy as quickly as possible because things were changing rapidly due to new roads being built into the interior. Large blocks were being purchased by speculators for resale, Biddle noted. He encouraged the use of credit if necessary, but gave a stern warning about what he called "wildcatters." He told the pair that they should only do business with banks that have established offices in Detroit, and to use notes issued by those recognized institutions as currency.

"High interest in Michigan Territory land is resulting in unscrupulous men preying on settlers who don't understand financial and legal issues, and who often can't read or write. These men are making generous offers for loans with high interest rates that often can't be paid back. They also sell notes that are worthless as money. The result is that families are losing their farms to these shysters when they cannot make a loan payment. These men travel the countryside looking for potential victims. They seek out the young and impatient, or those who are in financial trouble. Don't be fooled by them."

The friends thanked Biddle for the information and advice. As they departed, Jacob commented as to how difficult the process would be for someone who lacked any education, or who did not speak the English language.

A stop at the storefront office from which the road building projects were managed followed. Seeing the long line of men waiting to talk with the project overseers was worrisome, as the pair had no idea how many workers were being hired. They need not have worried. Once able to speak with the supervisor, they learned that workers were badly needed and that being young, dependable, and strong were the primary desired qualities. At ninety cents per day, wages were better than most other laborer jobs. Working on road projects meant living in camps that occasionally moved forward. Additional workers were being hired for the Chicago Pike, the Fort Gratiot Road, and the new St. Joseph River Road. Construction was set to begin soon on the Saginaw Trail, improving it beyond the Village of Pontiac.

Living in camps along a roadway was not exactly what either man wanted, so they spoke with other officials in the government complex. One of the men told them to talk with a Detroit city official about work. Finally locating the office, they inquired about employment.

"We are hiring people to clean the streets, removing manure and carting it away. You can start today."

Turning down that option, they inquired about other work. The man then told them about the large sewer digging project the town was about to undertake. He said that the job required laborers and stonemasons to dig and construct an underground network to carry sewage and wastewater to the river. The official said that it paid well and was a long-term project. When Jacob mentioned his prior work at a quarry, the official said that this experience would be beneficial, as the project involved tunneling through limestone bedrock. The man told him that if he qualified as a stonemason, his pay would be a dollar per day, as opposed to ninety cents for the common laborer position at which he'd start.

Given their desire to stay in Detroit long enough to earn some money and establish credit, the choice of work seemed clear. Neither looked forward to the backbreaking labor involved in tunneling, but it paid well, and work was available for as long as desired. Neither man planned to be around to witness completion of the construction project, intending to go their own ways as the owners of their farms long before then. They signed the necessary paperwork, and work assignments were made as a long and momentous day came to an end. The foreman wanted them to start the next day, but they insisted on a day to settle in. Project managers were under pressure from city officials and medical personnel to complete the sewer system as quickly as possible. It was an important long-term step for the future of a rapidly developing city.

Billowing storm clouds brought on twilight early. Thunder rumbled and lightning flashed west of town. To cap off a busy and successful day, both agreed that a celebratory beer was required. Since they were near the waterfront, and it was well known that the best pubs were on the waterfront, they decided to check out the bustling area where ships docked. Their first view of the river brought the same awe they'd felt at Buffalo. Sailboats and steamboats lined the shore at docks that seemed too flimsy for the job. Everything appeared to have been thrown together in haste. A recently arrived steamboat was still unloading passengers who appeared dazed by the dramatic changes taking place in their lives. Other ships were off-loading crates filled with the various supplies newcomers purchased in Detroit prior to setting off into the remote areas of the territory. The scene made Jacob anxious as it occurred to him that hundreds of people must be passing through Detroit every week on their way into the interior. Competition for land was going to be fiercer than he'd imagined.

A number of establishments near the water's edge were available for drinks and limited food offerings. They chose one that, based on the appearance of the men inside, seemed to cater to incoming settlers. Thinking it might be a good place to glean information, they entered just as the rain began to fall. The room was dark and smoky, too few lanterns losing the fight with the darkness brought on by the storm. The reason for the tavern's popularity was evident: cheap beer that was almost cold when served! The secret, they discovered, was a small brewery next door where they brewed the beer, then kept the barrels stored in the river where the cool water kept contents significantly cooler than the midsummer's heat. The beer was clearly a hit with customers, as reflected by the packed room.

The main topic of conversation among the patrons was the troubles with Indians near the Mississippi River. Chief Black Hawk's small revolution had caught the attention of the federal government in Washington. As a result, military reinforcements were on their way, soon to arrive at Detroit for a brief stop on their way to Lake Michigan. Rumor had it that General Winfield Scott was to arrive in a few days with reinforcements.

Though the uprising's effect in the Detroit area was negligible, the men were concerned that, if not quickly quelled, the fighting would spread. And if the troubles moved east of Lake Michigan, they feared interest rates rising, or less credit available for land purchases, if not actual bloodshed. Beyond the issue of Black Hawk's War, most conversation was about land in the territory beyond Detroit. Whether to go west or north was the question debated in many discussions. Land west of Detroit, along the Chicago Pike, had already proven to be fertile, but was any good land left? Land to the north, even all the way to Saginaw, was said to be a gamble because of the many unknowns. Was that part of the territory really malaria-infested wetlands? One man claimed to have known a friend who served at Fort Saginaw ten years earlier and warned that no one should think of staking out land in that uninhabitable swamp.

The alcohol-fueled conversations and arguments were going nowhere, so Jacob and Mick tried to find a quiet corner to talk about their plans. Given the makeup of the crowd, it was clear that no young ladies would be found to join them, and it wasn't the sort of place that would appreciate music, so talk focused on the issues of accumulating enough money and credit to allow them to pursue their land claim goals as quickly as possible. They agreed that they made the wisest choice—working on a project that would exist longer than they would need to work there, with guaranteed work and good pay.

In addition to their own plans, they had promised Mrs. Du Bois that they would start on the needed repairs on her small farm the next day. Since it was going to be a busy day, they decided that a long night's rest was wise. The walk back to their rooms in the rain was a silent period where each was deep in thought as to the future—it seemed so close that they could almost touch it.

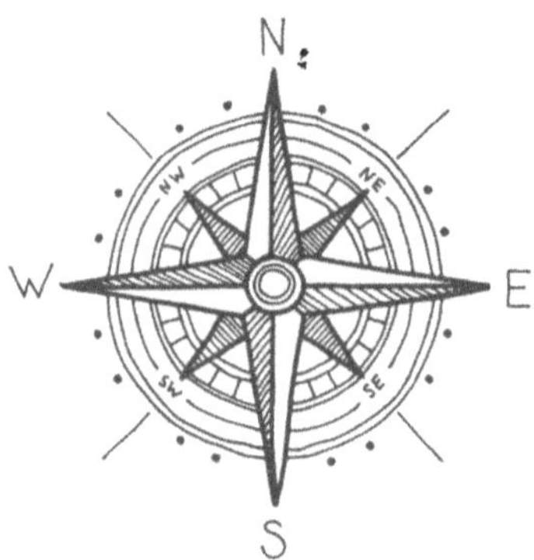

Chapter 11

THE NEXT MORNING DAWNED FRESH and clear, cleansed by the rain. After an early breakfast, they walked into town to further explore the idea of obtaining credit at a bank. Two businesses had signs identifying them as banks with loan services. The meetings at each were short, as the boys learned that they were putting the cart in front of the horse. There were two requirements before they could seek credit: earn money for at least half of the cost of land they wished to purchase, and then obtain a legal survey description of that land from the government land office along with a letter that confirmed their claim on the property. The loan company would then transfer the remaining funds necessary for purchase to the land office. Failure to repay the loan meant that the bank would sell the land to recoup their investment.

The scheme put Jacob on edge. He knew that it would be two years before any newly cleared land would become profitable.

He feared it would be difficult to make payments during that period, putting him in danger of defaulting on the loan and losing the land he had worked so hard to clear. He thought that this part of the arrangement is what caused many settlers to lose their land within a few years of purchase. Having money on hand to make payments during that period of no or low income was a crucial, but oft-ignored, necessity. For his part, he told Mick, he intended to work long enough to put aside a nest egg to cover expenses and payments during that initial unprofitable period of building the farm.

Returning to the Du Bois farm, they made a quick lunch and then spent the afternoon fixing fences, repairing leaky roofs, and taking care of other needs on the farm. The tasks came naturally to both, and they found it emotionally satisfying to do that type of work again. At the end of the hot afternoon's labor, they were pleasantly surprised by a dinner that their host prepared for them. After the meal, she asked if Jacob would play his violin. He gladly complied, playing some old-world classics. When he finished, Mrs. Du Bois thanked him with tears in her eyes, explaining that her deceased husband had also played.

Early the next morning, the pair arrived at the designated location to begin their work. A dozen or more other men were already there, and more soon arrived. All were young and strong, suited to the task at hand. The objective was simple: excavate a tunnel and brace the sides and top with timber that was being brought in from nearby forests. Teams were assigned to all the aspects of construction. Some dug, some cut rock, some moved the spoils to the outside, and others cut and installed the timbers. The work boss informed them that the jobs would be rotated on a weekly basis so that everyone could learn to do all the tasks, as well as breaking up the monotony of the work.

A nearby tent served as a kitchen where food was prepared for lunch. Like every aspect of the job, workers took their lunch on a rotating basis. The effort had the look and intensity of a military operation. Work was long and hard in the summer heat and on the hard, stony ground. Jacob groaned that once again he was spending his life cutting and carrying stones. Work left little time, and no energy, for the pair to do much more than help a little on the farm and rest when not working. Days passed in an indistinguishable blur, the young men mostly unaware of much of what was happening around them.

JACOB, MICK, AND THE OTHER town residents were not fully appreciative of circumstances at their doorstep that were about to change their lives. Initially, only government officials and the few doctors who lived in Detroit knew of the advance of a deadly but invisible enemy. A cholera plague, brought in from travelers arriving from eastern port cities, was about to change everyone's life in a manner few could imagine. The dreaded disease was coming west. The consequences of the arrival of disease-laden ships, and the unsanitary conditions that expedited spread of the disease, were on the horizon. Most Detroit residents had no inkling of impending disaster. Newspapers and other flyers covered the issue, but only briefly, aiming to avoid causing panic and economic collapse. On July 2nd, the steamship *Henry Clay* and three other ships left Buffalo en route to Detroit, carrying 370 soldiers destined to quell the uprising by Chief Black Hawk. Unbeknownst to everyone was that a handful of these soldiers were sick with the deadly plague. Men who were viewed as protectors of the frontier were unwittingly bringing one of the deadliest invasions the area was to ever see.

On July 4th, the *Henry Clay*, General Winfield Scott's fleet flagship, stopped in Detroit for supplies and fuel, and to off-load sick passengers. To the great regret of all, those passengers were sick with cholera, and by the next day, deaths were occurring in the city. As this was happening, the steamship *Sheldon Thompson* anchored next to the docked *Henry Clay*. General Scott and forty of his officers and staff boarded the *Sheldon Thompson,* under command of Captain Walker. It was a tragic mistake, spreading the disease to Walker's vessel and then to points beyond Detroit.

When more soldiers got sick and died, Detroit officials ordered the ships to move from the dock to nearby Hog Island. As the disease continued to spread amongst the crews, the ships moved on. The *Sheldon Thompson* went upriver first to Fort Gratiot, then to Mackinac, and finally to the village of Chicago, dispersing the deadly disease with every stop. The *Henry Clay* sailed back to Cleveland, with predictable results. Disease and death followed. While at Hog Island and Fort Gratiot, many soldiers deserted and tried to reach Detroit on foot. Less than half arrived alive. The invisible enemy entered an unprotected city, killing scores. Within weeks after the soldiers' arrival, over two hundred residents were sick, half of them dying within days, some within hours of the onset of the disease.

Desperate to halt the invasion, the Detroit Board of Health implemented instructions designed to prevent the spread of cholera. To that end, residents were instructed to avoid crowds of strangers, clean their yards, drain stagnant pools, and follow strict hygiene procedures. Detroit's mayor and city physician issued orders affecting ship traffic on the Detroit River. The regulations stated that no passenger or cargo ships from other ports could come closer than one hundred yards to Detroit's shores, and passengers could not disembark until inspected and approved by a health officer. Eventually, armed guards were stationed on roads and trails leading into the city to prevent unauthorized entry.

Few people had any idea of how cholera was spread. Unfortunately, blame was wrongly assigned. It was not *miasmas,* it wasn't ethnicity, it wasn't moral weakness or God's wrath. It was much more down to earth. Crude sewage disposal methods and nearly absent hygienic practices exposed people to the disease. Unsafe drinking wells contaminated by polluted groundwater, and exposure to other persons who lacked means of sanitation created prime breeding grounds for the bacteria. As a result of these conditions, the disease spread rapidly. An individual's exposure to disease-carrying items, food, or people, and their own body's reaction, determined their fate.

JACOB AND MICK AND OTHER workers had no way to know that items used to prepare lunch in the company tent were infected. They didn't know that one of the cooks contracted the disease the prior evening, and that his unwashed hands spread potential death to everything he touched. Thus it was that by the end of a workday in mid-July a few workers showed symptoms of cholera. Within days, two previously healthy young workers died. Their deaths caused much turmoil at the work site head-quarters. Laborers began to refuse to work.

Ignorance about how the disease spread fueled near-riot conditions in parts of the city. A frightened population cast the blame net broadly, unfortunately missing the actual causes of the disease. Being new on the job and needing the income their work provided, Mick and Jacob continued to show up for work, as did most other workers.

Officials and doctors responded to the extent of their knowl-edge. A makeshift hospital was set up on the edge of town. An emergency center at the mayor's office was established from which they coordinated the enforcement of regulations and responses to reports of sickness and deaths.

On an oppressively hot and humid night in late July, Mick woke with a sickness such as he never felt before. His gut was on fire, and uncontrolled diarrhea left him so weak he could not stand. At sunrise, Jacob went on a desperate search for a doctor, but none were to be found. At the makeshift government command center, Jacob was told that it would be impossible to find a doctor to tend to his friend; there were just too many sick people in town for the few doctors that were available. One harried official warned Jacob to stay away from anyone showing symptoms, as being near a sick person could cause him to also become seriously ill.

Returning two hours later, he was met at the door by Mrs. Du Bois, whose face told the story. Mick's condition had worsened. It was clearly useless to try to give him food during the day, though Mick did have an insatiable thirst. Jacob ignored the advice he received about not going near Mick. He told Mrs. Du Bois that he would take care of him, but that she should not go near him. He tried to cool the fever with wet rags and by keeping windows and doors open. The long day evolved into a stifling evening, and Mick's condition showed no improvement.

In a rare lucid period, Mick called for his friend. Hearing Mick's voice cheered Jacob. He responded quickly, taking a lantern into Mick's dark room to talk to him. Actually seeing Mick took away any short-lived hopes Jacob had about his condition having improved.

"It's about time you woke up, Mick! We have work to do!"

"Hey friend," Mick said with difficulty, "I have a huge favor to ask of you. Things aren't looking good my boy, and I don't want to die without my family knowing where their son is buried. And besides," he added with a faint smile, "Colleen might want to come to see me."

Mick went into a coughing fit while Jacob tried to dismiss the seriousness of his illness.

"No, you gotta listen, Jacob. I'm dying. I know it. You must listen carefully and write this information down so you can send my parents a letter."

Jacob found a piece of paper and charcoal pencil. With much difficulty, Mick eventually provided Jacob with the necessary information to notify his family in Ireland. When Mick finished, he was exhausted. Laying back on the bed, he smiled and told Jacob how grateful he was.

Jacob occasionally dozed off during the sweltering night. He frequently tended to his friend's needs, keeping him as comfortable as possible. Near dawn, he awoke suddenly, aware that the sounds of moaning and movement from Mick's room had ended. He jumped up with a smile, certain that Mick had overcome the worst of the fever and was finally sleeping calmly. He lit the lantern and went into Mick's room, where he could see him lying peacefully on the bed.

Wonderful, he thought as he approached the bed to see if anything needed to be done for him. It was not until he reached the bed that he realized that something was wrong. There was no sound or movement whatsoever, Mick was deathly still and silent. In a frightened panic, Jacob nudged Mick's shoulder to awaken him, but reality soon became horribly clear: Mick had died in his sleep. Jacob was gut punched. He staggered out of Mick's room, bumping into the kitchen table and knocking a dish on the floor. Mrs. Du Bois came to the door of her room and knew immediately from Jacob's actions that something was gravely wrong. Jacob sat hard onto a chair and put the lantern on the table.

"He's dead," he told her, his voice breaking badly. "Mick is dead! How can someone like him die at the beginning of his life?"

He put his head on his arms and wept. They sat in silence in the dark.

Jacob said that he would take care of Mick's things and go into town after sunrise to see what they must do. She cautioned him to not go back in the room, fearing that if he touched the body or anything in the room, he would also likely become seriously sick in the same manner. Unsure what to do, they felt that the safest thing was to leave the house until they were able to remove Mick's body. Mrs. Du Bois said they should spend time outside on her farm until they received word as to what was to happen next. They went out to sit on the porch until morning.

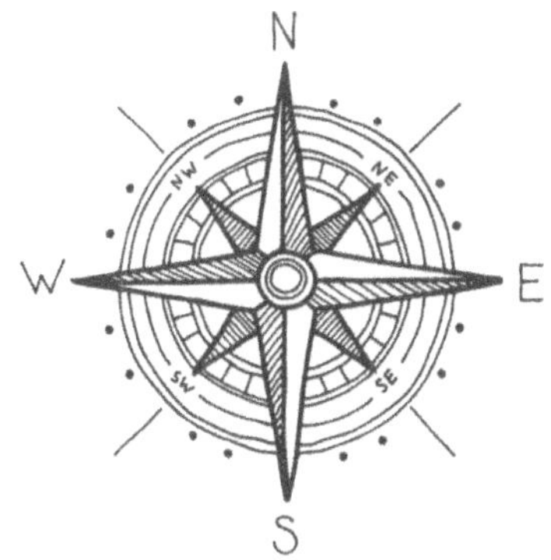

Chapter 12

JACOB WAS IN A DARK fog of grief as he walked into town. His memories of Jim's sudden death on the ship were still raw in his mind. Though he'd only known Mick for two months, the spirited, fun-loving Irishman had quickly become a close friend. His personality, strength of character, and zest for life were unlike anyone Jacob had ever known. It dawned on him with a crushing blow just how much he depended on Mick's advice and support, and how empty his world was going to be without him. For the first time since leaving home, he felt utterly alone.

Upon arriving at the city hall, he found an official to report the death to. Jacob was asked if he had any contact with the body, clothing, or anything else that Mick might have touched. Jacob felt it wisest to say that he had not. He provided all the information he knew about Mick for documentation purposes. The man told Jacob that a team of workers would be at the house that afternoon to take the body, along with all clothing and bedding. Mick and his belongings would be taken out of town and buried in a mass grave. He further ordered Jacob to whitewash and, with lye soap, carefully clean everywhere in the house that Mick might have been in the last week. The official also warned Jacob about sources of the disease, advising him to stay away from crowds and public water supplies. He told Jacob that city officials recently issued an order outlawing gatherings of all types.

The unbearable heat drained what little energy and emotion Jacob had left. He began the walk home, avoiding people and public wells, though he was desperately thirsty. He stopped at his work site to tell them what happened, only to find that a notice was posted at the entry stating that the site was closed until further notice. The sign stated that workers should show up daily to check their work status. The uncertainty of his return to work added another layer of frustration for Jacob. Every day that he was unable to work meant no income and a delay to his plans.

Returning to the farmhouse, he filled Mrs. Du Bois in on what would happen to Mick's body and belongings, and of the necessity to thoroughly clean everything. He then went to the well behind the house and drank deeply. He felt an overpowering need to wash away the evil that befell them. Emotionally drained and feeling more despair than he'd ever felt, he sat in the shade of a large chestnut tree and lost himself in thought. The sounds of a wagon and team of horses arriving at the house shook him from his reverie. Knowing why they were there, to take away the body of someone much like himself at the beginning of his life story, brought all his emotions to a boil again. He went into the house to see Mrs. Du Bois directing two men, fully covered and wearing gloves and a cloth over their face, to Mick's room. The men directed them both to stay outside while they took the body and everything else in the room out to the wagon. Jacob was glad that he had hid Mick's books. He would save them and one day read them himself.

Completing their unpleasant task, they confirmed Mick's information and prepared to leave. Jacob asked where they were going and what would happen next. They informed him that there was a mass grave dug outside of the city where victims were taken for burial. To avoid the spread of the disease, even members of local families were buried without public ceremony. In response to his final question, the men said that under no circumstances could he accompany them or otherwise go to the burial site. Fearing that Jacob would become a carrier himself, the men made it clear that he would be forcibly removed from the town should he go to the burial site.

Lacking an adequate supply of lye soap and quicklime, Mrs. Du Bois gave Jacob some money to go into town to purchase both necessary cleaning products. With extensive deposits of limestone nearby, Detroit was fortunate to have small mining and production companies to produce lime and quicklime. Mrs. Du Bois kept a small amount on hand for use on the farm, but more was needed to clean the entire house. They carefully washed all rooms and surfaces that Mick might have touched. Before long, their hands were raw from the powerful alkaline lime and lye solutions. Using a bucket and rags, they covered everything with whitewash to finish the germ-killing process. The arduous work on a hot, humid afternoon helped take their minds off Mick's fate, and the plight of hundreds in town that might be infected. They knew that everything had changed. According to Mrs. Du Bois, this situation was as impactful and life-changing as the great fire of 1805 when much of the town burned, and when the British captured Detroit a few years later during the war.

Jacob's thoughts wandered. Even at his early age he knew that there were no guarantees. People he knew in Vermont, people he'd encountered on his trip to Detroit, right up to the present day—everyone's life was impacted by forces they were powerless to control. At a gut level, Jacob knew he must somehow move on. He was bitter just the same. In just two months, he had faced the storm on Lake Erie, witnessed Jim's death, and now a cholera epidemic that took the life of a friend. The permanence of death haunted Jacob. During their time together, the friends knew that they would go their own way at some point. But they had both expected that they would be able to communicate and even visit on occasion. Now that wasn't ever going to happen. Mick would never own his farm nor marry Colleen.

"It's just goddamned unfair!" Jacob angrily declared, slamming his fist on the table.

Mrs. Du Bois gave him a shocked and disapproving look.

"Fairness has nothing to do with anything in life. If you haven't learned that lesson yet, you'd better grow up and learn it now. *C'est la vie.* There is no fair or unfair. There is only what fate brings you and what you do with it as a grown-up. *Are you a man or a child? Sois un homme!*"

"You and my father would have gotten along well," Jacob said in response with a repentant smile.

Mrs. Du Bois and Jacob felt it safest to avoid other people as much as possible. For a week, they stayed at her house with almost no contact with others. During that period, Jacob wrote a letter to Mick's parents and walked into town to mail it. Neighbors occasionally spoke to them from the roadway, passing along rumors. Many of the rumors were falsehoods about the cause of the sickness. With erroneous beliefs guiding the actions of many people, lack of sanitation, and spread of bacteria by infected persons at public places, it was guaranteed that the disease would spread.

The absence of credible information as to what was happening on a broader basis was adding to Jacob's worries. When and where would he be able to find a job again, when could he collect pay due to him from time spent on the sewer project, when would it be safe to interact with strangers again? These were just some of the issues that Jacob needed answers for. His confidence and clarity of plans morphed into doubt, uncertainty, and anger over the seeming wrongness of it all. Now that he was truly on his own, balancing his wants and needs with the vagaries of an uncaring fate, he knew he had to plot a new course. He could not stay in Detroit.

DAYS PASSED. JACOB WAITED FOR possible options to materialize and pondered his future steps. He told Mrs. Du

Bois that he would take care of the animals and do other work on the farm in the meantime. It provided a chance to be alone and clear his mind. The smell of lye and powdery lime dust in the house was strong and lasted for many days. As a result, they ate their meals outside whenever possible. The aroma of freshly baked bread and stew brightened their evenings as they sat in the fresh air of the porch to eat. On past evenings, there would have been music, jokes, and chatter. Mick's endless supply of jokes and witty comments would have brought tears of laughter to their eyes. Neighbors would have joined in the music and laughter.

Only unknowing crickets and birds broke the dreary silence of twilight after Mick's death. The livestock in the Du Bois barn were as happy as ever when Jacob brought their food and cleaned their stalls. Animals and birds were unaware of the evil that darkened the town.

Jacob became more depressed and solitary. He spent as much time outside as he could, avoiding human contact as much as possible. He decided to sleep in the barn or on the porch to be alone. Solitary brooding led to a deeper level of anger, frustration, doubt, and depression. Jacob knew where street peddlers sold home-brewed whiskey. A week after Mick's death, he walked the dark, quiet streets to the waterfront. There were groups of men arguing about the epidemic, unaware or uncaring that their very gatherings were exacerbating the problem. Angry blame was cast, and loud curses uttered. Jacob found the whiskey seller and parted with his precious money.

He avoided people as he slowly walked back to the farm, drinking steadily. He slept in the barn that night, and the next.

With little activity or work to diminish his depressing thoughts of death and hopelessness for the future, more money was spent on whiskey. Many days culminated in drunken depression, wallowing in dark thoughts of Jim and Mick and the daily reports of death in the city. Mrs. Du Bois's efforts to bring Jacob out of his melancholy failed. His health was noticeably deteriorating, and it was clear that he'd abandoned hope for his future, investing instead in the false relief of pain-killing alcohol.

After two weeks of Jacob's self-defeating behavior, Mrs. Du Bois knew she must do something, or he was going to throw away everything he had worked for. One day, Jacob woke up late in the barn's hay mow, his head pounding and his stomach in revolt. Walking to the house for an expected breakfast, he instead found all his belongings piled on the porch. He stumbled to the door and tried to open it. It was locked. He yelled and pounded on the door but there was no answer. Eating little during the past week, Jacob was hungry, as well as angry. He went to the back door and found it likewise locked with curtains drawn. Windows were similarly locked and covered.

Jacob cursed and sat down next to his collection of worldly belongings. The sun rose in the sky and his stomach growled. Hours later, having dozed off in the summer heat, he decided that he would at least spend some money for food. He dug out his shirt with the hidden money pocket to get some coins, but the pocket was empty. There would be no food or whiskey. Not wanting to leave his valuables unprotected, Jacob slept on the porch.

During the night, thunder pounded and lightning split the skies as heavy rain fell. Jacob moved as far back to the rear of the porch as possible, but rain was still blowing on him and his possessions. He realized that his precious violin was uncovered on top of the pile, with mist blowing on it. A brilliant flash of lightning illuminated the porch, allowing Jacob to see what his situation had become. He and his belongings were wet, he was hungry, and sick, and worst of all his violin, which meant more to him than any other possession, was exposed to the rain and possibly damaged. He covered the instrument as best he could with his clothes.

In frustration, he leaned against the wall of the house and wept with a mix of anger, sadness, and hopelessness. *How had it all come to this?* He cursed the epidemic and the fates that seemed so against him. He fell into fitful periods of depression as the rain fell and he felt all his hopes and plans fading away. *How can this be happening! Who could have foreseen the terrible circumstances and events that have tested me to the core?* Jacob slipped in and out of sporadic sleep, episodes that ended with nightmares of people falling off masts on a ship and of dead bodies in beds.

The glaring light of the morning sun in his eyes woke Jacob with a start. With every part of his body aching, he walked to the barn to relieve himself. Never had he felt worse. He ate a few half-ripe grapes and a dirty carrot pulled from the black soil, and then took care of the animals and cleaned up some storm damage. His thoughts turned inward as he worked and took an introspective look at his current life. He knew he must do something, or the life that he worked so hard to achieve would come to an end that day.

Why are these things happening to me? No one could have

foreseen and overcome such ill fate. Or could they? Didn't my own grandfather nearly lose his life and our farm fifty years ago during the war? And didn't my own father see death take family members through sickness and accidents? They faced the same troubles and dangers that I have, but they stood up like men and conquered them. These are exactly the sorts of things that my father tried to warn me about!

"I'm a goddamn fool," he muttered. *I'm acting like a pathetic helpless boy, unable to take care of myself, just like my father said would happen. Everyone warned me that it would be hard and dangerous. What am I doing? Mick would be ashamed of my behavior and Jim would call me a weakling. I need to grow the hell up and become a man, a real man, not the child I've been acting like. If I don't, I'll never have a farm of my own. I'm not going to allow myself to fail and go back to Vermont in disgrace! There must be meaning and reason in all that has happened. I can't allow it to all be for nothing!*

What was that Irish word Mick told me about back in Buffalo, about having the strength of character it takes to carry on against the odds? Misneach—that's what he called it.

"Well, Mick," Jacob said aloud as if explaining his thoughts and making sure that Mick could hear him, "I will prove to you and everyone else that I have the backbone and character to see this through. Thank you for the great advice."

Jacob sat down in the quiet of the small cattle barn to ponder his situation. The shed was one of his favorite getaways since they'd begun boarding with Mrs. Du Bois. The few livestock in the barn seemed to enjoy his presence. They would approach him the way a friend welcomed someone who had been away, though with a nuzzle from a damp snout rather than a handshake or hug. Sitting in the quiet space with the gentle sounds of the animals, he realized anew that this was his dream. This is what he wanted.

I had damned well better get my act together if I'm going to achieve my dreams. Jacob realized with stark certainty that his parents and everyone else who tried to warn him were right: it was going to be difficult, with unexpected trouble at every turn. It was up to him to stand up to the troubles and overcome them, or be smart enough to avoid them.

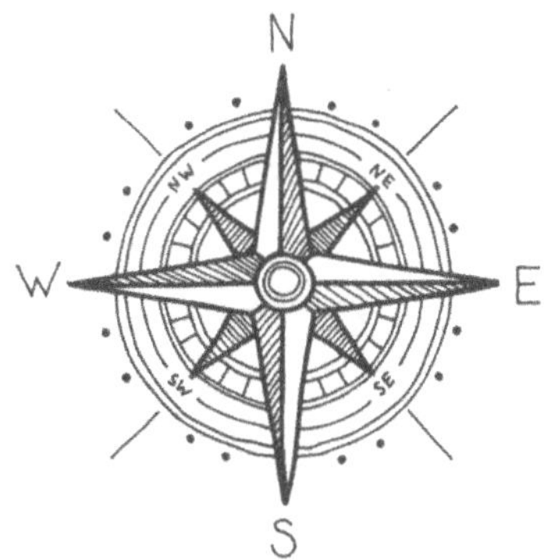

Chapter 13

JACOB FELT LIKE A NEW person. He washed up with a bucket of water from the well and made his way to the porch. He assumed that Mrs. Du Bois was inside the house and could hear him. Knocking on the door, he told her that he was sorry for his behavior. That it was over, and that he was ready to move on with his life again. The door slowly opened. Mrs. Du Bois looked at Jacob with a penetrating stare. Satisfied, she led him to the kitchen for some breakfast. After eating, they talked. They both agreed that he must leave Detroit as soon as possible rather than wait around to see how things worked out. He must seek work elsewhere, possibly on one of the roads that were being constructed in the interior of the territory. In short, he must get on with his plans, but do it away from Detroit, the epidemic, and the memories. Mrs. Du Bois apologized for hiding all of Jacob's remaining money, but it was for his own good, she insisted. Jacob agreed, thanking her for saving it from waste.

While talking, it occurred to Jacob that his family might have heard about what was happening and could be very worried about his safety. They might even think he had died in the epidemic. He must get word to them by means of a letter. After breakfast, he told Mrs. Du Bois that he would go to city hall and other government offices to find out what was happening. He would also send a letter to his family at the post office. He assured her that for both of their safety, he would take all precautions to avoid close contact with other people, avoiding crowds and gathering places in general.

On his way to the center of town, he passed his work site. The faded sign was still posted. It cast doubt on the chance that work could resume soon. At city hall, he spoke to Doctor Houghton with the health bureau. More knowledgeable than many, the doctor explained the pathways of the disease, giving Jacob confidence that he could resume life by following the practices he and Mrs. Du Bois had implemented. An official in the mayor's office confirmed Jacob's fears that the sewer project would not resume until the epidemic ended. When asked about back wages, the official said Jacob would have to come back the next day when the man overseeing the project would be there. That foreman could recognize Jacob and pay his due wages.

Leaving city hall, Jacob went to the post office to mail a letter home. The clerk asked Jacob if his family knew that he was in Detroit and Jacob confirmed that they likely did, as he informed them in an earlier letter that Detroit was to be his destination. Hearing that, the clerk suggested checking backlogged mail that arrived in recent weeks in case a letter came for him. He explained that letters often arrived in outposts on the frontier addressed only with a person's name and the nearest town.

Emptying a bag of letters on the counter, they both began to sort through them. Several minutes later, the clerk gave a cheer, showing Jacob a badly weathered envelope with his name on it. Recognizing his mother's handwriting, Jacob felt his heart beating rapidly, dizzy from the surprise and anticipation of hearing the latest news from home. He quickly opened the envelope.

His mother wrote that she prays that her letter will reach him somehow, thanked him for sending his letter from the Maumee River location, and asked questions about his plans once at Detroit. She noted that everyone was in good health, though they all missed him. She hoped he was well and that everything was going according to his wishes. She either was not aware of the cholera epidemic or chose to not bring the topic up in her letter. She closed by saying that they all send their love, and that Sally stopped by two weeks ago and inquired about him, noting that she sends her warm regards.

The letter was one of the best things that Jacob could have imagined happening in those dark days. He was thrilled beyond belief. The insight that he could communicate with his family, even on the frontier, gave him a new view of his situation. Yes, he was far away and unable to see those he loved, but he could still be in contact with them. This realization gave him a new sense that he was not alone; he was just away.

On his way back to the farm, Jacob decided to go to the office that was overseeing the road building projects. They were told earlier that this was a high priority project with government money behind it. Therefore, he thought, because road construction was an important priority, and because construction was occurring in remote areas away from people, it meant that road projects wouldn't be affected by the epidemic.

Mr. Boyd, the project manager appointed by the Michigan Territorial Legislative Council, confirmed that while certain precautions were in place limiting contact with recent arrivals, road building was continuing. Active projects included the Chicago Pike, the Fort Gratiot trail, and the Saint Joseph River Trail. Boyd added that the Saint Joseph Trail was still sometimes referred to as the La Salle Trail because of its historic nature. A blank look on Jacob's face suggested that he was not aware of the French explorer's history. Jacob inquired as to the locations and ultimate destinations of each new trail improvement project. The official explained that existing roads, which were little more than Indian foot paths or improved trails constructed by the earliest settlers to allow limited use of horses and wagons, were being upgraded so that a team of horses pulling a wagon could routinely traverse them. In swampy places, this meant building a corduroy road, similar to what Jacob had experienced on his trip north to Detroit. In other places, construction meant cutting trees, removing stumps, grading the roadway, and digging ditches alongside. It was demanding work but paid well for as long as one was willing to work. Jacob was sold. He saw working on one of the road projects as the key to once again earning money for his ultimate dream: purchasing land for a farm.

He asked Boyd if he had any opinions about the quality and availability of lands near each new road. Boyd told him that most development so far has occurred along the Chicago Pike. Other regions of the interior were still unsettled, though just recently surveyed and thus available for purchase. He suggested speaking to the government land agent about questions of land quality and availability.

Since that office was nearby, Jacob went directly there. He didn't know it at the time, but this decision changed his life. The agent opined that if it were him, he would choose one of two routes into the interior. The first option was to go west on the St. Joseph Trail, referred to as The Territorial Road—one of multiple trails using that title, being carved through the forest west of Detroit. The agent explained that the road was also called The Second Tier Road because it would cross the territory through the second tier of recently defined counties. He said that reports he heard from road workers and surveyors were that the land west of Detroit would make excellent farmland. Two small villages providing basic services were taking form on the route of the St. Joseph Road: Ann Arbor and Jacksonburg. He said that further west on the trail there were reports of large prairie openings, making the conversion to cropland easier.

Northwest on the Saginaw Trail was his second recommendation. He explained that the land lying between the villages of Pontiac and Saginaw was less well known, but from what travelers and surveyors said, there were large areas of forested lands that would eventually make good farms. A crude road was carved out of the wilderness by the Army a decade earlier to supply Fort Saginaw, he said, but the road was abandoned and overgrown since the fort closed in 1823. A few settlers cleared land and built log cabins in the Pontiac area and further north where the Saginaw Trail crossed the Flint River, the agent revealed. Jacob had a great deal of information to process.

He realized that there were in fact options and opportunities available. He would have to give them serious thought, make decisions, and get on with his life.

Jacob came to the realization that he did not begrudge his time in Detroit. What he learned there was invaluable. He could not have successfully pursued his goals without the skills, knowledge, and maturity that life in Detroit provided him. He realized just how ignorant he was merely two months earlier when he'd been so confident that he knew everything he needed to know. Going back to the farm, he told Mrs. Du Bois of all that he learned. When he described the Saginaw Trail, she inexplicably smiled.

"The Saginaw Trail is now famous."

"Famous? How so?"

"Last summer, the neighbors told me that two French noblemen were at the newspaper office. I went into town to see them, hoping to talk to them about my home country, and find out what they were doing in Detroit. I had a wonderful conversation with them. They were doing a tour of America. They came to Michigan to explore the Saginaw Trail, intending to follow it all the way to the outpost of Saginaw. They wanted to see the wilderness before it was gone and meet Indians still living like they used to.

"They were going to write a book about their time in Michigan. They told me about what was going on in France and that they were here on an official mission on behalf of the French government to learn about America. Their names were Alexis de Tocqueville and Gustave Beaumont. They were perfect gentlemen—so handsome and brave. I will never forget the time I met two French counts."

"What an interesting story! I'll keep the fame of that trail in mind when I decide what to do. I'm going to meet with the government man tomorrow to get more information and likely sign up for work on one of the new roads."

Sleep didn't come easily that night as Jacob lay awake contemplating his options. None of the paths ahead of him were "wrong," and that was part of the difficulty. Knowing that his choice of road project would likely determine where he—and potentially his future family—would live for many years weighed heavily upon him.

Finally dozing off, he awoke with a start as a thought came to his mind that clarified everything. He needed an ongoing project. That ruled out the Saginaw Trail, which did not have the current construction status of the other three. He wanted to avoid the crowds of settlers, which ruled out the Chicago Pike project. He knew nothing of the Fort Gratiot trail and the land that lay in that direction. But the agent's description of good land and promise of progress along the St. Joseph River Trail seemed to fit exactly what he had staked his dreams on. West into the interior it would be.

Jacob met Mr. Boyd early the next morning, telling him that he was interested in work on the St. Joseph Road. Laborers were needed, and it was clear that Jacob could perform the difficult work. After processing the paperwork to place Jacob on the payroll, an account was set up for Jacob at the nearby bank where his pay would be deposited while working in the wilds. The bank provided the same service to current road workers.

The bank also worked on a regular basis with the government land office, processing payments for land patents. Overall, it clearly seemed the safest way to protect his investment, although letting someone else keep his money ran counter to his life experiences up to that point. *I'm not in Vermont anymore, so I'd better get used to doing things differently,* Jacob thought to himself as papers were signed.

"Take these papers to the Sheldon Inn at the settlement called Sheldon's Corners, which is where the new road begins. It's a long day's walk west of Detroit on the Chicago Pike. Take everything you need with you, because once you get west of Sheldon's Corners, there isn't much out there except trees and mosquitoes. You'll be working hard all day, cutting trees, moving stones, and digging dirt. I hope you don't mind hard work!"

"I'm used to it," countered Jacob, as he left the office.

Before heading back to the Du Bois house, Jacob walked to the post to mail a letter home. He felt much satisfaction in that he was finally able to provide some detail about his plans. He doubted that his family had any idea where the Chicago Pike or Territorial Road were, but he could fill in that lack of information for them. It also occurred to him that, when his family does eventually hear about the cholera epidemic in the west, it will be comforting to them to know that he had left Detroit and was heading into a safe area unaffected by the disease.

After mailing his letter and checking for any additional mail from the east, he started the walk back to the farm to tell Mrs. Du Bois about his new job. It would mean leaving the hospitality she generously provided. Jacob knew that living on the road was going to be difficult to get used to after the comfortable home life he'd gotten used to.

God, I wish Mick were here, Jacob sadly thought. *By rights, he should be the one doing this. He knew what he wanted, and nothing was going to keep him from his dreams, nothing except the damned cholera. I know you can hear me Mick: I might be calling on you for help again.*

Jacob made a final stop at city hall where he met with his former supervisor on the sewer project. The supervisor gave Jacob his back pay in the form of bank notes from the same Detroit bank where he'd just arranged an account for. The supervisor assured Jacob that the bank notes were honored everywhere in the territory. His activities in town all taken care of, Jacob returned to the farm. Mrs. Du Bois was clearly happy for Jacob as he told her of his plans. She had enjoyed having the pair there to talk with and help take care of the farm. She loved Jacob's music-making and Mick's optimism and attitude. She missed Mick and knew she would miss Jacob, even though it had only been a few weeks since they'd moved in.

Jacob said he would stay on one more day to make sure everything on the farm was taken care of. He felt bad about leaving, knowing that the many chores would once again fall on Mrs. Du Bois's shoulders. He knew she loved the small farm that she and her husband had run for many years, and that she would continue to run it if her health allowed. They both knew all too well, however, that the farm's days were numbered. Detroit was growing, and what remained of the old French ribbon farms would soon be lost to development.

The morning of his departure dawned with no clouds or

breeze. Conditions pointed to a stifling day for the long, lonely walk west to Sheldon's Corners. Mosquitoes and flies buzzed aggressively around the cattle pens as Jacob took care of every-thing for Mrs. Du Bois a final time. He had much on his mind as he worked, ruminating on the reality of what was to come.

Jacob could smell breakfast meat frying, the aroma over-powering the heavy smell of farm animals in the pens. Upon finishing the various tasks, he washed up and followed the mouthwatering fragrance of cooked food to the kitchen. It was truly a meal fit for minor royalty, he thought, as he poured maple syrup on freshly baked biscuits and cakes, served alongside fresh sausage and eggs. A cup of coffee, which Jacob knew was a costly treat for the widow, capped off the feast. Jacob savored his breakfast, knowing it would be the best food that he would eat for many months.

Despite his happiness at being able to continue pursuing his dreams, he knew he'd miss Mrs. Du Bois and the neighbors with whom he'd spent enjoyable evenings talking and singing. Jacob had been grappling with a major nagging issue in recent days but had not yet found a satisfactory resolution. It was what to do with his fiddle and bow. Though he knew there would be occasions while working in the road camps that he would have time to play it, he also feared for its well-being. There were many threats along the road, from storms and floods to theft and inadvertent damage. While working in the shed that morning, a solution occurred to him.

After he ate and helped clean up the pans and dishes, he asked Mrs. Du Bois if he could request an important favor of her. He explained his conundrum about his fiddle, asking Mrs. Du Bois if he could leave the instrument with her for safekeeping while he worked on the road crew. His plan, he explained, was that he would come back to pick it up when he returned to Detroit to purchase his homestead from the land office. He said that he did not think it would take more than six or eight months to earn enough money, and establish necessary credit, to make a land purchase. He was confident, he said, that in less than a year he would be a landowner working to clear his new farm.

Mrs. Du Bois said that she had no plans to leave or move elsewhere and that the violin, as she referred to the instrument, could be safely kept at her home during his absence. That was a huge weight off his mind, and he thanked her profusely. He said that his only fear now was that he might have to relearn how to play the instrument after so many months.

With that issue satisfactorily settled, Jacob carefully wrapped and stored the fiddle. He gathered his gear, which he had carefully cleaned and packed the day before. Mrs. Du Bois went into the kitchen to get a package containing bread, cheese, and jerky for the journey, surprising Jacob. The load was less cumbersome without the fiddle, but still a heavy weight on his back and shoulders. Grasping his gun, they went out onto the porch. Giving Mrs. Du Bois a hug and kiss on the cheek, he bid her adieu and walked out to the roadway. Waving goodbye one final time, he turned to the west, shifted his load on his shoulders, and focused his mind on what lay ahead.

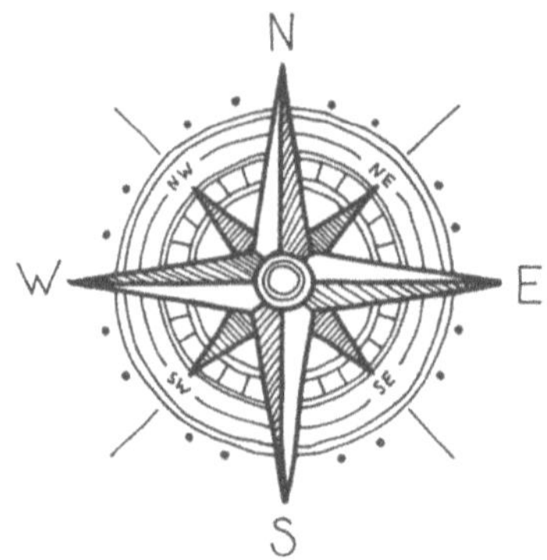

Chapter 14

IT TOOK AN HOUR TO reach the Chicago Pike. The sun was overhead by the time he arrived. Though trees along the roadway provided shade, the heat was oppressive just the same. Insects were a nuisance, especially the deerflies circling Jacob's head as he walked. They had an annoying habit of waiting for an opportune moment to alight on his neck or bare arms and quickly bite before being brushed away. The occasional team of horses raised dust that lingered in the windless heat. Near Detroit, the ancient Indian trail was already transformed into an up-to-date road capable of handling teams of horses pulling large wagons. He was surprised by the number of people using the road as he walked westward. The road construction official in Detroit explained that at Sheldon's Corners, the Chicago Road veered southwest then west near the Ohio border. It was clear that development along the ancient pathway was occurring rapidly. The new St. Joseph Road, Mr. Boyd had explained, was being built straight west, beginning at Sheldon's Corners, then diverging from the Chicago Pike into primarily unsettled territory.

In the early afternoon, Jacob stopped near a small creek to eat some of the food that Mrs. Du Bois had given him. He drank deeply of the fresh water, refilling a stoppered jug he carried with him. Ripe berries and grapes supplemented his lunch. He picked a supply to eat later.

Midsummer daylight lingered late. Jacob's fascination of the woodlands was reawakened as he walked in the evening twilight. Bird and animal sounds were everywhere, as were fireflies, which filled the darkening landscape with a dazzling display. Just before darkness, Jacob settled in for the night. He spread his tarp on the ground near a spring under the branches of an ancient maple tree, placing his gear on the tarp. Cleared brush and stone fire circles made it obvious that others had camped in this location over the years. Resting his head on his backpack, he wrapped himself in his light blanket to escape the mosquitoes. A whippoorwill and an owl in a nearby tree provided background music as he dozed off, soaking in the peaceful splendor that surrounded him.

Jacob woke early from a deep and restful sleep. The eastern horizon was just starting to show a faint pink light. He sat quietly in the darkness, conscience of sounds that did not seem right. After several minutes, he was certain he could hear faint voices. A slight breeze then carried the unmistakable smell of smoke from a campfire. Now fully awake, it occurred to Jacob that he should not be surprised that other travelers were camped nearby. He should have expected as much, he thought to himself.

After washing up at the spring, he finished eating most of Mrs. Du Bois's food. He packed his belongings, drank heavily, and refilled his water jug before leaving. Shouldering his pack, he made his way toward the nearby campsite, intending to briefly speak with them prior to continuing his journey west. When the other travelers came into sight, Jacob was shocked. Expecting to see a lone traveler or a family group, he instead saw a group of about fifteen Native Americans, including women and children. They eyed him cautiously, having been aware of his presence since the prior evening. Jacob said hello, feeling foolish because it immediately occurred to him that the Indians likely could not understand him. To his surprise, a young native about his own age responded with a heavily accented greeting. The two strangers were able to communicate enough for Jacob to explain his destination. He was surprised to learn that the Indian band was en route to Amherstburg in Upper Canada near Detroit to meet with British officials. They made the trek annually to receive payment resulting from treaty agreements with the British.

The travelers parted company amicably, Jacob continuing his westward trek. Pondering his encounter with the Native Americans as he walked, Jacob felt humbled by how much he didn't know of the world around him. It also occurred to him just how "recent" history was on the frontier. The situation was far different than in New England.

Seeing that it was going to be another hot and humid day, he accepted the long, tedious walk ahead of him. He mentally set a goal of arriving at Sheldon's Corners by late afternoon. Jacob had not walked very far when he was overtaken by a team of horses pulling a freight wagon. He stepped off the roadway to allow the teamster to proceed, but the team stopped next to him. While the two horses angrily swished their tails and swung their heads to chase off biting flies, the driver hailed Jacob and asked how far he was going. Jacob explained his destination, and the driver said he would be stopping there himself before continuing west on the Chicago Road. Introducing himself simply as Red, a tag made obvious by his plentiful reddish hair and beard, he offered Jacob a lift. Readily agreeing, Jacob put his belongings in the back of the wagon and climbed up to sit next to Red, whose bulk took up most of the board.

As he did whenever possible, Jacob took advantage of the situation to obtain information that would be helpful in his quest. After filling Red in on his purpose for going to Sheldon's Inn, he wasn't disappointed in Red's response. Meeting him truly was a stroke of good fortune. Red explained that he had lived in Detroit for three years and made his living hauling freight and supplies to customers along the Chicago Pike. His knowledge of the area was extensive. He said he frequently carried supplies to Sheldon's Corners for use by the builders of the new road. Red gave names of key persons responsible for the project to Jacob and provided details about how the project was being implemented. The man in charge, he explained, was a Mr. Callahan who often spent time at Sheldon's Inn to meet with territorial officials, keep track of workers, file reports, and handle payments. Jacob filed the information away in his mind, hoping that it would prove valuable once he arrived at the inn.

Well beyond the town of Detroit, they continued to frequently encounter other travelers. Near midday, they stopped where a small creek crossed the trail, allowing the horses to drink and graze. Jacob saw a rabbit hiding in the brush. He quietly retrieved his gun from the back of the wagon and loaded it. A single shot to the head killed the rabbit, which Jacob retrieved and cleaned. A fire was quickly started, and the carcass roasted above the flames, spiced with juniper berries picked from a tree. Brambles provided tart raspberries and large blackberries in abundance. With their hunger satisfied, the needs of the horses met, and water containers refilled, they continued their westward journey.

Lazy clouds floated overhead, unmoved by a breeze on the sultry day. They were both grateful for the shade provided by large trees lining the sides of the road. Before long, the rhythmic sound of the rolling wheels and steady clop of the horses' hooves lulled Jacob into a deep sleep. Red also dozed off, leaving the horses to use their judgment and follow the obvious trail, which they had traversed many times. A hard jolt rudely awakened Jacob just before falling off the seat onto the hard ground. Red nearly fell on top of him, grasping the side of the wagon to break his fall. The cause of their situation was immediately obvious by the sight of the right front wheel: two spokes snapped in two and the rim having bent when they hit a rock on the trail.

"Damn it!" shouted an angry Red. "Well, let's get to work. This is going to take a while."

They unhitched the horse team, securing the animals in a shaded location off the trail. Red took his axe and cut a stout branch to use as a lever, instructing Jacob to find a large rock or stump. Jacob told Red about his prior experience fixing busted wagon wheels, and that he knew what had to be done. With the necessary tools gathered, they lifted the front of the wagon, resting it on the stump. Red then removed the wheel.

Jacob took the saw to cut two spokes of appropriate length and a section of wood to fit in the broken outer rim. He located a nearby hickory tree and cut the necessary branches. With Red's spokeshave tool, he quickly transformed the strong branches into spokes. In the meantime, Red pounded the iron rim with a heavy hammer until it was once again properly shaped. With the spokes and rim section cut, Red assembled the pieces with the skill of someone who had obviously performed the same type of repair many times. With Jacob's help, it took just over an hour to fix the wheel and be underway once again.

"Someday," observed Red, "this road will be smooth enough so that people won't have to worry about rocks and stumps in the trail."

Tired, hot, dirty, and sweaty, the men rode in silence in the afternoon heat. Jacob dozed off a couple times, but immediately awakened with every bump in the trail. Eventually, Red said that they were almost there, and a few minutes later, Jacob saw a large house with smaller service buildings and stables along the road a short distance ahead. Once in the immediate vicinity of the complex, Jacob noted that there was much commotion generated by men and horses, the most he had seen since leaving Detroit.

"We're here!" Red declared with obvious happiness.

Jacob helped Red stable the horses and provide them with food and water. After the team was taken care of, they stopped at a well where they both drank heavily and washed a layer of dirt off their hands and faces.

With thirst satisfied and once again reasonably clean, they made their way to the inn. "Let me introduce you to some folks that you should meet," Red said.

Other teams were tied to hitching posts in front of the building, and owners milled around the entrance. Red led the way into the inn, explaining that it was a privately owned house providing lodging and tavern services to travelers. They were about to enter the door when a loud voice called out.

"Hey Red, you card-cheating rogue, who let you in here?"

It took a few seconds for Jacob to realize that the man making his way toward them was laughing, not angry.

"Hello, Tim! How the hell are you? Where is the brains of this operation?"

"If you mean my wife, Rachel, she's in the kitchen starting supper preparation for undeserving bums like you."

Red turned to Jacob. "I want to introduce you to one of the most important men in the territory," he said, introducing his friend as Timothy Sheldon, owner of the home and inn.

"This inn is making settlement of the interior possible. When people bring their families to settle near here, they need a place to sleep and eat while traveling. That's what Mr. Sheldon is providing. When you're out there living in the woods building the road, you'll wish there were more places like this available!"

"I'm sure I will."

But privately, Jacob was concerned that if such a place were available, he'd spend all his money there trying to have the comforts of home. *Just as well*, he thought, *that I'll be roughing it and eating company food; at least I can save my money rather than spend it in places like this.*

Red said he was going to go say hello to Mrs. Sheldon, telling Timothy that Jacob might have a few questions for him about the new road. Appreciative for the opportunity to glean information, Jacob asked Mr. Sheldon if he had a few minutes to spare and was elated when Sheldon replied in the affirmative. Jacob explained his upcoming job as a worker on the road, asking if the supervisor, Mr. Callahan, might be there. Sheldon said that they expected him in a week or so, explaining that he usually stopped at the inn around the first of each month to take care of business. Noting that Jacob was uncertain about what to do since the boss was not around, Sheldon explained that other new road workers that passed through the inn just continued west on the new trail until they reached the current location of the project headquarters.

"You can't miss it. The camp is a collection of buildings that they tear down and move every month or so as they progress further inland. It will be where they keep equipment and where you will sleep and eat. That is where you will find Mr. Callahan in the next few days. They're about ten miles west of here right now, near to the village of Ann Arbor."

"So, are you saying that the road workers sleep in a bunkhouse, not camp along the road? I've been resigned to living in my tent for the next year."

"You might wish at times that you were sleeping by yourself in a tent, but you will spend most nights in the bunkhouse. It's more efficient to have everyone together for morning and evening meals, and to go to and from the work site together."

Since day was quickly slipping into evening, Mr. Sheldon

told Jacob that he was welcome to stay there for the night before heading down the trail.

"Either camp outside or splurge a bit and spend the night inside if you wish, it's up to you. There is a well near the stable for water, and you can sleep in the barn or outside, or inside the inn, whatever you choose."

Jacob chose a middle ground. He would camp to save money, but take advantage of the inn's food, as his own supply was running short. The smell of the supper meal was wafting through the house and porch, enticing people from outside. Following their example, Jacob left his stack of belongings in a corner and found a seat at a long table occupied by a family with children and a variety of solitary men.

Supper was hearty, filling, and delicious. Trays of venison and pork, fresh vegetables, freshly baked breads, and pies were passed around. Conversations mostly had to do with the plans of the people at the table—where they were heading and what they planned to do upon arrival. Most were seeking land like Jacob, though some of the men were businessmen like Red. Almost all the land seekers were heading west on the Chicago Pike. The father of the family noted that he already purchased land six months earlier, and that his family was just now moving onto the land to clear it and build a cabin and sheds before winter. Their loaded cart, he said, was waiting outside, along with a team of oxen in the corral near the stable.

Jacob was the only road worker, though Mr. Sheldon said that more single men, and even entire families, were passing through to the new road. He explained that an improved trail had existed, formed by settlers traveling on the old Indian trail.

Early explorers and settlers cut trees and widened the trail as necessary to get small wagons and horses and even cattle through, he said. Now, he explained further, workers were widening and straightening the road, following the surveyed route approved by the territorial legislature.

After supper, people remained in the large parlor, relaxing and sharing stories. Jacob wished that he had his fiddle with him so that he could play for what he was sure would have been an appreciative crowd. Before darkness fell, he said goodbye to Red, thanking him for his help, and went outside to find a good place to camp. He chose a spot in the nearby woods, away from the road and stable noises. He felt good; the more he learned, the more certain he was that things were falling into place for his future. Rising early, he went into the inn before leaving to inquire about postal services. Mr. Sheldon told him that they did indeed have mail picked up weekly for delivery back east. Paying for writing materials and postage, Jacob sent a letter to his family updating them on his plans. He suggested the village of Ann Arbor as the best post office location for future correspondence. Confident and satisfied, he bid Mr. Sheldon goodbye. Shouldering his pack, he began the final phase of his journey west through the woods on the new road.

JACOB ATE THE LAST OF his provisions, including a large slice of bread he'd saved from the prior evening's meal, for lunch under a majestic chestnut tree. Crows loudly protesting the presence of a nearby hawk provided entertainment. He was fascinated by the antics of the crows, uncertain as to whether they were very brave or clueless as they dove at the hawk, even pulling feathers from its wing and tail. Helpless to fend off the bothersome crows, the hawk eventually sailed the thermals to a quieter part of the forest. With one adversary chased away, the crows focused their attention on Jacob. Realizing it was because of a nest they were guarding in the chestnut's dense foliage, no doubt with a couple of fledglings not ready to be on their own, Jacob chuckled and assured them that he'd soon be on his way. A fox sneaking down the trail, unaware that it had been spotted, and the distant drumming of a pileated woodpecker provided additional entertainment. The beauty of the wildlands put Jacob in a festive mood, happy to be alive and pursuing his dreams. After a brief nap, he resumed his walk, hurried along by ubiquitous insects.

Jacob noticed that the landscape was slowly rising in elevation as he traveled west, enough so that it was a tiring walk. After a few miles, he came to a significant dip in the road and saw the unmistakable presence of buildings next to a small stream. It was quiet as he approached the facility, which made sense, he reasoned, since everyone would be out working on the road. He peeked into the largest building and saw cots and a table. Making his way further into the camp, he saw a stable and corral, along with a building whose chimney was spewing smoke. Assuming that this was the kitchen, and that kitchen workers were already preparing supper, Jacob entered. The heat in the building was almost overwhelming, as was the smell of smoke. Jacob entered and yelled out a greeting, met with a curt response that supper was still two hours away. Jacob introduced himself as a new worker and asked where he would find Mr. Callahan.

"They'll be back in a couple hours. In the meantime, go to the bunkhouse and find yourself a place to sleep tonight," the cook said crossly.

Jacob piled his gear on a vacant cot. Once his belongings were secured, he made his way to the creek. After satisfying his thirst, he took his clothes off and entered the marvelously cool waters to wash off days' worth of sweat and dirt. The sound of a gunshot startled him momentarily, though he relaxed as he assumed that it was a nearby settler shooting a deer or other wildlife. When he finished bathing, he washed his dirty clothes, laying them on the bank to dry.

Jacob realized that the next couple of hours would likely be the last alone time that he would have for himself, so he put on a pair of undergarments and went back to the bunkhouse. Lying on the cot he had selected, he dozed off in the stifling heat. The echo of a second gunshot in the nearby forest woke him after an hour or more of sleep. As he slowly awoke, he heard much commotion outside the building, and a group of young men noisily entered the bunkhouse. Jacob noted that they ranged in age from about eighteen to at least thirty years old. Some laid on their cots, others stripped and went back outside to wash in the stream.

One young man with a bunk near Jacob's looked at him and

said simply, "New guy?" Jacob confirmed that he was, saying he had paperwork to give Mr. Callahan.

"Well, you won't find him in here with us bums, he's got his own office over by the kitchen." Jacob had noticed the small building on his walk. He thanked the man, and getting his papers from his pack, he went back to the creek, put on his now dry clothes, and then set out to find the boss. While at the creek, he saw a man dragging a deer and carrying a large turkey, both recently killed. "Tomorrow's dinner," the man said as he took the animals toward the kitchen.

"Yeah, what do you want," was the unpleasant response to Jacob's knock on Callahan's office door. *Hell, I'd be tired and grumpy too if I just got done working all day,* thought Jacob, giving Callahan the benefit of the doubt.

"I have papers from Mr. Boyd in Detroit. To be a worker on the road."

After noisy movement in the office, the door finally opened and a large, bearded man drying himself off with a towel stood in the doorway.

"Let's see your papers." Jacob handed the forms to Callahan, who quickly scanned them. "Well, everything looks in place. I hope you are ready to start tomorrow morning." Jacob confirmed that he was and that he already found a place in the bunkhouse. "Welcome aboard, Mr. Hart. When the chow bell rings don't be late, or you won't get anything to eat. We leave early in the morning."

Jacob met a few of the more talkative men in the chow hall that evening, including Tom, the youth who'd briefly spoken to him earlier. They all shared the same story; working a temporary job to earn money to buy land. Some of the older men had left families behind who would join them once they purchased their future homestead or farm. After eating, most of the men found a place in the shade to rest. A few played cards in the bunkhouse, with all doors and windows open to cool it down. It was clear that after an exhausting day of digging and chopping, the men wanted to simply relax in preparation for the next hard day of work.

The eastern sky was just beginning to glow when a loud bell woke Jacob. The men silently dressed and made their way to eat breakfast. Jacob was impressed with the size of the servings, and when he commented on it, he was told he'd better eat it all because he will work it off. After eating, everyone helped hitch up teams of horses onto two flat wagons loaded with various tools. A box containing bread, dried meat, and jugs of water was loaded onto the wagon for midday lunch. Once ready, everyone climbed aboard the wagons and made their way west on the newly built roadway. They had not gone far when they crested a small hill. Jacob could see the new road carved arrow-straight through the forest for at least a mile. During the short ride to the work site, workers applied a variety of potions to deter mosquitoes and other biting insects. Animal fat, especially pork, served as the basic deterrent, along with a variety of home remedies comprised of various ground-up roots and grasses. Some tried bottles of patent medicines sold by druggists and traveling peddlers. On his first day out, Jacob noticed that most of the other workers were wearing long-sleeved shirts and pants with cuffs sealed at their boot tops. Upon asking why, he was simply told that he'd find out. The next day he dressed similarly. Being hot was better than falling victim to the scourge of insects they dealt with.

Eventually, the crew reached the point where the improved trail ended. A rough, narrow trail continued, curving through the dark forest. Tom explained that earlier settlers had widened the original meandering footpath, but that the work crew hadn't followed the old trail very much, instead following a straight line marked by surveyors.

"We've been told that from here it gets a lot harder, because of hills and large swamps near a river," Tom said. "East of here," he continued, "the land was flat and mostly dry, so clearing it was easier. Plus, winter is getting closer every day, so building the road is going to get a hell of a lot harder soon!"

Without having to be told, workers spread out with their tools. Some had axes and small handsaws, some teamed up with two-man saws, and a few, including Jacob, carried picks and shovels. The sawyers went ahead to fell trees, which workers then cut up to move off the roadway. Others dug out stumps and rocks, dug roadside ditches, and carted gravel to fill holes. It quickly dawned on Jacob that it was going to be a slow and laborious process. It also became clear that he, too, would only want to rest at the end of the day.

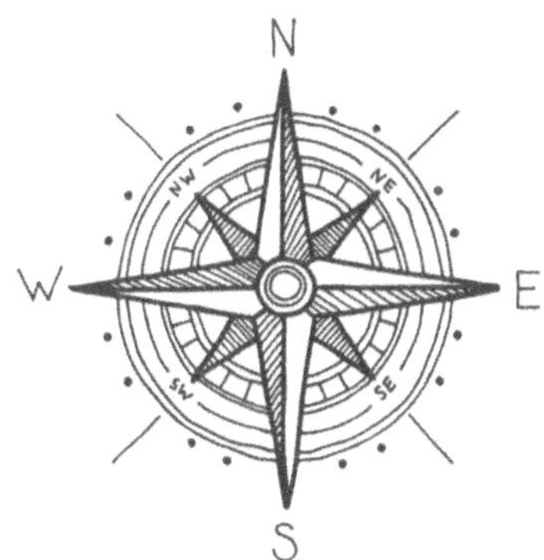

Chapter 15

WORKING IN THE FOREST ALL day and then eating and sleeping at the base camp became Jacob's life. The base camp was moved westward every three or four weeks. Mr. Callahan occasionally made trips back to Sheldon's Inn and to the territorial government offices in Detroit seeking additional funds for the road, as well as more workers. In his absence, he assigned a seasoned worker to manage the work crew. It didn't take long for Callahan to recognize Jacob's capabilities and appoint him as one of the lead workers. The extra pay made the difficulties of managing the work crew worthwhile, though no less frustrating.

On a day much like any other, screams for help from the tree cutting crew were heard. Everyone ran forward to see two workers frantically trimming off large branches of a tree. It turned out that the two-man team felling the centuries-old tree misjudged its lean angle and the oak unexpectedly came crashing down on top of them. The trapped sawyers were two of the older, more experienced men that everyone knew well. They could be seen under the branches, though neither man was moving. Everyone grabbed axes and saws and began the dangerous job of cutting branches that were themselves as large as some trees. It took an hour to cut down to the men, only to find them already dead from the crushing injuries they received. They helped move the bodies back to the wagon, which Callahan had already hitched to the horses. The crew followed behind the wagon, back to the camp. Mr. Callahan continued to Detroit where he turned the bodies over to officials. He was back at camp the following morning.

Accidents and less serious injuries were common, as was the resulting turnover in workers. Injuries occasionally required transporting an injured man back to Sheldon's Inn or to a doctor in Detroit. Laborers kept most injuries secret because being removed from the work team meant the end of their employment and future plans. Arguments and disagreements were likewise frequent, but seldom turned into physical confrontations. Everyone was too tired and sore to fight and knew that there was too much at stake to risk being fired.

As they slowly progressed toward their Lake Michigan goal, the seasons turned, and trees lost their leaves. As predicted, the land became more varied. A series of hills and swamps made progress on the road more challenging. The workers no longer followed a straight course through the forest. Instead, they found that the most logical route coincided with the trail that natives created generations earlier. It followed the high ground rather than attempting to follow a straight line. Avoiding large swamps and steep inclines was more important than following a surveyed line across the countryside.

Upon topping a final hill, the river they had anticipated came into view. Mr. Callahan said the stream was called the Huron, named after Native Americans that lived in the region. It took two more weeks of challenging work, however, before they arrived at the top of the bluff on the east bank of the stream. The route of the new road curved northerly, following the water.

Eventually, the improved road reached the bustling settlement of Ann Arbor, formed at a powerful set of rapids in the river and already home to nearly a thousand residents. Two sawmills, built by the Geddes brothers and Robert Fleming, used the rapids to power their mills, providing lumber for the villagers. A grist mill was situated a short distance away where a tributary cascaded into the main river. Many homes and small shops, including a post office, had sprung up on both sides of the river. Area forests were being rapidly cleared for farmland. The road crew was surprised and pleased to see that a substantial bridge was constructed earlier that year at a shallow crossing that had historically served as the fording location. Located below the mills, the new bridge was the logical place to cross the river. This placed the road and bridge in the heart of the village, guaranteeing that Ann Arbor would soon become a prosperous town.

The landscape made building the road in the vicinity of Ann Arbor difficult. Conditions necessitated moving the base camp to the west side of the river. As a result, the crew spent much time in the vicinity of the rapidly growing village. Anxiously checking at the small post office on the first occasion he had,

Jacob was ecstatic when Postmaster John Allen informed him that there was indeed a letter waiting for him, mailed two months earlier. Written by his mother, she said that they were happy to have received his letter. They heard about the epidemic and numerous deaths. Learning that he survived, she wrote, was wonderful news, and they were all glad that he found work away from the city. She confirmed that all was well and that the growing season had been successful. She wrote about the activities of family members, including a note that they see Sally often at church and that she was also doing well and sends her greetings. Writing a quick response, Jacob described his life over the past several weeks and asked that they send the next letter to the new village of Jacksonburg, where he should be in a couple of months.

Road workers were pleasantly surprised to find that a newspaper was printed in Ann Arbor. They read every copy of the *Michigan Emigrant* that they could find to catch up on the news. The paper discussed local issues and provided helpful information for emigrants. It also had a correspondent in Washington, D.C., who covered national affairs, sending weekly updates to Samuel Dexter, the publisher. The workers heard many rumors and claims from various people they met along the road. The newspaper allowed them to read articles written by people more likely to be knowledgeable.

THE YEAR 1833 ARRIVED WHILE the crew was in the Ann Arbor vicinity. Some workers took advantage of that fact and spent much of their hard-earned money in local taverns to celebrate. Jacob and a few others participated, but with more caution than other revelers. Regrets were commonplace the following morning when hangovers and empty wallets made their presence felt.

It took a week to move the camp buildings and supplies west of the river and rebuild the camp. With additional boards provided by the sawmills, some of the buildings were built with new lumber rather than moving the entire old base camp. Once everything was established west of Ann Arbor, work on the road continued. With winter firmly established, cold and blustery weather became the norm. Because the ground was frozen and too hard to dig, they focused on felling trees and clearing stumps. Fire was an important tool in this process. Another crew would arrive in the spring, according to Callahan, to level the roadway and dig adjacent ditches.

Work was difficult and comforts few as the crew worked their way west. The landscape alternated between gravelly, unfertile hills, large swamps, and flat lands that gave the promise of excellent farmland. Jacob saw many places that he would have been happy to call home. However, he kept close track of his bank account, and knew that he had to work more before he could afford the amount of land he wanted while still having a cushion for hard times.

Winter turned to spring as they slowly progressed, following the original Native American trail on high ground between swampy areas and ponds. Just the same, the prevalence of wetlands and numerous small streams required making corduroy roads and building many bridges. This difficult task meant moving heavy tree trunks into place and filling the gaps between them with small stones and dirt. Even with the help of mules, it was backbreaking work. On many days, the distances accomplished were frustratingly short. The number of settlers and land seekers they encountered increased noticeably as the weather warmed. Jacob viewed each family and every young man with the same plans as his as competition. He was beginning to wonder if there would be any good land left for him once he was financially able to stake a claim. Weeks turned into months, and the crew found themselves at the settlement of Jacksonburg, located at a fording location on yet another river. The swift current was critical for the sawmills and grist mills that formed the basis of the new settlements, providing lumber for homes, barns, businesses, and the means of flour production.

Jacob found an opportunity to check at the small postal office in the village located in a home that also served as a tavern and inn. He was sorely disappointed to discover that no mail awaited him. The inn owner explained that mail delivery was highly irregular and undependable in places as remote as his village.

"Times are changing though," said the optimistic businessman. "Soon, we will receive mail on a daily basis! Our village is going to prosper because of the new road and the river, which flows all the way to Lake Michigan! Indians that live nearby still call the river Owashtanong, or some such, but everyone else calls it the Grand River.

"Small steamboats will soon use the river as a highway. We might even be the new capital when Michigan Territory becomes a state in a few years. Our town was named after President Jackson, and many people here agree that the name should be changed to simply Jackson. It sounds much better than Jacksonburg! People are moving into this area every week. It will soon be a modern city with shops, businesses, and government offices. A city where the mail will be dependably delivered."

Time passed in a blur, and it was soon June. Flatter land made the work easier in the forests and oak savannahs west of Jacksonburg. Six miles west of that village, they came upon the budding settlement of Barry. Like virtually all early settlements, it was situated on a stream that provided waterpower for a sawmill. A half-dozen new homes had been already built along the old trail.

Two residents of the tiny village, Sam Thompson and Benjamin Dalton, enthusiastically met the road crew as they neared the settlement. Thompson identified himself as the original settler at the location three years earlier, and Dalton described how he bought up more land and platted it as the Village of Barry the prior year. They were ecstatic because they knew that the road would bring more settlers into the area.

Plans were already underway for construction of a church and school, which they planned to have completed within the year. Fields were cleared nearby, with corn and wheat growing in the dark loamy soil, though there were still many stumps in them needing removal. Proud of the community they started, the two men boasted of its bright future because of the quality of the soil and the presence of sandstone to use as a building material. And now, most importantly, a passable road leading directly from the docks on the river in Detroit to this remote location.

As the road crew worked on the trail in the Barry area, a level of almost uncontainable excitement was building in Jacob's mind. For a month, he calculated and recalculated his figures. Jacob knew that he was now financially able to stake a land claim.

Why not right here? thought Jacob. *There is no reason to wait any longer! I've been working my tail off for nearly a year. It's the middle of June already, and this place has everything that I was dreaming of. If I act now, I can buy the land and have a small cabin built by winter.*

Jacob had witnessed other road workers quit their job to stake land in the Ann Arbor and Jacksonburg areas. He was sorely tempted to do likewise but knew that his finances were still a bit shy of what he felt was a truly adequate amount. The fear of running low on money before his farm became profitable caused Jacob many sleepless nights. He wasn't taking any chances of that happening. He would not allow his farm to be lost to the creditors and banks.

The additional weeks of income achieved by working until reaching the village of Barry provided the cushion Jacob felt was adequate. Confirming in his own mind that he had arrived at his desired homesteading location, Jacob met with Mr. Callahan to discuss terminating his employment. Callahan told him he was aware that Jacob would be quitting the road crew soon and was surprised he hadn't bought land somewhere before this. The foreman said he would go to Sheldon's Inn in a couple of weeks, and that Jacob could ride with him back to the inn. From there Jacob knew that it would be easy to get a ride back to Detroit.

In the meantime, Jacob had to make the most important decision of his young life: exactly what land he would stake and claim. Land in the immediate vicinity of the village was already claimed and was being cleared by would-be farmers. Sandstone bedrock exposed by the creek discouraged Jacob from that immediate locale. He knew the soil would be thin and poor in areas with surface bedrock. He spent days walking in the area's forests. A mile north of the village, beyond the clearings, Jacob came across gently rolling land with oak openings. Digging in the area showed rich, dark, well-drained soil. A damp area at the base of a small hill indicated the presence of accessible groundwater.

Jacob was thrilled. This was exactly what he was looking for, and his calculations supported his ability to make a purchase of 160 acres—half with cash, half on credit—while still having enough to purchase necessary equipment and see him through the early lean years. He recalled everything that he learned from various land agents and other people who had provided him with advice in the past year.

With the help of two local homesteaders, he began the process of staking the desired parcel of land. Finding blaze marks left by government surveyors on trees, and section corner markers, they carefully measured and marked his choice of land in what surveyors recently labeled Sandstone Township. With lumber from the sawmill, Jacob built a temporary one-room cabin on the land. He wanted to make it clear that the parcel was claimed to discourage squatters, but also so that when he arrived back to his land, he would have a place to live while he began building a permanent home. The possibility of someone assuming possession of his staked parcel prior to his return was of great concern to Jacob. He was aware that it was a problem for which there were few recourses other than forceable removal.

Dramatic changes followed the westward progress of the road. Within weeks, commercial interests appeared. There was word that a post office was to be established in the coming months. Among the people moving westward in relative comfort in horse- or oxen-pulled wagons were land speculators, blacksmiths, small businessmen, and entire families seeking land. One of the businesses that occurred almost immediately was that of cartage and coach services. No longer did a person have to walk into the wilderness carrying their belongings; they could pay someone to transport them from Detroit to any desired point along the road.

This transport system allowed Mr. Callahan and Jacob to return to Sheldon's Inn where Jacob's employment documents were finalized, and payment approved. Another teamster transported Jacob to Detroit, with the first stop being at the government land office and the neighboring bank. The crowd in the office gave him a start. With improvements made to roads into the interior, settlers and land developers were beginning to pour into a territory that was long avoided because of its alleged shortcomings. But no longer. Detroit now boasted the busiest government land office in the country.

SO IT WAS THAT IN July of 1833, in his 21st year, Jacob acquired ownership of his dream. His next stop was at the house of the widow Du Bois, who greeted him with tears and a motherly warmth.

"It has been longer than I anticipated since seeing you last. I feared for the worst, that you were injured or the victim of some calamity," she said.

After dinner, they spent an evening on the porch, sharing a bottle of her homemade wine while Jacob filled her in on the many events of the past year. She happily agreed that he should stay with her while taking care of the many things he had to do in the city before leaving for good.

His first stop the next morning was at the post office. Upon searching through a large backlog of mail, the clerk did indeed find an old letter from his family. A thrilled Jacob read the long letter, which was written under thinly concealed concerns for his well-being. They had not received anything over the course of the winter; his mail from Ann Arbor had not made it through.

Written as usual by his mother, she implored him to write as quickly as possible so that they knew he was okay. With the hope that he would receive the letter, she also filled him in on the latest news. Sally Baldwin was engaged to Charles Smythe. The reality of her marriage to another man was difficult for Jacob to accept even after being apart for over a year. But he knew that bridge was burned and there was no returning. The fortunate groom was an old acquaintance who would make an excellent husband. He was happy for them. Jacob wrote a long letter, congratulating the future Smythes, and briefly explaining his activities of the past year. A sizable portion of the letter concerned the details of his land claim. Uncertain as to when Barry would have dependable postal service, he instructed his family to send mail to his attention at Jacksonburg.

Jacob's next priority was equipment and supplies. Flour, saws, axes, hammers, clothing, powder and shot for his gun, and other basics were needed. Detroit's key role at that point in time was to fill the many and varied needs of settlers. Several businesses catered to providing supplies. Jacob eventually found everything he needed, though costs were higher than expected due to demand. With his expanded possessions filling a room at the widow's home, Jacob next arranged transport. There were a half-dozen small cartage businesses to choose from. Anxious to get to his new home, Jacob scheduled a teamster and wagon to leave early the next morning. Possessing a chivalrous spirit at his core, he then set aside an adequate amount of time on his final day to take care of any needed repair work on Mrs. Du Bois's house, sheds, and fences. He fed the animals one last time, giving each a playful rubdown. After a bountiful supper, they again spent a long evening on the porch talking—Mrs. Du Bois about her past, and Jacob about his future.

Breakfast came early and the teamster arrived as scheduled. Finishing up loading his supplies, Jacob gave Mrs. Du Bois a long hug. He knew he would miss this dear lady, so much a part of Detroit's unique past; a time that would soon be just a memory as progress rushed pell-mell into an unrecognizable future.

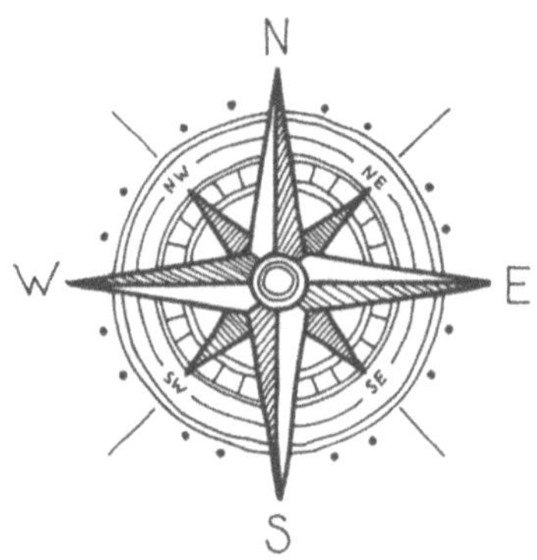

Chapter 16

"Timothy, you brat!" Mary Fischer screamed when she discovered the slimy wriggling earthworm in her dress pocket, livid at the latest prank of her younger brother. Having to ride with him in a cramped wagon on a bone-jarring road was bad enough, but finding a worm when reaching for her handkerchief was the last straw. Their age difference made this sort of disagreement as to what constituted cleverness inevitable. At nineteen, Mary was in every way a poised young woman—finished with school and ready for everything that came with being an adult. She was beyond finding such pranks the least bit humorous. At fourteen, just two months away from fifteen, Timothy was a prankster—one of the cleverest, in his mind. Unfortunately, for the last month Mary had been the primary recipient of his less than cunning comedic attempts.

Mary's parents never fit in well in New York City. Their conservative faith and ancestral agricultural roots made the transition to the metropolis difficult at best. Married while still living in rural Bavaria with its long-standing traditions, the reality of their new life in America did not pan out as they hoped. The dramatic culture shock of New York resulted in challenging circumstances for the family. They dearly missed the open fields and beauty of their homeland, and the familiar and safe environment that their Mennonite community had provided. Old World norms suited Max and Edna Fischer's viewpoint on one's role in life. New World customs did not.

Max Fischer loathed his work in a butcher shop. He also felt guilty that his wife Edna, an accomplished musician, had to work at an orphanage as a laundress to help make ends meet and to set some money aside for a better future. When the company's workload dropped and Max was notified that he was being let go, the Fischers viewed the news with as much relief as worry. That evening, in their small apartment, the family talked about their future. Max and Edna felt that the time was right to revive the dream of owning their own farm in America.

"We have been blessed with an opportunity to achieve what we have long dreamed of," Mrs. Fischer said. "We must not forsake it."

"There are two conditions to guide us," noted Max, reflecting long-held cultural beliefs they would not abandon.

"First, we will not move into a portion of the country that allows slavery. It is an abomination. Secondly, since we cannot afford to buy an existing farm, we will have to move to the frontier as homesteaders. We will clear our own land and create our own farm."

Since both children were born before emigrating to America,

neither felt a particularly close connection to New York. Just the same, Mary was conflicted about leaving. The city was where she assumed she would live out her life. Having finished Normal School, she was going to teach at the local elementary school.

She also expected that quite soon she would marry someone in her community. Blessed with sparkling blue eyes and long blonde hair, she was a lovely woman by any definition. But there was much more to her than simply being pretty. She was a highly confident, capable person, having no doubts about her abilities and anticipated future accomplishments. Mary was a trained vocalist and piano player, taught at home by her similarly skilled mother. She was of age for marriage, however, and some optimistic local youths already vied for her attention. The thought of moving west to start a new life left her simultaneously fearful and fascinated. After careful consideration, she decided to move with her family, certain that demand for schoolteachers and a plentitude of young bachelors would exist wherever they moved. Mary had one inflexible condition: that she could take her collection of textbooks and novels. An avid reader, Mary would rather go without other necessities than leave her precious books behind.

Timothy was torn. He did not want to move away from his friends, but the idea of moving into the wilds excited him. After much discussion, the family confirmed the idea of homesteading in the west, somewhere in the Great Lakes region. Selling what could not be taken on their journey, including a treasured piano, and with what savings they were able to accumulate through years of frugal living, they left the city behind on a fateful day in the spring of 1833.

Like so many others making a similar emigration west, the Fischers planned to take the Erie Canal to Buffalo. They paid a teamster to take them to Albany to begin their journey. The trip on the post road was almost enough to cause the family to change their minds. Heavy rains had made the rough road a quagmire, and several times everyone had to help free the wagon from deep mud. The horses were straining almost beyond their limits, and what enthusiasm Mary and her family had for the decision to move quickly evaporated. Upon arriving, they were shocked at the crowds they found at the Erie Canal lock. To make matters even worse, it took three days before a packet boat became available with space for them. *We are being tested,* thought Mary. *But we cannot give up now.*

The journey on the canal passed slowly but uneventfully, one day being much like another. At each stop, Mary and Tim exited the boat and walked around to relieve the boredom and muscle cramps. While on the packet, Mary covered her head with a scarf for protection from the burning rays of the sun and read books. *I can't wait for this trip to be done*, she thought silently, trying to not be an additional burden for her parents. Mr. Fischer took the opportunity to speak with as many other travelers as he could, hoping to learn the process of homesteading. His strong accent and limited fluency with English made it difficult for Max to communicate with others or read documents. He depended on Mary to serve as an interpreter when necessary.

Most other passengers were in the dark about the steps they needed to take and were optimistically hoping for the best. Mr. Fischer didn't share his concerns with his family, but he worried greatly about what the future held for them. *Have I made a terrible mistake*? he pondered, as they slowly made their way west on the canal. All of their possessions were packed in boxes, and they had no definitive plan for the future—not even where they were going.

The pilot eventually announced that they were nearly to Buffalo and that everyone should prepare to disembark in an hour. Mary was ecstatic when they arrived and could leave the cramped boat for good. Upon departing the boat in the bustling town of Buffalo, they gathered under a shade tree to discuss the next phase of their trip.

Getting to Buffalo was the easy part of their journey. The family had no clear idea what their next move should be.

Lacking knowledge about homesteading on government lands, Mr. Fischer said that they must locate a government office and speak with an official before making further plans. He silently prayed that the government man could provide the necessary information and guidance they needed to plan their course of action. Before leaving the vicinity of the canal lock, Mr. Fischer asked the captain where the government offices were located. Having encountered the same situation many times, the captain assumed that Mr. Fischer needed to go to the land office. He gave the appropriate directions to that frequently-asked-about agency. Following his directions, the Fischers made their way through the crowded, muddy streets. The government building was easy to locate, but unfortunately one of the busiest offices in the city. They waited in line until called.

The agent did a thorough job explaining the process of home-steading, detailing each facet of the procedure.

"The first question you must answer is where you want to go.

There is currently much interest in prairie lands in the region from Ohio to Illinois. The most fertile land in those states has largely been claimed. But keep in mind that the Michigan Territory and other unexplored lands further north or west are becoming available because of Indian treaties."

Getting to the most crucial issue first, Mr. Fischer inquired as to the cheapest farmland available.

"If you were here ten years ago, I would have told you to go to Ohio. But the best lands in Ohio are taken, and some are already being resold at high prices. If you want land that is still affordable, and you are willing to work hard to clear it, I recommend going north into the Michigan Territory, which will mean dealing with the land office in Detroit."

The agent explained the legal process of purchasing government land, and the timetable of the process. He also explained the concept of using credit to cover part of the costs.

"You must allow enough time to get to your chosen destination in the territory, meet with a bank, locate and stake unclaimed land, then travel back to the land office in Detroit to make the purchase. Because your whole family is moving, you will need to construct a cabin or find other lodging before winter sets in. It is going to be a tight race. I encourage haste on your part."

Looking at his wife for affirmation, Mr. Fischer said, "Then that is what we shall do. How does one get to the Michigan Territory?"

Mary was disappointed when the agent said that they must go to Detroit by way of a sailboat across the vastness of Lake Erie. She remembered well the frightening storms encountered when they sailed from Hamburg to New York.

Thankfully, the voyage across Lake Erie was calmer than their trip across the North Atlantic. Upon arriving in Detroit, they sought lodging for as long as it would take to prepare themselves for the next phase. They arranged a meeting with Major Biddle at the land office who provided further information about local conditions. Making use of the large wall map that showed all unclaimed lands, he suggested that the greatest likelihood of finding high quality land would be to travel west on the new road toward the small village of Jacksonburg.

"You should find available land anywhere in that area that will suit your purpose. When you do, stake it, and come back to my office to file the patent claim. If you lack the money to pay for the land in full, then go to the bank before you leave to file for credit so that you will be able to make the purchase when ready."

Using more of their savings, the Fischers bought a team of oxen and a wagon from a Detroit livery. Mr. Fischer decided on the oxen because he knew that they could not only pull the wagon as well as a team of horses, but that they had more usefulness when pulling stumps or performing other heavy work connected with clearing land and building structures. *And in an emergency*, he thought to himself, *the meat of an ox will keep a family alive during the winter.*

SO IT WAS THAT MARY found the earthworm in her pocket while in a wagon traveling west of Detroit in the heat of a summer's day. The condition of the newly constructed road impressed the Fischers, as did the number of people traveling on it. Loaded wagons pulled by teams of horses or oxen, many with some livestock trailing behind, were commonplace. Their lives had changed so much, Mary mused, in the time since they left New York City with all the belongings they could carry.

However, the crude settlement of Jacksonburg did not impress Mr. Fischer. Accustomed to the neat farms of Bavaria, this region bore the look of quickly raised rough buildings with fields of stumps. Mr. Blackman's small store was the only business. To make matters worse, there were reports of people in the village sick with the plague, which Mr. Fischer took to mean cholera. Though anxious to find a homesteading location, the Jacksonburg site did not seem right.

"Let's travel one more day to see what awaits us," he suggested to his family. Camping overnight for a final time, they proceeded west at daybreak, arriving at the settlement of Barry at noon. Stopping to water the team in the stream that flowed under a newly built bridge, they rested in the shade and enjoyed lunch in the tranquil setting. Mrs. Fischer commented about the pleasantness of the area and Max supported her impression, noting that the land looked fertile.

It was there that talkative Mr. Thompson encountered them. He bragged of the promise of the community. Extolling the fertility of the land, the nearby deposits of sandstone, and the settlement's access on the recently finished road, he boasted, "Nowhere in the territory will you find a more promising homestead. Whether you want to start a business or a farm, this is the place to do it. We are building a school and a church, and soon everything that a family needs will be here."

It was a stroke of immense good fortune. Mr. Fischer asked further about the school and whether they had yet hired a teacher.

"Not yet, but we will soon. Even before the building is finished, we will hire a teacher to meet with children in their homes. There are a dozen children here already and they need a teacher! Their parents are too busy building homes and clearing fields to do it themselves."

Upon overhearing the conversation, Mary decided that she had possibly found her future in the most unexpected place and manner. Reaching into her canvas luggage, she extracted her Normal School certificate. Walking self-confidently over to Mr. Thompson, she showed him the impressive-looking document.

"Perhaps your search has succeeded, Mr. Thompson. And I am fluent in three languages. Am I correct in assuming that many of the settlers here are from Europe?"

With a surprised look, Thompson took the document and reviewed it.

"Why, you just might be exactly what we are looking for, young lady! Let me gather a couple more gentlemen from town and we can settle this question before the sun sets." Pointing out his nearby home, he asked, "Would you folks be kind enough to join my wife and I, and some neighbors, for dinner this evening so we can discuss this matter further? In the meantime, you may wish to explore the local area and see what Barry has to offer your family."

Hitching the team once again, the Fischers continued west on the road for an hour, following trails leading off the road into freshly cleared fields and locations where cabins were being built. Upon digging test holes as they moved west, the fertility of the land was confirmed. The fact that the dark, rich soil was deep, with few large boulders and no bedrock outcroppings, satisfied a crucial factor in their analysis. Stopped in the shade of an ancient oak, the family discussed the feasibility of calling this area their home. The location, the quality of the land, an adequate water supply, and the scenic surroundings, all near a promising new town, were enough to convince them that they should give it high consideration. By the time they arrived at the Thompson's home for dinner, they agreed—this was the location that they would call home.

The Thompsons welcomed them, introducing four couples from nearby farms. They enjoyed a hearty meal, and conversation focused on the community and its promising future. The need of a good teacher for their children was clearly a priority topic for the locals. It seemed obvious to Mr. and Mrs. Fischer that this was more than a friendly dinner gathering; these people were anxious to apprise Mary's abilities and moral standing as a teacher and, if she passed their review, attempt to convince them to stay.

After clearing the table, the hosts shared a bottle of wine with the guests. Mrs. Fischer, noting the presence of a piano in the large home's parlor, commented as to how painful it was to leave their piano behind in New York. Mrs. Thompson inquired as to whether she played, and Mrs. Fischer responded that she had since she was a child. Mr. Fischer added what his wife was too modest to claim—that she did not just play the piano, she was an excellent pianist.

The Thompsons asked her to play for the gathering, which she gladly consented to do. She played some short pieces for practice and then announced that she would play and sing a tune called "I Know a Bank Where the Wild Thyme Blows" from Shakespeare's *A Midsummer Night's Dream.* She asked Mary to accompany her in the duet. Their rendition of the piece left everyone spellbound, their musical abilities far exceeding expectations. The Fischers all knew that the piano was out of tune but politely kept that fact to themselves. Mrs. Fischer relinquished the keyboard and thanked the Thompsons for the opportunity to play once again.

"It is we who are in debt to the two of you for such beautiful music!" exclaimed Mr. Thompson. "It was wonderful, and we would be honored to be able to hear you and Mary again."

Clearing his throat, Mr. Thompson continued.

"I won't beat around the bush, Mr. and Mrs. Fischer, and Mary. We all met earlier this afternoon to discuss this matter. We agreed that if Mary were indeed the sort of upstanding young lady that this town needs as a teacher—and everything we saw this evening confirms that she certainly is—we are proud to offer her the job as Barry's schoolteacher. You no doubt saw the school that we are building just a short distance west of here. After meeting all of you this evening, we are pleased to offer you the job, Ms. Fischer, and hope that you accept. We also offer whatever assistance we can, Mr. Fischer, in helping you locate and file a claim for land nearby, and assistance with the establishment of a home for your family."

Turning to Mary, Mr. Fischer told her that the final decision belonged to her. Mary looked around the room at the expectant faces.

"I am proud to begin my life work here. Yes, I accept the opportunity. But inform your children that I will be a hard taskmaster!" Her words were met with a resounding cheer.

With the help of families already established at Barry, the Fischers located a parcel of land on the west side of the settlement, near the new school. After staking the desired 80-acre parcel of land, Mr. Fischer made a hurried trip to Detroit to make ownership official. The Thompsons insisted that Mrs. Fischer, Mary, and Tim stay with them until their own home was built.

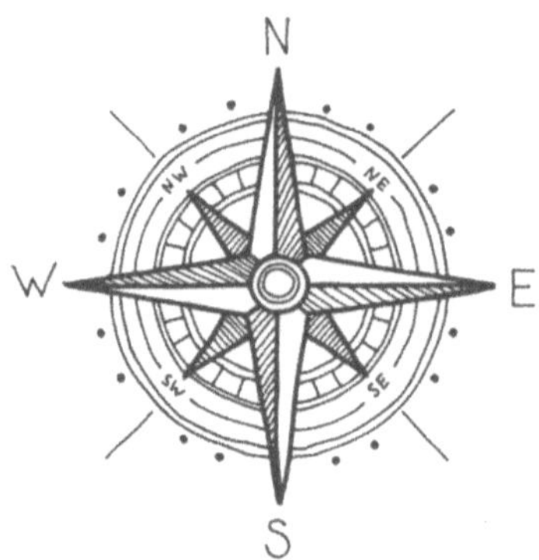

Chapter 17

WHAT A DIFFERENCE THE NEW *road makes*, thought Jacob as they traveled from Detroit to Ann Arbor on the first day. He felt pride in his contributions to making the road what it was. The hills and winding road slowed them on the second day, but by the third evening, they arrived in Barry. Being too late in the day to venture back to his property, they set up camp along the main road. Regardless of the long, tiring day, Jacob spent most of the night listening to the sounds of the forest and admiring the display of stars in the dark night sky. Being so close to his dreams overpowered all other thoughts and made sleep impossible. He arranged for the teamster to assist for one day after arrival. The horses had to be utilized as pack animals, carrying everything on their backs to his land because the trail was not yet improved enough for wagons. By midmorning, everything was carefully and securely loaded onto the unhappy horses. Leading them by the bridle, Jacob led the way north to his land. His heart was pounding.

It took over an hour to lead the horses through the windfalls, stumps, and thick brush before arriving at the small shelter he had built. He was extremely happy when he saw that everything looked in place with no sign of squatters or other problems. With a joyful heart he carefully unloaded his belongings, which nearly filled the small hut. He paid the teamster who led his team back through the darkening woods to the village. Jacob sat against an oak and stared around him at his domain.

"Mom, Dad, Robert, Sally—how I wish you could all see what I'm seeing right now."

Opening a bottle of whiskey bought just for the occasion, he poured two small glasses and said "*Slainte*, Mick. I wish you were here to see this." The unanswered howl of a distant wolf was the last sound Jacob heard as he finally dozed off under a brilliant celestial display.

The following weeks were difficult but fruitful. He dug a well and lined it with stones. With his water supply secured, Jacob constructed a root cellar to store perishable foods. Numerous trees were cut, trimmed, and stacked nearby for use in building a cabin. He was careful not to cut any sugar maples. Living off the land, he shot game which he cooked over an open fire, and harvested the plentiful wild blackberries, chokecherries, and blueberries. Dandelion leaves, roots of wild carrots, and other edible plants provided additional nutrients. Nuts in the forest litter from the prior year's mast crop were collected and stored by the bushel. Bergamot tea provided a relaxing drink at the end of long days. Jacob occasionally saw some of the other settlers from nearby parcels. On two occasions, visitors stopped by to introduce themselves and talk. On other occasions, he saw strangers following the section line further north, looking for land themselves. With the end of summer looming, everyone focused on their work with little time for socializing.

When the first hints of autumn arrived, Jacob knew that the point at which he needed help had arrived. It was time to lift logs into place and to construct a stone fireplace, critical steps that he could not do alone. Once finished with the exterior walls and roof, he would go to the sawmill to obtain planks to finish the cabin's interior.

Jacob left early one morning to visit other young settlers he knew in town and on nearby farms. He understood that it was critical to make arrangements with them to work together in the coming weeks to finish all their building projects before winter. He spent three days visiting as many of the locals as he could. He intended to make arrangements to band together for the remainder of the year, traveling from one homesite to the next, building cabins and barns.

Jacob's travels eventually took him to the Fischer homestead, just west of the village. He was impressed to see the entire family, including a young lady near his own age, hard at work on their new home. Jacob gladly accepted their invitation to take a break from his travels to share their midday meal. The history of each person he encountered in his travels west never failed to fascinate him. The Fischers were no different, their story being so similar to those of others seeking a new life on the frontier. Mary Fischer, with her sparkling personality and intelligence, particularly impressed him. *She will make an excellent schoolteacher*, he thought, appreciative of the role a teacher would play in the success of a new community.

A comment by Mrs. Fischer during their discussion about how much she missed the piano they sold prior to leaving New York caused Jacob to realize how much he also missed the joy of playing his fiddle for the delight of others. Though he played occasionally at the end of the day, he was usually too tired and focused on other critical issues to spend time with the instrument.

I've been focusing too much on the land and cabin, it's time to enjoy life again. I know what Robert, Jim, and Mick would have done—they would've spent less time cutting trees and more time with people. Hmmm, what if....

"Mrs. Fischer, I don't play the piano but I'm a fair fiddle player. One day I could bring it and we could celebrate our new lives here with some music. Maybe even invite nearby settlers and have a party."

"That is a lovely idea, Mr. Hart. We must plan to do that."

Lovely idea, indeed, thought Jacob as he left. *And I would surely like to get to know Mary better.*

Jacob spent the fall helping neighbors. They in turn helped him build his cabin and a small barn to be used for a horse and, eventually, cattle. He became close friends with two of the men. One of them was Isaac, a single man a couple of years older than himself who owned land along the creek. It was his intent to start quarrying the sandstone to meet demand for the building material which he was certain would soon be present. The other was Jerome Walker, a young family man with a wife and child, who was clearing land just south of Jacob's. Jerome reminded him much of Mick with his irrepressible good humor. His wife, Helen, was a charming, bright woman and active partner. She learned women's hair styling skills in New Jersey before marrying Jerome and moving west. Her skills were sought by many of the local women.

The Walkers also raised a highly sought-after breed of dog, black and tan terriers, for sale. Farmers highly prized the dogs for their ability to kill vermin, protect fowl and sheep from predators, and for hunting birds and small game for food. Knowing that he would need one, Jacob claimed the pick of a new litter.

It was several weeks of demanding work traveling from farm to farm helping to build homes and barns. When the work was completed, Jacob decided the time was right to visit the Fischers once again. Before doing so, he visited his friend Jerome. Hat in hand, he asked Helen if she would cut his unkempt hair and neatly trim his equally unruly beard. Cutting a man's hair had to be easier than the difficult process of styling a woman's long hair, Jacob assumed, and no barber had opened a traditional shop yet. Living in the woods and focusing on matters of immediate importance had caused him to ignore his personal appearance. He knew that if he wanted to impress the Fischers, and Mary in particular, he must make himself look like the responsible, intelligent young man they would respect. His appearance was currently a long way from that.

His motives were not lost on Helen.

"What young lady are you trying to impress, Jacob?" she said with a teasing laugh. "Could it be Miss Fischer?"

Jacob's face flushed, visible despite his suntanned features.

"No! I've been living in the woods for months and look like a wild man. I just need to have my hair cut and my beard trimmed so I look like a civilized person again. I look so bad that even you and Jerome wouldn't let me in your house if you didn't know me."

It was obvious that he didn't convince her of his motives. After she finished, he once again looked like a responsible young man that even his own strict father would find acceptable. He thanked her profusely, leaving some loin chops from a deer he recently butchered as payment.

Wasting no time, he walked over to the Fischer homestead, trying to brush the hair clippings off his clothes. Finding them at work outside, his heart fell when he realized that Mary was not present. Much progress was made on their land-clearing efforts, and a modern board house had been partially constructed since his last visit. In the ensuing conversation he learned that Mary already began her teaching duties. Until the new school was completed, she traveled to local homes where children gathered three days per week. Not wanting the idea of a musical gathering to be forgotten, he raised the concept again. He suggested a Christmas Eve get-together as an opportunity for the many newcomers to celebrate the holiday for the first time in a new land. They wholeheartedly agreed. Jacob was delighted when Mary arrived home just as he was about to leave. They shared a few comments, and he left feeling embarrassed because he feared that he came across as an awkward child.

"Damn! I wish to hell I had Robert's or Mick's charms when it came to talking to women!" he angrily mumbled to himself after he left.

Before making his way to his cabin, he stopped at the Thompson's. They not only had a piano, but their house was the largest in the village. If a social event was to be held in the winter months, it was best suited for the purpose. The Thompsons thought it was a great idea and immediately endorsed it, committing to spreading the word to neighbors.

Helen had mentioned earlier that his pup was weaned and ready to be claimed. Jacob stopped again at the Walkers to take possession of the dog. He named it Spot because of a large white patch on its head. Jacob, carrying the pup, made his way back to his cabin in the subdued early winter twilight. The path back to his land was becoming a well-used trail. He and other nearby settlers gradually cleared section line roads perpendicular to the St. Joseph Road, now commonly called the Territorial Road. These section line trails, running north and south from the east/west axis of the main road, allowed access to parcels located some distance inland. What began as footpaths were for the most part now traversable by horses, even horse-drawn carts in many instances.

WITH WINTRY WEATHER SETTLING IN, Jacob spent much time cutting firewood for use in his fireplace and the small cookstove he had purchased before he left Detroit. Maintaining an adequate supply of firewood was a difficult, time-consuming task. Cutting pieces small enough for his stove was especially challenging. He recalled that during the first few days on his land, when digging the well, he noticed what looked like coal near the surface. At the time he didn't give it much thought, since he had enough firewood to last many years. But the advantage of coal was becoming more apparent as he labored with a saw and axe to stockpile wood. He knew from his days in Vermont that coal was superior to firewood for use in smelteries and foundries as well as in stoves found in homes for heating and cooking.

It dawned on Jacob that coal would soon play a vital role in the local economy. Its presence on his land could represent a significant financial opportunity if it were present in a large quantity. At the first opportunity, Jacob dug in the area near his well. He did not have to go very deep before running into a significant coal deposit. Digging along the seam of coal, he found that it followed a distinct path, slowly getting deeper underground as he progressed downhill.

Jacob knew he had confirmed the presence of enough coal to make it profitable. That evening, warming in front of his fireplace, he pondered what this meant to his future. It became clear to him that the coal had little value if he used it just for himself. Mining and selling it, however, was an option, and the timing was right. Blacksmiths, and other small industries that might take root in Barry or Jacksonburg, would need coal. The level of development was reaching the point to make a coal business profitable. Owners of homes built on platted village land did not have access to free firewood; they had to purchase it. These homeowners would no doubt prefer coal because of its efficiency and ease of handling. Most of these immigrants were more familiar with the use of coal as the fuel for heating a house and cooking. It was the fuel they used prior to moving.

A comment by a neighbor that a blacksmith had recently opened a shop in the village only strengthened the case in Jacob's mind. Jacob understood that if he acted quickly, he could place himself at the forefront of supplying coal for local use. The new, unanticipated idea of going into business was overwhelming. Such an undertaking would be an enormous gamble. Could he do both—clear land and sell coal at the same time? *What the hell*, he thought. *As Robert used to say—nothing ventured, nothing gained. Good fortune has blessed me, and I shouldn't throw away this opportunity. I will do it.* Jacob realized that to take full advantage of the situation, he would have to make the necessary investments. The first was transport capabilities.

Jacob lay awake much of the night thinking and plotting his course of action. By morning, a bold plan had materialized, a plan that required much work to implement. He left home after a quick breakfast. As the sun was just clearing the eastern horizon, he set off on a long walk. He first stopped at a farm near Jacksonburg where he knew horses and equipment were sold. Finally agreeing on a price, he purchased a horse and harness, a small wagon, and a supply of hay and grain. The mare was a Morgan, a bit older than he wanted, but affordable. She had many years of service ahead of her as both a workhorse and a rider. Jacob's father and many of his neighbors in Vermont owned Morgans, a good, all-purpose breed.

Jacob then went to the new blacksmith's shop in Barry. He met Isaiah Woodbury, a young ironworker recently resettled from Massachusetts with his wife and two small children. It was his first attempt at running a smithing business by himself, having previously served as an apprentice for two years. They got to know each other a bit and then Jacob inquired as to where the smith bought the coal he used. Woodbury explained that while in Detroit, prior to moving west, he'd spent much time investigating how to obtain the coal he would need. He said that there was a company there that brought coal from Pennsylvania mines to Detroit. They then sold it to local homes and businesses. Woodbury described contracting with a teamster that agreed to cart the coal west to his shop on a monthly basis. A load had been delivered three weeks prior to Jacob's visit. Woodbury said that it was an expensive and cumbersome process, but having eastern coal shipped in from Detroit was the only available option.

Jacob made a proposal that the ironworker agreed to consider. He promised to deliver in two days' time a load of coal for the smith to inspect. Jacob promised that if Woodbury found it acceptable, he could guarantee a dependable source and delivery as needed, at a significantly lower cost. Jacob further stated that they would discuss cost only after Isaiah inspected and approved the coal.

Arriving home just before dark, Jacob spent the remaining daylight making the shed an acceptable home for his new horse, whom he decided to name Molly. With the horse taken care of, Jacob took time to relax after a very long day. After a meal of potatoes and venison, he lay in his cot and quickly fell asleep. Awakened by the pre-dawn cold, the next morning came much too soon. He had slept so soundly that he failed to replenish the firewood during the night, resulting in the fireplace turning cold. He decided that he would research the best use of coal in his own fireplace, mixing it with wood to produce the hottest, longest burning fires.

Jacob spent much of the day digging out coal. He separated poor-quality pieces from the top of the seam from the higher quality coal below it. He carried a supply of low-value crumbly chunks into his cabin for his own use. About two hundred pounds of hard coal rocks were loaded into his wagon and covered with a tarp for transport the next day. Finding that digging the mineral with a shovel was difficult, he decided that the next step would be the acquisition of a pickaxe. The idea of bartering the coal in the wagon for a pickaxe made by the blacksmith seemed a logical approach, since he was quite sure that he would not find such a tool for sale nearby.

Jacob awoke to a wintry landscape. Though it was snow covered, the trail into the village appeared passable. He hitched the horse to the cart and hoped for the best. With no other tracks to help guide him, staying on the trail was difficult at times. It took considerable control to keep the horse on the correct course, avoiding hidden stumps and holes. The trip into Barry was a time of deep thought for Jacob. He assumed that if he found coal on his property, the mineral would certainly be found on other nearby properties. It would only be a matter of time before other property owners discovered it and tried to sell it to local businesses and homeowners. If he was the first to discover a coal deposit, he must take advantage of that fact and move quickly and decisively. Today was the day to make the first and most important deal. With luck and focus, more could follow.

Jacob eventually saw smoke from village homes, providing

guidance through the now heavily falling snow. He found the blacksmith hard at work in a shop behind his house. He welcomed the opportunity to spend a few minutes in the hot workshop to rest and warm up. Jacob then brought in an armload of coal for inspection. Isaiah inspected it closely, comparing it with the eastern coal he used. Putting some chunks in the fire and watching it burn, Isaiah was satisfied that it burned with heat adequate for all but the most demanding forging projects requiring maximum temperatures. For infrequent ironworking projects that required the highest temperature fire, hard, eastern coal from his stockpile could be added.

Jacob knew that the time to make a deal was now or never. He asked how much Isaiah paid to have a load delivered. Isaiah went to his desk to locate the shipping invoice. Viewing it, Jacob proposed to deliver all the coal that Isaiah needed at one-half the price stated on the document. Isaiah estimated that a wagon load would be about a thousand pounds. Jacob said that he could also provide that amount monthly, with the first load available in a week's time.

Isaiah pondered the proposal. When Jacob then told the blacksmith that he could have all the remaining coal in the wagon if he made him a pickaxe, the deal was sealed.

Isaiah invited Jacob to stay for lunch and meet his wife and children. Over lunch, they talked about the future of their community. Though freezing weather dramatically slowed the movement of immigrants, it was still quite common to see a family making their way west. At least a half-dozen families purchased lots for a home in the village. Other immigrants were staking claims in the local area for farmland. The sight of trees being cut and the burning of brush piles and stumps were commonplace. Construction was nearly completed on both a church and the school. Small shops and businesses were starting up. Isaiah mentioned that he already found it hard to keep up with orders for farm tools and sundry items needed in a household. Jacob suggested finding an apprentice.

As he said it, Jacob realized that he would soon need a helper himself. Once spring arrived, it would be almost impossible for him to do all the farm work that would be required along with running a coal mining and distribution business.

After lunch, Jacob hitched his empty wagon and made the cold ride back to his cabin. There were many things to consider and actions to take if his plans were to come together. His priority was to honor his agreement with Isaiah, which meant excavating a wagonload of coal for delivery within the next week. He also had another looming commitment. If he was going to play his fiddle as promised at the upcoming Christmas Eve celebration, less than two weeks away, he needed to practice. After Christmas, weather permitting, he planned a trip to Jacksonburg. The success or failure of his plans in that neighboring town would greatly impact his future.

But first things first—Jacob spent the next two days excavating coal. With the wagon loaded, he covered it with the tarp to keep the coal dry and secret. The next day he delivered the load to Isaiah. With payment in hand, Jacob went to the equipment dealer near Woodville, three miles to the east, to buy a saddle for his horse.

Back home, he took care of maintenance on his cabin and small barn, and spent time digging up as much coal as he could in the likelihood that excavation would not be possible once a hard freeze settled in. If his plans were successful, he would need two tons of coal ready for transport. In the evenings, he practiced his fiddle. Realizing that he did not know any traditional Old World Christmas carols caused a panic, but he knew he could do nothing about that situation now.

Jacob was the first to arrive at the Thompsons' home on the afternoon of Christmas Eve. After putting Molly in their barn, he brought his carefully wrapped violin into their house to warm up. He helped them get everything set up as neighbors gradually arrived. The house filled well before the 8:00 dinner time. The arrival of the Fischers brought a smile to Jacob's face. The thought of playing his violin accompanied by Mrs. Fischer on the piano intrigued and excited him. While he had played as part of a duo with Mateo back in Vermont, he had no experience being part of a duet with such a skilled musician as Mrs. Fischer. Knowing that Mary would sing as they played made the dream complete.

As neighbors arrived, the musicians made their way into the home's parlor, where the piano was located. Mrs. Fischer sat down and did some quick drills on the keyboard. Her fears were confirmed upon finding that the piano was still out of tune. Being discreet, she asked the Thompsons and her husband to speak with her in the parlor for a few minutes. Once there, she explained the problem. The Thompsons said that they weren't surprised, since they had not been able to have the piano professionally tuned since they moved into the house. Mrs. Fischer informed them that that wasn't a problem because her husband was able to tune pianos. He'd learned the skill in Germany and had used it while in New York City, both for extra income and to keep his wife's instrument in tune.

Already aware that the Thompsons' piano needed tuning, the Fischers had discussed the issue before leaving home. Mr. Fischer brought the necessary tools with him that evening in case his skills were needed.

"All we need is your permission to proceed," Mrs. Fischer said.

The Thompsons cheerfully agreed, leaving Max to do his work.

The dinner exceeded all expectations, and compliments flowed freely for Mrs. Thompson and the neighbors who helped her. Following the meal, everyone except Jacob, Mary, and Mrs. Fischer relaxed near the blazing fireplace.

The musicians reconvened in the parlor. There they discussed which holiday tunes to play. Jacob confessed his lack of knowledge of traditional European Christmas carols, which came as a surprise to the Fischers. As a result, he and Mrs. Fischer spent the next hour practicing four tunes: "Joy to the World," "Silent Night," "We Wish You a Merry Christmas," and "Hark the Herald Angels Sing." Feeling ready, they opened the parlor door and invited guests in. Barry residents talked about the special night for years. With Mrs. Fischer on the piano, Jacob on the violin, and Mary soloing, it was a performance worthy of the best venue in a large city. Besides the Christmas hymns, Jacob and Mrs. Fischer both played a mix of tunes from Europe and the eastern United States. Everyone agreed that in the cold wilds of a Michigan winter, the performance brought warmth to their hearts.

Most of the guests left after season's greetings were shared after midnight. The Fischers remained a bit longer, allowing Jacob an opportunity to speak with Mary. They could have gone on talking late into the night, but her father eventually insisted they leave, as they had more than a mile to ride in the cold darkness. When Jacob prepared to leave, Mr. Thompson suggested that he spend the night there, rather than risk traveling on horseback with his violin through the dark snowy woods. Jacob reluctantly agreed, but once rolled up in a blanket in front of the fireplace, he was glad for the offer of overnight lodging.

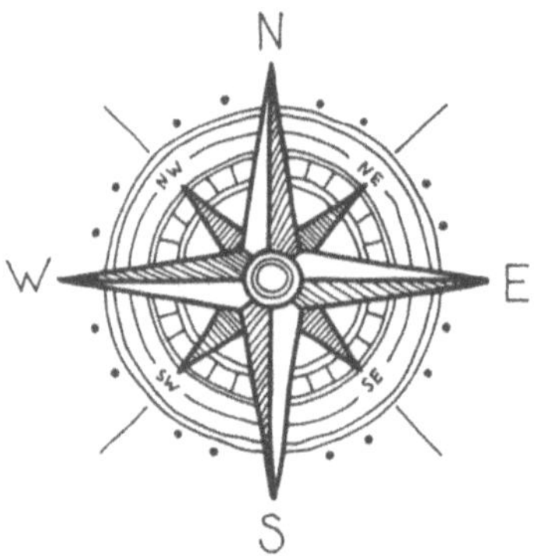

Chapter 18

THE YEAR 1834 DAWNED CLEAR and cold. It was a time of unbridled optimism in the territory. New villages in what had been wilderness just a few years earlier were prospering. Forests in the southern portion of the territory were being converted into farms, and roads and trails were extending into hitherto inaccessible regions. There was even talk of railroads and canals. Interest in land in the Michigan Territory was higher than ever, and the influx of settlers resulted in the demand for goods and services. The economy and population were rapidly expanding. Jacob witnessed this progress from the village of Barry. A post office opened in a newly built general store shortly after Christmas. The stars seemed aligned and prospects bright. Jacob believed that the new year would be an excellent one with opportunities for those willing to aggressively pursue their dreams.

In early January, Jacob took his next daring step. Dressed as warmly as he could, he left home in the cold early morning snow. A bag secured to his saddle had several chunks of coal in it. His destination was Jacksonburg. Upon arrival, he stopped at the blacksmith's shop, located on the river just south of Territorial Road. Heavy smoke from the shop's flue made it easy to find. James MacDonald could not have been more different than his Sandstone Township counterpart. Twice Woodbury's age and size, MacDonald had been a metalworker in Scotland since his youth, learning the trade by working at his father's side. He and his family emigrated in 1830, making their way to Jacksonburg a year later. Jacob stood by silently while the smith finished shaping a piece of molten metal into the shape of a plow point. Looking around while waiting, Jacob noticed a large pile of what looked like hard Pennsylvania coal.

When finally finished with the project, MacDonald looked at Jacob with a "what do you want" expression. He personified the living definition of gruff and taciturn, and his bulk made it clear that one made him angry at one's own risk. Jacob introduced himself, quickly getting to his point. As with Mr. Woodbury, he told the smith that he could provide him with a dependable supply of coal at a significantly lower cost than he was currently paying.

"Pish!" Spitting on the floor, MacDonald continued. "Just how the hell do you propose to do that! Do you take me for a damned fool?" with an accent so thick Jacob had difficulty understanding him.

Taking a direct, no-nonsense approach, Jacob simply said, "Because I know a source of good coal that is a hell of a lot cheaper than what you're paying. You are buying coal mined in Pennsylvania, shipped to Detroit, then carted from Detroit to Jacksonburg. Am I right? I am here to tell you that I have a much closer source for coal, and as a result I can sell it to local businesses like yours for much less."

"Where is this source of yours?"

"If you buy coal from me, I may tell you. But not before, perhaps not even then, because I must protect my property. I have a source. I own it, and if you want to discuss the details and reach an agreement, I can guarantee delivery at about one-half of what you are paying right now to purchase coal from five hundred miles away."

"Prove this nonsense that you're claiming!"

"I have a sample of the coal with me. If you wish to discuss my offer, I will bring it in for your inspection. I will tell you right now that my coal is suitable for most of your work. If you make steel items, you may need the hard coal you purchased from the eastern mines. But for most of what you do my coal is totally suitable."

"Bring it in."

Jacob brought in the bag of his coal and gave it to MacDonald. The smithy's lifetime of experience at the forge showed.

"This is softer coal than what I buy from Detroit. It isn't as good."

Jacob was glad that he had met with Isaiah Woodbury first and had an opportunity to calmly discuss the needs of a typical blacksmith. Knowing what a blacksmith needed for fuel, based on the types of work being done in the local region, gave Jacob the knowledge and confidence to state his case intelligently.

"As I said, this coal will burn hot enough for every iron

product you make. If most of your work is horseshoes, plow points, tools, and other iron products, this coal is totally sufficient. There may be a small portion of your work that will require mixing some of the harder eastern coal in with mine. But why pay for a type of coal that you don't need, from mines 500 miles away, and pay for all that shipping and carting, when I can provide coal that will perfectly suit your needs from nearby at a much lower cost? Why not keep the money you work so hard for, rather than give it to strangers for shipping your coal hundreds of miles?"

"I just received a load of coal a couple days ago, so I don't need any right now. But I may be willing to give your coal a try. How much are you charging?" Based on information he had obtained from Isaiah about his costs for having a half-ton of hard coal delivered from Detroit, Jacob made certain assumptions about what MacDonald paid. Considering the additional distance involved in carting coal from his farm to Jacksonburg, Jacob gave an amount that he assumed would be about 55 to 60 percent of that estimate.

"I will try one load. But I won't need any until March. If it works as well as you claim it does, I will buy more from you. If it doesn't work as well as you say, then you needn't come back here again."

"I accept. I also have no doubt that you will find my coal will meet your needs and you will find that my word is dependable. I will be back on March 15 with a half-ton."

Returning to Barry, Jacob stopped at the new general store and post office. There, he planned to carry out the second step of his plan. In small villages across the territory, the postmaster was frequently one of the most important people in town. Developing a relationship with them had benefits. Jacob had an additional goal for this visit.

After introducing himself to Horace Johnson, the new postmaster, Jacob wrote a letter to his friend Robert in Vermont. From discussions they had prior to his departure, Jacob knew that Robert also feared that the future held little for him in his current situation for many of the same reasons Jacob had felt. Jacob believed that Robert could have a good future nearby. In the letter, Jacob assured him that good land was still available nearby to purchase for a farm. Jacob also shared with his friend the discovery of coal deposits on his land and outlined his idea for the two of them to team up and operate a coal-selling business. He explained that there would be a strong demand for coal soon, and that if they acted quickly, they could capitalize on this need by being the first to supply the fuel.

For the next two months, Jacob focused on land clearing activities. As was the case on neighboring farms, the process of burning piles of branches and stumps was unending. The smell and sight of smoke served as a daily reminder of farmers' struggles to get fields cleared for the spring planting season. Burning unwanted slash from clearing of woodlands created serious wildfire dangers when the ground was not snow covered, thus winter was the time when this task most commonly took place.

Jacob took time to deliver loads of coal to Isaiah each month as promised. In January, he gladly received the pickaxe requested during his initial meeting. Testing it as soon as he arrived back home, he was extremely pleased with the tool. It was much more efficient and easier to use than a shovel to extract coal. During his February delivery to Isaiah, the smith told him that a general store had just opened, and that it would house the post office for the village. Jacob told Isaiah that he was aware of the store and post office, but the smith was ahead of him. "The store will need coal to burn in their stove," Isaiah suggested with a wink.

Jacob just smiled and nodded his head. He didn't feel it necessary to explain to Isaiah that he had already thought about this possibility. Given his current situation, however, Jacob felt that he could not take on any new buyers yet. It was going to be difficult to mine and deliver the coal shipments that he already had to guarantee. For the time being, the blacksmiths would remain his only customers.

Just as Jacob and other new settlers were preparing their land and building necessary structures, their lives became more complicated. A new rule required all able-bodied men in each township to work a certain number of days on road construction. Though Congress or the territorial legislature provided funding for the few main roads in the region, there was no means or money allocated for construction of local roads. These township roads, primarily built on section lines, served as the routes from farms to markets and connected residents and towns to other communities. Though the work was hard and interfered with the lives of residents, the payment received was valuable and the broader benefits of transportation were substantial. Road building income from the local government carried many new farmers over the period when no income was being generated from the farm. Once farms were producing, getting produce to potential customers by means of the new road network was critical. For his part, Jacob and nearby farmers now had access to all area homes, businesses, and farms, making commerce possible. Few were aware that the money used by township officials to pay residents for working on roads came from the sale of properties that had reverted to the government after homesteaders had failed to pay their taxes.

Jacob's coal deliveries during March included the promised shipment to the Jacksonburg blacksmith. MacDonald was true to his word and cancelled his contract with the Detroit supplier. It appeared that both smiths were satisfied with the quality of his coal, as well as the cost and dependability of deliveries.

Returning to Barry, Jacob went to the general store. It took a lot of explaining on Jacob's part, but in the end, he successfully explained to Mr. Johnson of his need for replacement violin strings. To make Johnson's job easier, Jacob was able to provide the name of the store in New York City where they could be ordered. Johnson said he would work with his wholesaler to accomplish the unusual request. Jacob thanked him profusely.

Observing Johnson struggle with the act of bringing wet firewood in for his stove, it seemed clear to Jacob that the owner would prefer the ease of burning coal to heat the building. He almost brought the idea up, but didn't, knowing that he would have trouble honoring one more coal delivery request at the current time. He made a mental note to talk to the owner when he could honor any new coal selling agreements.

But not yet, Jacob thought. *Besides, I feel a bit of ague coming on. After all the work I must do in the next few months is finished, and I have some help, I'll expand my business.*

Inquiring if there was any mail for him, he was pleased when the clerk found two letters. One was from home and the second from his old friend Robert. He read the letter from Robert first. It had been written almost a month earlier. A broad smile came over Jacob's face as he read. After thinking about Jacob's offer, Robert agreed. He would take care of necessary affairs at home, and then move west. He thought that he would arrive in late March. He asked Jacob to stake out a nearby eighty-acre parcel of land; that was the most he could afford. Robert noted that since the number of land buyers would increase dramatically in the spring, he hoped that Jacob could preserve some good land for him. Jacob was exultant. He knew of a parcel of land nearby that would fit Robert's needs. If it weren't for other plans, he would ride to it that very day to do necessary measuring and staking. But he had other plans for what would be a long and hopefully productive day. He put his mother's letter in his pocket to read later in his cabin.

Leaving the store, Jacob rode the short distance to the Walker homestead. Almost all settlers found that they needed to depend on savings or have an alternative source of income during the first two years of homesteading, before the sale of produce was possible. Homesteaders utilized a wide variety of income-producing enterprises, from selling eggs to market hunting. Helen Walker's hair cutting business was doing well, and Jacob (and other local men) were all too happy to take advantage of her barbering skills. This time he was prepared to pay her with money, instead of venison. Rather than accept the money, Helen asked if he could stop by in two or three days to help Jerome install a beam in the barn he was building. Jacob happily agreed and promised to be there.

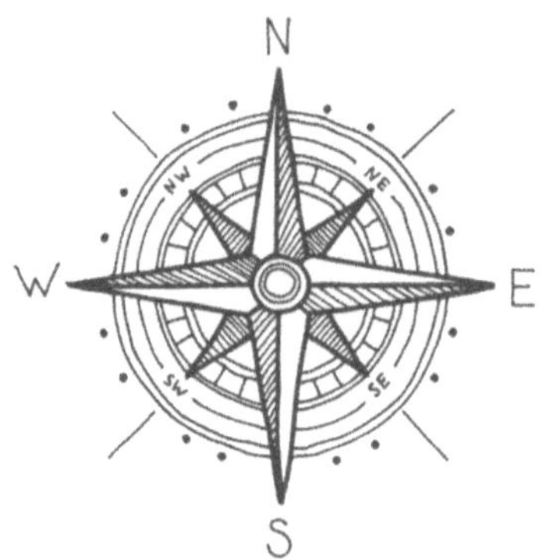

Chapter 19

LOOKING MORE DAPPER THAN HE had in years, Jacob rode west to the Fischer residence. He had two reasons to visit them. One personal, the second involved business. Securing his horse to the decorative hitching post, Jacob was amazed at what he saw. The large house was finished. A small barn in the rear of the yard was also new since his last visit, replacing the crude lean-to. A horse that shared it with the two oxen was also new. He saw young Timothy in the side yard, splitting firewood. Looking at the two substantial chimneys, he surmised that keeping a supply of wood for such a large home would be nearly a full-time job. He greeted Tim and asked if his parents were home, to which Tim confirmed that they were, and that they would be happy to see him. Hearing the two of them talking, Mr. Fischer came to the porch and invited Jacob inside.

Upon entering, he was greeted by Mrs. Fischer and led into the living room. She noted Jacob's cough and suggested that he sit near the fire for warmth, then excused herself to prepare refreshments. Seated in chairs on either side of the fireplace, Jacob and Mr. Fischer discussed local matters. Upcoming spring planting activities were a major concern for both landowners since it was to be the first year for their crops. Neither felt fully prepared. Mr. Fischer said that the equipment dealer in Jacksonburg will sell seeds for corn and oat crops, as well as for vegetable gardens. A nursery near Ann Arbor was selling varieties of fruit trees. There was so much work to do during this initial spring of their farming aspirations that both men wished they could begin the necessary work immediately. It was too early in the year, however. In March, a farmer can only plan and prepare, not plow and plant.

Mrs. Fischer brought a tray of coffee and snacks into the living room, taking a seat next to her husband. She told Jacob that she put a bit of brandy in his coffee to help with his catarrh. One of the many conversation topics was the mutual desire to organize another event such as the Christmas Eve party. They agreed that something to welcome the upcoming spring would be most appropriate.

During their conversation, Jacob couldn't help but wonder where Mary was. He hoped that she would be home since it was a Saturday, and he didn't think she would be teaching. At an opportune time, Jacob asked if he could discuss a business issue. Breaking the ice with an easy one, he asked if he could pay for the use of the oxen team for a day to drag stump remnants out of the first field he had cleared. The Fischers said they could certainly arrange that. Jacob's second proposal involved Timothy, now a strapping youth nearly sixteen years of age.

Jacob inquired about hiring their son to help with various tasks that Jacob would lack the time to do once warm weather arrived.

Explaining that he would be kept busy on their own farm, the Fischers inquired about how many days per week or month Jacob had in mind. When he said it would only be about one day per week on average, it eased their concerns. Mr. Fischer said that it was Timothy's decision, and he called his son into the house. Upon hearing Jacob's proposal, Timothy readily agreed. The idea of making some money of his own excited him. He then excused himself, going into the kitchen for a snack.

The sound of a door closing upstairs and footsteps on the stairs caught everyone's attention. Looking toward the sounds, Jacob smiled when he saw Mary come into the room. He rose to greet her and offer her his chair, which she declined, taking a nearby seat instead. She apologized for not coming down sooner, explaining that she had many student assignments to check before Monday.

"Some of the essays about the War of Independence are quite interesting!" she laughingly declared. "As are some of the answers on the last mathematics test."

"I am so glad that it is you doing such difficult work, Mary," noted Jacob, "because I would have no idea how to teach children to write, read, and do math. I have enough difficulty with those things myself."

Mr. and Mrs. Fischer excused themselves, citing various tasks they had to do. Mary remained, and for the first time, the two took advantage of an opportunity to talk alone on a personal level. Jacob learned more about Mary's passion for teaching and for music. She discovered Jacob's love of the land and desire to be a successful farmer. She came to learn that he also shared a passion for the important things in life, though Jacob would probably never describe it in exactly those words. He derived true joy from achieving dreams and not being restricted to what others believed things should be. Much like herself, she concluded.

It was late afternoon when Jacob finally departed for home. He knew it would have been wise to leave sooner, as he was feeling quite sick, but he had no intention of cutting his time with Mary short. He begrudgingly declined the Fischers' offer to stay for supper. A cold drizzle and gray clouds portended an unpleasant trip, and he preferred to have some daylight remaining as he made his way through the slush and mud to his cabin. Jacob was pleased to learn that Timothy had taken Molly into the barn for food and shelter. Bidding the family farewell, and promising to plan another musical event, Jacob departed into the gloom of the late winter twilight. He rode only a short distance when he realized that his dress, adequate for midday wear, was totally inadequate for the cold, wet ride home.

Soaked from the cold rain and shivering uncontrollably, Jacob arrived home well after dark. It required extraordinary effort to care for Molly before finally making his way into the cabin. It was nearly as cold inside as out, but at least it was dry. He labored urgently to get a fire started. Once that was finally accomplished, he changed into dry clothes. Forgoing supper, he chose to sleep instead.

THE NEXT MORNING, JACOB STRUGGLED to get out of bed. His throat was on fire and his lungs hurt from bouts of uncontrollable coughing. He built up the fire and warmed a broth but was shivering so badly he had trouble drinking it. Before laying down again, he retrieved the letter from home that was folded up in his coat pocket. Fortunately, it was still legible, though wet. Upon opening the letter, Jacob hoped that there was no bad news contained within his mother's missive. He did not feel up to reading bad news. In fact, as he suppressed another fit of coughing, he struggled to recall ever feeling so lousy. The letter described life events that were common in every family and repeated endlessly across the centuries. They were all doing well, though his brother Joe slipped on ice and broke his arm. His uncle Lou, his father's brother whom Jacob didn't know well, had died. There was concern about what was to happen to Lou's family and farm. Jacob's oldest sister, Jasmine, was engaged to be married to the Carlson's son Fred. The rest of the letter continued in the same vein, providing an update on life in Jacob's home community. After another coughing outbreak, Jacob put the letter in a box with the others. He then put on another layer and laid in front of the fireplace, experiencing a dire need to feel warm again.

After a brief period of sleep, Jacob awoke feeling even worse. A sense of desperation overcame him. He knew that he must get up and take care of Molly and bring in some water and prepare food to eat. His horse took priority. He drew a pail of water from the well, using it to replenish Molly's water trough. He cleaned her stall, adding dry straw, and gave her a supply of fresh hay. Satisfied that Molly was okay for the rest of the day, Jacob filled the water pail and took it inside the cabin. He placed some venison in a frying pan to grill, adding some water and vegetables. He didn't feel hungry but knew that it had been a full day since eating the few hors d'oeuvres that Mrs. Fischer prepared, and that he should eat something.

The terrifying ordeal was repeated for a week. Jacob's daily goal became simply to care for Molly the best he could, ignoring his own needs. On the sixth day, Jacob was unable to even get up to take care of his precious horse. He gasped for breath, in pain from the endless coughing. Unable to go for help, Jacob knew his situation was perilous. What most Vermonters back home called the Winter Fever had been the cause of death of several people he knew back home. He knew he had it, and that death was the likely result. Anger and frustration were fueled by the helplessness he felt. Struggling mightily, Jacob got up one last time to take care of Molly. That done, he added wood to the fire and laid down for what he knew was likely his last time, with Spot at his side.

More than a week after Jacob assured Helen he would help with the barn building project, he had not shown up as promised. This seemed out of character, but Jerome knew that he was busy. Cutting trees along his property line, Jerome noticed that the trail to Jacob's cabin did not show signs of recent use. Now concerned, Jerome decided to walk back to his friend's place.

Seeing no sign of activity near the cabin, Jerome walked directly to the barn. Seeing the horse without food or water, he knew something was very wrong. *A tree has probably fallen on him in the woods*, Jerome thought to himself in a panic. He scoured the area for any sign of his friend, calling Jacob's name as he fruitlessly searched.

Now very concerned, he made his way back to the cabin, which was the last place he thought to search. Knocking on the cabin door, Jerome was surprised to hear Spot bark from inside. When Jerome forced the door open, the famished dog came racing out, desperate for food and water. With the light of the open door, Jerome saw Jacob on the floor in front of the cold fireplace. The scene of the cabin made it obvious that it was where Jacob had been for several days. The worst possible situation seemed obvious. Rushing to check his condition, he was overjoyed to hear a rattling breath. He tried to wake Jacob but was unsuccessful.

Acting quickly, Jerome hitched Molly to Jacob's wagon. He then carried Jacob out and laid him on the wagon, covering him with all the blankets he could find. He gathered up Spot, and holding him in his arms, proceeded to his house as quickly as he dared on the rough trail. On arrival, he ran inside to get Helen. They carried Jacob in and laid him on the floor in front of the fire. Upon discussing what must be done, Helen said that in the past, Mrs. Thompson had mentioned treating sick friends. She might be the only person in the area who knew what to do. Jerome put Molly in his barn, assuring that her needs were met. He took Spot to his familiar kennel.

He then saddled his own horse and hurried to the Thompsons'

home, quickly explaining the situation. The Thompsons said that they would be there as fast as possible, and in the meantime, they should do their best to get Jacob to drink something.

With Helen's help, the two of them were able to hold Jacob upright enough to get him to drink some warm broth. He drank two cups by the time the Thompsons arrived. Mrs. Thompson asked Jerome to remove Jacob's coat and shirt. She rubbed a foul-smelling compound on his chest, then covered him with layers of clothing again. She also assisted in forcing him to drink more water, into which she added brandy. They then covered him well and left him in front of the fireplace. Mrs. Thompson explained that they must apply the salve at least three times per day and force him to drink the water and brandy mix several times each day. This scene was played over the next few days. Each morning showed a slight improvement. Jacob's color and appetite slowly returned, and his raging fever gradually receded.

The actions of Jacob's friends that day saved his life. He slowly regained strength and the desire to get back to his life as his body overcame the sickness in his lungs. A number of nearby residents stopped by, offering words of support and food. As the calendar rolled to April, Jacob felt concern about the many tasks awaiting him on his farm, and guilty about being such a burden to the Walkers. They encouraged him to stay at least one more day, so that he was clearly healthy and strong enough to resume his normal activities by himself. That afternoon, there was another knock on the door. Helen answered it. Jacob could hear her speaking with someone on the porch, thinking nothing of it. Helen came back into the room, informing Jacob that he had a visitor. Jacob assumed that it was another neighbor. When he saw his old friend Robert walk into the room behind Helen, he was surprised and delighted beyond words.

Robert greeted Jacob as if they had never been apart.

"So, this is the life you've been living since leaving Vermont? Laying around, fat and lazy! All this time we thought you were out here working hard."

Jacob laughed until it hurt, already feeling the warmth he had long missed return to his life. "It's so wonderful to see you, Robert! Meet Helen and Jerome, I owe them my life."

Robert explained that he had arrived in town a couple hours earlier.

"When I saw the general store, I naturally went there to ask directions to your place, because store owners generally know everyone in the area. And if the store clerk didn't know, he could no doubt suggest someone who would. It was strange though. The storekeeper got a funny look on his face and told me that I should talk to the Thompson family. He pointed out their house down the road, so I walked over there.

"When the Thompsons told me that you were staying here with the Walker family for a while, I couldn't help but think that something unusual was going on. This close to spring planting and all, why would you not be at your own place? Helen just now briefly explained the situation on the porch before I came in. It's so good to see you alive and well, my friend. I understand that it was a mighty rough go for a while!"

"Yes, it was. But for Jerome, Helen, and Mrs. Thompson, I would not be here. Jerome found me half-dead in my cabin, and Helen and Mrs. Thompson cared for me like I was their child. It is a powerful and humbling experience to owe your life to others. I will do my best to repay my debt. But for now, I think it's time for me to go home and get my life back in order. I have so much to do! And I must apologize to you for failing to stake the parcel of land for you, as you requested."

"Don't you worry about that. Once we get you situated back in your own home, we can take care of it. And I have a bit of news to tell you. Remember the lovely Fiona Campbell, that young lady that I used to try to impress with my wit and good looks? Well, over the past two years she still hasn't learned what a rascal I actually am, and in fact, she is going to move out here once I have a home built. And, she has agreed to marry me!"

"Of course I remember Fiona! She was one of the smartest and prettiest girls in the village. We all used to wonder what the hell she saw in you! That's wonderful. Congratulations! This means we need to get to work as fast as possible on your land and home. If you wait too long, Fiona might come to her senses in the meantime."

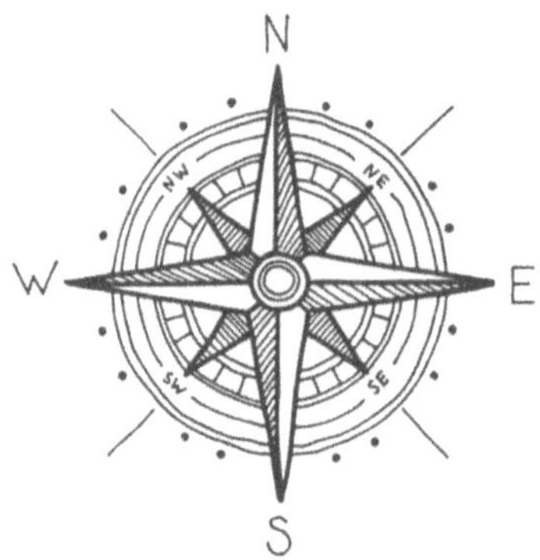

Chapter 20

MARY FISCHER WAS UNCERTAIN ABOUT what she should do. Word of Jacob Hart's illness spread throughout the village. When he was well enough to receive visitors, the Fischers, like most other neighbors, made a brief stop at the Walker home to see if they could help and to wish Jacob the best. Mary felt that she should go see Jacob, not as a daughter of the Fischer family, but on her own as a grown-up friend. She was a twenty-year-old young woman who had developed deep feelings for the interesting violin-playing farmer. The fact that his interests extended well beyond the farmstead that he carved out of the wilderness intrigued her. Mary admired his broad, inquisitive view of life. She appreciated that he, too, was an admirer of intellectual and artistic values. She felt that he was much like her in that regard. Walking home from the nearby residence where the area children gathered for lessons that day, Mary decided to briefly stop to see how Jacob was progressing.

She knocked on the front door, which Helen Walker opened. Seeing Mary on the porch brought a bright and knowing smile on her face.

"Such a busy afternoon! Welcome, Mary, come in."

Mary hesitated a moment on the porch, removing her muddy boots, while Helen walked into the living room, informing Jacob that he had another visitor. A few seconds later, Mary entered the room where Jacob, Jerome, and Robert were seated talking about farm and weather-related matters. When he noticed Mary enter the room, happiness overpowered Jacob for the second time in a half hour. He rose to greet her.

"Hello, Mary," he stuttered. "It's so wonderful to see you. Thank you for coming. Meet my good friend Robert. He just arrived today from Vermont!"

Mary's visit lasted only a few minutes. It was an important step for her, and its healing value for Jacob was inestimable. Even more so than Robert's surprise appearance, despite the difference in distance that each traveled.

Jacob convinced Jerome and Helen that, with Robert's help, he was fully capable of returning to his cabin. He thanked them profusely for their assistance and promised that one day soon he would pay for the expenses they incurred to care for him, Molly, and Spot. He also assured them that he, and likely Robert, would be back soon to help finish building their barn, as he'd originally promised.

Helen packed a freshly baked loaf of bread, cheese, and other items for the pair. Goodbyes finished, Robert hitched Molly to the wagon and retrieved Spot from the kennel. With a final word of thanks to Jerome and Helen as they waited on their porch, the friends slowly made their way to Jacob's cabin. Traversing the trail north allowed Robert to take a good look at the sort of land that was available, and made him even more anxious to get a parcel staked so he could make the necessary trip to Detroit to make it all legal.

It took the remainder of the day to get Jacob's cabin and barn back to the proper condition. By the time the work was done, and they cooked supper using Helen's provisions, it was nearly dark. They spent the evening talking about the coming days in front of the warm fire. Jacob filled Robert in on his plans for a coal supply business and the crops he planned to plant in the coming months. He was thrilled to once again see his world filled with promise, opportunities, and friends. Robert spent the night at Jacob's cabin. They talked late into the night about their future.

The next morning dawned bright and clear. Nature, it seemed, was in lockstep with their plans. Finishing Helen's food for breakfast, they laid out the day's busy schedule of tasks. They agreed that locating and staking a claim for Robert was the highest priority. It was also an undertaking they could quickly accomplish. Once done, they could move on to other pressing issues. They made their way through the forest to the area that Jacob had told Robert about. It was obvious from the tree cover that the soil was rich—plenty of black walnut, ash, and maple. As they walked, they used their shovels to dig into the forest litter in numerous locations, ensuring that the soil was indeed deep and rich. Satisfied with the condition of the land and soil, the pair then located the necessary surveyor marks to determine exact borders. This accomplished, they marked trees and drove stakes around the perimeter. Twilight settled over the land as they wearily made their way back to the cabin, having completed a life-changing day's work.

They agreed that Robert must leave for Detroit as quickly as possible. Jacob explained that he needed Molly and his wagon to make promised coal deliveries. Since the first delivery would be made to Jacksonburg in two days, Robert noted that he could easily hire transport from there to Detroit. They spent the next day loading coal, and the following morning, departed for Mr. MacDonald's shop. In Jacksonburg, Robert arranged for transport to Detroit, telling Jacob he would see him again in about ten days after he took care of the land office and bank business.

Upon arriving home late that afternoon, Jacob loaded another shipment of coal for the Barry blacksmith, which he delivered early the next morning. With an empty wagon, Jacob went east to Jacksonburg where he purchased seeds and a small plow. He then went west to the Fischer farm. There, he made arrangements to borrow the oxen team for the next day, along with the help of Timothy to clear stumps.

Robert returned less than two weeks later, official paperwork for his eighty-acre parcel in hand. It was currently forested, but within a year it would be a farm. He was amazed at what Jacob accomplished in his absence: a field was cleared, and the sod broken, making it nearly ready for planting corn and oats. A portion of the field was set aside for hay as food for Molly and the cattle that Jacob intended to purchase soon.

Robert and Jacob used Molly and the wagon to get lumber from the sawmill in Barry. With boards cut to size, and with Jacob's help, Robert was able to quickly build a small cabin without the need to trim and stack tree trunks, greatly speeding up the process and reducing the labor involved. With a cabin and wood stove for cooking and heat, Robert was able to spend more time clearing trees for fields.

Molly more than earned her keep in the coming months. Fields were prepared, crops planted, and loads of coal delivered. Timothy's occasional help was invaluable. On a day when there were no critical tasks waiting to be done, Jacob saddled Molly and rode to town. He had an idea to coordinate another musical gathering, and a July 4th celebration offered the perfect rationale. He would have to act fast, as the date was only two weeks away. To make his idea happen he must also get the Thompsons and Fischers on board.

Jacob's first stop was at the general store. He was ecstatic when Mr. Johnson told him that his new violin strings had arrived. After thanking Johnson for his efforts, he paid and made his way to the Thompsons' home. He found full support for his July 4th proposal. Riding to the Fischer residence, he was happy to see Mary sitting on the front porch, reading a book. She smiled warmly as he secured Molly to the hitching post.

"Are you studying a textbook, or reading a story book for fun?" Jacob asked as he approached.

"I'm reading for enjoyment, though I must say it is quite serious. This is a book of poetry by English writer Agnes Strickland. It's called *The Seven Ages of Woman*. I'll start preparing classroom lessons again next month, so I'm doing some light reading while I can. To what do I owe this surprise visit? I'm going to guess you didn't come all this way to discuss poetry."

"Well, maybe not poetry, but I would enjoy discussing books

with you some day. I don't have much time to read, but that doesn't mean I don't enjoy it. I have three books from an old friend of mine that I have carried with me for the past year. I've been meaning to read them. However, I did come to discuss an idea with you and your mother that involves something else you're very good at: music. What do you think about putting on another music show for the village?"

"What a wonderful idea! Let's go in and talk to Mother about it."

Mrs. Fischer and Mary both supported an Independence Day event at the Thompsons. Mary said it was perfect for her, because after that, she would soon spend much of her free time preparing lessons for the students. They agreed that it might be best to play different tunes, rather than trying to find the time to learn the same songs. Jacob thought that was sensible because it meant he could practice on his own. The Fischers said that they would arrange to spend a few hours at the Thompsons to practice their songs on their piano. As Jacob was preparing to leave, Mary walked out to the porch with him.

"Tell me about your friend, the one who loaned you those books you mentioned. Was that Robert?"

It took Jacob a moment to gather his thoughts. "Let's sit down."

Jacob told Mary about Mick and of the brief but life-changing period of friendship they had. After relaying the story, he realized that he had never told anyone else, not even his close friend Robert. Only Mrs. Du Bois, and now Mary, were aware of the short but intense period of friendship that the pair had shared.

Mary wiped tears from her eyes as Jacob finished the tale,

describing the terrible day when city workers came for his body and belongings. He described hiding the books of which Mick was so proud so they wouldn't be destroyed along with all of his other belongings.

"I'm so sorry," Mary said as she hugged Jacob affectionately. "What a terrible loss…. I would love to see those books and read them someday if that's okay with you."

"That would be fine with me, and I know Mick would be proud to have you read them. I will bring a couple of them with me to the July 4th party. I believe I will start reading one of them myself, like I always meant to do."

Though his reason for going to the Fischers' house was successfully accomplished, Jacob didn't want to leave. Mary was also in no hurry for the special opportunity to be together to end. Sitting in the shade, they spent an hour talking about a variety of topics. As the afternoon shadows lengthened, Jacob apologized for taking up so much of her time and said he should leave.

"I suppose I'd best get back home before dark. There is always so much work to do."

"No need to apologize. It's been a pleasure visiting with you. I will see you on the fourth at the Thompsons."

The pair shared a goodbye hug. Jacob felt powerful emotions as he rode Molly home through the woods. Reawakened memories of Mick were painful. Talking with Mary about him, however, had a healing effect. The conversation took an emotional load off his chest.

Viewing Mary as a close enough friend to share the story with put her in a new place in his worldview. He'd been fond of her since they'd first met, but it felt like a line had been crossed. She was more than an acquaintance he admired. She was a true friend in whom he could confide deeply personal emotions. As Jacob rode through the quiet evening forest, he wondered if Mary wasn't more than just a friend. It occurred to him that his feelings for her were more intense than what he'd felt for Sally before leaving home. Instead of friendship based on mutual expectations, this seemed different. He was strongly attracted to Mary's overall qualities and her captivating personality. Jacob experienced an epiphany as he rode through the quiet world to his home. It concerned Mary Fischer. *So much has changed so quickly. My new life is even more different than I thought it would be and I want Mary to be part of it.*

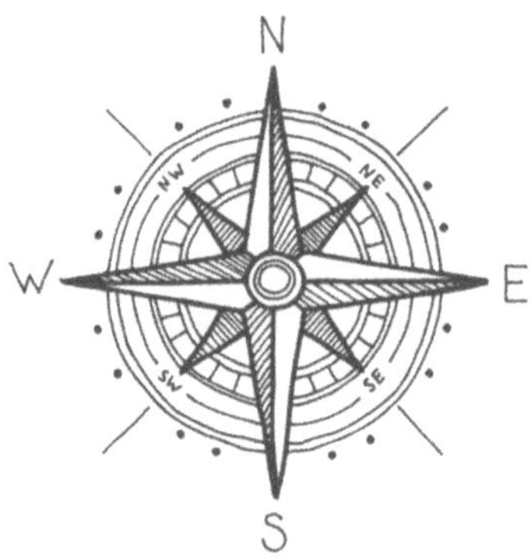

Chapter 21

JULY 4TH DAWNED CLEAR AND mild at Jacob's farmstead. It was a perfect summer morning signaling a pleasant day ahead. Birds and small animals chattered as they searched for food in the tall grass of the open yard. The knocking of a nearby woodpecker echoed in the morning silence. A flock of passenger pigeons squabbled loudly in the tops of sugar maple trees in Jacob's yard. Normally he would shoot a few of them, as all settlers did, for the evening meal. But not today. There were other things on his mind. He carefully packed his violin and two of Mick's books for Mary, then rode Molly down the familiar trail to the village.

The holiday gathering was an important community event. It offered a rare opportunity for people to get to know each other better, given how busy everyone was establishing a future for their families. The number of children in the community had nearly doubled in the past year. It was agreed that a second teacher, and likely a second school building, would soon be necessary. After a potluck supper, the music began. Mrs. Fischer and Mary made a delightful duo as Edna played the piano and Mary sang popular songs of the period. Jacob's energetic violin solos had everyone clapping and tapping toes in time with the lively tempo.

The period following July 4th found everyone even busier than before. Crops and livestock needed care and the summer months found settlers hard at work clearing wooded lands to serve as fields for the following years' crops. Jacob had an additional task—mining coal and expanding his coal-selling business. Robert agreed to help as much as he could, earning a portion of the profits for each load delivered. Jacob met with Horace Johnson, owner of the general store, reaching an agreement to deliver coal beginning in October. Word of Jacob's coal business spread. The minister of the new church expressed an interest, stating that a coal stove would be more efficient and safer than firewood in an open fireplace. The committee overseeing the school felt likewise. With these contracts in hand, Jacob and Robert did not pursue any additional customers, as they felt that honoring the commitments they now had would take up all of their available spare time.

Summer and fall were busy seasons of harvesting. As was the case with other aspects of developing homesteads, neighbors traveled from farm to farm to help with the harvest. It had been a good year. Yields were bountiful, and the new road guaranteed access to the port at Detroit and shipment on the Erie Canal to profitable eastern markets. It was an especially busy period for Jacob and Robert. Digging and transporting coal took much time and effort, in addition to other tasks related to development of their farmsteads.

Jacob tried his best to send occasional letters home, a task made easier with the post office at the general store. A September letter from Vermont brought a mix of news; Jacob's grandfather died suddenly one day while working in the field. It was painfully sad news for Jacob, who'd always felt close to his grandfather, feeling a closer kinship with him than with his own father. Jacob's mother added a P.S. letting him know that the Smythes were going to have a baby near Christmas.

Life settled into a pleasant routine in the cool days of autumn. More new settlers moved into the area, and "old-timers" like Jacob and Jerome helped them with their homes and barns. Additional fields were being cleared for crops, and some homesteaders constructed fences for cattle. Everything about the steady progress seemed in line with the collective dreams of people like Jacob who risked everything on their quest.

With the end of summer, the first school year in the new school building was underway. Though Mary was aware of the extent of a teacher's responsibilities, the reality was more than she anticipated. Her duties included cleaning and taking care of the building, as well as teaching all topics to children of various age groups. Though she focused on basic reading, writing, and arithmetic skills, Mary also made sure that the children learned about important topics such as art, music, and history. Conversations with parents made it clear that everyone thought highly of Mary, even her students.

Teaching was more than a job for her—it was her passion. Satisfying the school trustees regarding the topics that she taught was an unexpectedly frustrating challenge, however. She was surprised by the many different attitudes and expectations that parents had about what their children should, or should not, be taught. The unfortunate side of Jacob's busy schedule, and Mary's teaching duties, was that they rarely encountered one another. Their homes were far enough apart to make chance encounters unlikely. Jacob occasionally stopped at the Fischer home when making coal deliveries in Barry, but as often as not Mary was at the school building. On the occasions he delivered coal to the school, taking time to talk with the teacher was not an option. He envisioned pleasant talks on the Fischers' porch with her, or someplace more private, but that was proving to be a difficult goal to achieve.

AT THE END OF A hard day's work, sleep came easily for Jacob, and he wasn't easily roused from a deep slumber. Suddenly awakening on a dark late October night, he knew something was wrong. Once fully awake, the problem was obvious: he smelled the overpowering odor of smoke. The odor and sight of lingering smoke, especially on calm days, was a common occurrence, because of settlers burning stumps and piles of branches. But this seemed different.

Dressing quickly, he raced outside, his worst fears confirmed by the ominous glow of fire in the southwestern sky. That was the direction of the Fischers and other nearby families, as well as the new church and school. Jacob saddled Molly and grabbed a bucket, shovel, and as many other items as he could carry with him that would be helpful in extinguishing a fire. Jacob pondered taking the time to ride to Robert's homestead to warn him. Making his way through the forest and fields in the pitch blackness would be nearly impossible and take at least two hours to accomplish. By then, the fire could do a great deal of harm. Instead, Jacob raced down the trail toward the village, ignoring the dangers of the rough track in the darkness.

An overwhelming panic grew in his mind because the glow of the flames was clearly in the direction of the Fischer home. Riding much faster than reasonable, Jacob's heart pounded as he imagined the worst. This night was one of the coldest of the fall thus far, and most people would have started a fire for warmth. The dangers of fire in the homes and cabins scattered across the countryside were well known and greatly feared; fires were common, and the ability to extinguish them nearly nonexistent.

When Jacob reached the home of the Walkers, he stopped. After pounding on their door and yelling their names, he finally woke them. Jerome was stunned when he saw the nearby fire, which was now nearly due west. Towering flames were visible through the trees. Jacob raced away, with Jerome a few minutes behind.

Riding west on the Territorial Road, Jacob breathed a huge sigh of relief when it was clear that the fire was west of the Fischers' home, the church, and the school buildings. He saw many other people on the road heading toward the fire. Most were carrying rudimentary items such as shovels, axes, and pails.

A few carried lanterns, but most were invisible in the moonless night. As they neared the cloud of smoke, the worst fears of the residents were confirmed. The forest was aflame with a large, out-of-control wildfire. There was only a slight breeze moving through the trees, making it impossible to tell which direction the fire was most likely to spread, but everyone present knew that it would continue its unstoppable advance until extinguished by a heavy rain or by encountering large rivers or swamps in its destructive path.

Trying to create some sense of order in the darkness proved nearly impossible. There was no organized official response or presence, just local men and women fearing the worst and willing to do whatever they could to help. It was eventually agreed by those present that they must do everything possible to stop the fire at the road. If it crossed and headed north or east, the fire would unquestionably destroy homesteads that lay in its path, and much of the village itself. If it progressed northeasterly, the homes of Jacob, Robert, and the Walkers were in danger.

Digging a wider ditch on the south side of the road seemed the most effective effort, so several people began that task. A local resident said that there were two homesteads south of the road in the direction from which the fire came. It was agreed that as soon as dawn provided visibility, search teams must make their way past the fire to check on those families. Max Fischer asked Jerome to ride as fast as possible to Jacksonburg to seek the services of a local doctor and to recruit as many men as possible to fight the fire. Though he protested, saying that he should stay to help, Jerome's riding skills and his young child at home made him a logical choice to seek critically needed help rather than being on the front line.

Jacob decided that the best thing he could do was to help dig the firebreak. He asked people who were unable to dig to line up a bucket brigade extending to the creek located about three hundred yards to the east. He instructed them to gather every possible container, fill them with water, and bring them closer to the fire to protect the school, church, and nearby homes.

Everyone worked to the best of their abilities, aided by the few lanterns that provided small islands of light. Hearing Max and Timothy Fischer, Jacob worked his way toward them, finally locating them helping to dig the firebreak. Mr. Fischer said that they were all fine and that Mary was helping her mother pack important items should they have to flee their home. If the wind increased in speed and shifted from the west, the entire settlement was in grave danger. Evacuation would be the only option.

With daylight, the ability to communicate and coordinate efforts improved. The bucket brigade and firebreak efforts became more effective. Two teams went into the woods behind the fire to check on the families that would already have been caught in the flames. The teams followed the trail that led into the forest on the east side of the fire. Jacob and the blacksmith comprised the team that was to check on the eastern-most homestead. The other team would continue west to locate the second homestead. Everyone hoped that a westerly wind would not pick up until the crew made it back out. If the fire turned to the east, it would overtake them.

The lack of wind was beneficial in that the fire was moving slowly in the damp morning conditions. Smoke, however, hung thick near the ground, and the flames were dangerously hot. The simple act of breathing was difficult. With wet cloths covering their faces, the teams made their way toward the first homestead. As they neared the home the smell of the smoke changed. It was no longer the smell of burning wood and leaves, but something frighteningly different. The smell of burnt flesh became overwhelmingly noxious.

As they entered the homestead clearing, the destructive force of the fire struck fear into their hearts. They passed by the barn first, toward what remained of the house. The shed was destroyed, and the remains of horses and cattle littered the yard where a corral stood hours before. The smell of the burned animals was overpowering, nearly causing the men to be sick. Walking past the remains of the barn, Isaiah called the others over to show them the charred body of the farmer. He had no doubt gone out to save the animals but had become trapped in the flames himself. It was with deep grief that the second team continued westward toward the second homestead. They expected the same results.

Jacob and Isaiah hurried toward what remained of the cabin. Because of the use of fieldstones instead of tree trunks, the walls were still standing, though the roof was collapsed. Calling out as they approached the former home, they were shocked and happy to hear calls for help and cries of a wailing baby. Rushing inside, they carefully moved the roof beams that were covering the calls for help. They eventually saw a young woman holding a child of no more than one or two years of age in a dark corner. Ash and debris covered both of them, but they appeared to have no major injuries. The stone walls no doubt saved their lives.

"Chuck, where is Chuck?" yelled the woman as soon as she saw her rescuers. "He went out to let the horse and cattle out of the barn. Where is he? Did you see him outside?"

To get her mind off of her missing husband, Isaiah asked the distraught woman her name.

"Linda Watson," said the woman.

"Well, Linda, we're here to help. Why don't you take care of your baby and gather what you need to take with you. We will go outside and look for Chuck."

As soon as the woman identified herself, Jacob realized that he met the family at the July 4th event. The Watsons, just a year or two older than himself, arrived in the spring of '34. Jacob recalled how proud they were when talking about their new farm. Of the challenges Jacob encountered since leaving home, this was one of the most difficult. *How do we tell her that her husband died trying to save their farm, and now he lies burnt on the land that had been their family's dream? How do we tell her that her husband and the father of her child is dead?*

Once outside, the men agreed that they would not immediately tell Linda about her husband's fate. They would walk with her to the village where she and the child could be cared for. Then, after some time for her to grasp what happened, the minister could tell her about her husband's heroic death. *It is going to be a rough day for the newly arrived minister*, thought Jacob.

Going back inside, they told her that they could not locate Chuck, but that after they got her and her child to safety in the village they would come back to search further.

"He likely got lost in the darkness," Isaac suggested.

This wasn't a complete falsehood because they did indeed

plan to come back to retrieve her husband's body. The men were aware that the danger from the fire had not subsided but was actually growing in intensity as the morning breeze picked up. It was critical that they get out of the forest and back to the village to help fight the fire or help evacuate other families threatened by the flames. Likely understanding more than they realized, Linda agreed. She salvaged what they could carry and led the way to the village.

Walking out of the forest, Jacob's concern grew. A southwesterly wind was clearly gaining strength. Preventing the monstrous fire with the wind behind it from crossing the road would require a miracle. He didn't think there would be any divine intervention on this day, only death and destruction. Arriving back at the main road, Jacob and the others were so blackened by ash and smoke that they were unrecognizable. The easterly sun shining on the billowing smoke displayed a demonic scene. Flames were now moving from treetop to treetop, creating a roar seemingly straight out of hell. It was clear that there was nothing they could do to stop the fire. It was going to cross the road and go where the winds took the flames. Everyone agreed that the priority must now be to stop it from burning down the village.

By midmorning, help arrived from the east. Doctor Leepson and his wife with a buggy filled with supplies to assist the injured were a welcome sight. The school and church were converted to temporary shelters and hospitals for the injured and homeless victims. Food, water, clothing, and rags for bandages were gathered and volunteers did what they could for the casualties, led by Doctor Leepson. At least two dozen helpers arrived over the course of the morning, carrying as much as they could. Jerome had met several of them on the road already as he raced eastward for help before dawn. They had seen the glow of a fire and were already responding. Every resident was fully aware that an out-of-control fire was a threat to everyone.

The wind was pushing the fire across the road just west of the Fischer house. In response, focus shifted to the east side of the fire. A bucket brigade carried water from the creek to the east edge of the flames where a new firebreak was being dug. Brush and grass were drenched with as much water as possible to keep the fire from moving toward the village.

Jacob inquired as to whether anyone had seen Robert. When he learned that no one had seen him, he became concerned. Robert's homestead was almost directly aligned with the direction of the flames. Jacob's home was in the same area, but he couldn't bring himself to think about that possibility. At least he and Molly were safe, and the people he cared about were safe.

Robert can take care of himself, Jacob thought. *He'll know what to do.*

"And Mary is safe," he added aloud.

Jacob joined a team digging the firebreak extending north from the main road. The intent was to keep the fire as far west as possible because there were fewer homesteads in that area. Everyone knew that homes were going to be destroyed and lives lost, but they also knew there was nothing whatsoever that they could do about it. Hopefully residents in the path of the fire could find ways to escape during daylight hours prior to their homes being burned. That simple hope was the focus of thoughts and prayers of those who survived thus far.

When Jacob learned that the team that had checked the second homestead had not yet returned, he felt a deep sense of helplessness.

"They should have been out by now," he told Isaiah. "But it is suicide for anyone to go in there to try to find them until the fire subsides in that area."

Food and water were delivered to the workers during the day. The hours-long battle to keep the fire from spreading east toward the village seemed to be succeeding. Early in the afternoon, the second team that had entered the forest that morning emerged from the smoke. Their clothes were in tatters and the men were filthy and covered with scratches. Though they located the burned homestead, they could not find the family. Searchers told a harrowing story of nearly being trapped in the flames when fire circled around behind them, trapping them in the inferno. They were forced to dig a hole for shelter, narrowly escaping death. After being treated at the school for cuts and burns, they were on the fire line within minutes.

Chaos continued to reign while residents were doing their best to fight the inferno. On two occasions, homesteaders from the west stumbled out of the forest. They raced ahead of the flames during the night, eventually turning eastward, to try to get out of the danger zone and reach help. Jacob's confidence in Robert's abilities was justified when Robert eventually emerged from the woods, helping lead a young family from a homestead a mile to the northwest. Robert had likewise been awakened by the smell of smoke during the night. Seeing that the neighboring family was directly in line of the flames and likely not familiar with the landscape, he went to their aid before leaving the danger zone.

Later in the afternoon, the fire having moved further north, it was decided to try a second rescue attempt behind the flames to search for the missing family. Jacob agreed to go again. He felt that he had the least to lose. He had no family, and he could rebuild what he stood to lose because of the fire. His experience helping to locate the Watson family that morning would also help guide the team in the right direction.

Everything was going to look very different behind the fire.

Jacob and his bachelor friend Isaac agreed to go. They felt that having more searchers would only weaken the critical efforts of those on the fire line. Carrying containers of water and as much food and other supplies as possible, they followed the same trail into the forest that they had used in the morning. The second home, built by the Smith family—a young couple with two children—was located about a half-mile west of the Watsons. Unfortunately, there was no clear trail to follow once they began their westward trek. Upon reaching the Watson homestead, they turned toward the Smith family house, but only after covering Chuck Watson's body with a blanket.

As Jacob and Isaac struggled through the burned landscape, the intensity of the fire became obvious. Stumps, fallen timber, and underground roots were still burning. Great care had to be taken to avoid red hot coals and flames. Ash and an occasional branch fell from above. Both men covered their nose and mouth with wet rags to avoid breathing in the ash and smoke. *Nothing could have survived this fire,* thought Jacob. He kept his fears to himself. Neither man was going to quit searching for the Smiths until darkness made it impossible. Both searchers yelled as loudly as they could, but throats raw from the smoke and ash made it painful, and eventually impossible. The eerie, smoky silence of the ruined landscape, broken only by the occasional falling tree, was a scene of unimaginable destruction.

After struggling through the hellscape in silence for an hour or more, they saw what appeared to be the cleared homestead area ahead. For the first time since leaving the village, there was something positive to bolster their hopes. Both men found the energy to increase their pace until they reached a field. On the other side, they saw the unmistakable remains of a house and shed. They walked across the small, scorched wheat field toward the hulk of a destroyed chimney. Upon arriving, they called out until their painful throats made it impossible to continue yelling. Splitting up, they began to search the area of the burned house and barn. They were joyful that they found no bodies but surprised to not find the remains of horses or cattle. After thoroughly checking the debris that hours earlier had been the house and shed, the pair teamed up again, using the chimney as the focal point.

"The fact that there were no dead animals near the shed, and no bodies in the house, might be good news," Jacob opined. "Maybe they woke up in time to turn the animals loose and made their own escape."

"But," said Isaac, "if they fled north toward the main road, with the fire behind their back, it likely would have overtaken them in the dark. I fear that no one could have made it, let alone running in front of the fire in the darkness carrying two young children with them."

"We only have a couple hours of daylight left. Let's search a broader area while we still have some light."

They split up once again, agreeing to meet at the chimney in about an hour. Isaac was to search the area north and west. Jacob checked the burned over scrubland to the south of the former farmstead, calling out as much as possible. Jacob felt it ironic that as he walked south, the land became noticeably swampier. *This is the land everyone tried to warn me about*, he thought to himself. *Too bad it wasn't a big enough swamp to stop this damned fire!* The shallow water and mud of the swamp made walking difficult. Stopping to rest, Jacob called out one final time before moving further east. To his shock, he thought he heard a response. Calling again resulted in an unmistakable reply from about a hundred yards southwest. Jacob struggled through the thick brush and muddy conditions to the source of the yells. He soon saw a man desperately waving his arms for attention. The cries of young children made the situation clear as Jacob made his way toward them.

The sight of the family was a shock, even after what Jacob already witnessed that day. They weren't just muddy, rather, muck an inch thick covered every family member. As he got closer, Jacob saw that the woman was injured with what he suspected was a broken leg. One of the children suffered a deep gash on his arm that was badly bleeding. As he watched the man move, it was clear that he had a leg or ankle injury as well. Jacob gave them water and food and helped clean and bandage various cuts. There was clearly nothing that he could do about the more serious injuries.

As Jacob was doing this, the man, who identified himself as John Smith, described the harrowing account of their escape. As Jacob had assumed, Smith released their horse and two cows from the barn when the smell of the fire awakened them and they saw the terrible advancing flames. Knowing that they themselves had no chance of outrunning the fire, they pursued the only course that they thought could save their lives: run toward the fire into the swamp, hoping they got to the wetland before the fire.

Running in the pitch blackness through the treacherous landscape was not without danger or injuries. Mrs. Smith had injured her leg and Mr. Smith had a badly damaged ankle. Smith further explained that when they reached that spot, they lay down in the shallow water and covered themselves with mud. Though unimaginably hot according to Mr. Smith, lying in the shallow water covered with mud enabled them to survive as the flames passed overhead. Their condition made it obvious why they were not able to make their way to the village. Walking in the muddy and rough terrain was impossible for both adults.

After he did all he could, Jacob instructed them to wait while he went to get Isaac. It took a frustrating amount of time to locate him in the area north of the homestead. Isaac was amazed to hear that, though in desperate straits, the Smiths were alive. Once arriving back to the family, they discussed what the best options were. There was no question about getting the children out that afternoon. Fortunately, they were old enough—though just barely—to negotiate the terrain on their own and had not suffered leg injuries to hinder them. The condition of the parents made their situation much more problematic. It was agreed by everyone that they could survive another miserably cold, wet night in the swamp. Having Isaac or Jacob make their way to the village then back to the swamp before dark was also not possible. There wasn't enough daylight left for someone to get to the village and bring help. That meant Jacob and Isaac would have to help the parents walk through the rough terrain the best they could. It was going to be a long, painful exercise.

Though the ordeal meant the difference between life and death, it was a more difficult and painful undertaking than they imagined possible. Making their way through the burned-over landscape meant constantly tripping and falling. Jacob and Isaac were essentially carrying the parents, and when one person stumbled, they both fell. As they struggled back toward the Watson homestead, obstacles of every type made the trek nearly impossible. After what seemed like an eternity, they finally reached the Watson's home, where they planned to rest. Twilight had settled on the hellish landscape, highlighting the flames of still-burning stumps. The Smiths broke down in tears when they saw their neighbor's property and the dead livestock. Being of the same age and circumstances, they knew each other well. Jacob made sure that they did not see Mr. Watson's body.

The evening chill was having a life-threatening effect, especially on Mrs. Smith, who was shivering uncontrollably. Though the temperatures were dropping, everyone was sweating due to the exertions of the trek. Jacob went inside the burned dwelling to search for anything that could be used to keep the family warm. Remnants of burned clothing and blankets were the best he could find. They were invaluable to the Smiths, children and parents alike, all of whom were showing signs of hypothermia in the evening chill. They rested for several minutes. Upon attempting to continue their walk, Mrs. Smith collapsed when attempting to put weight on her one good leg. Jacob knew that neither of the adults would be able to make it out to the main road. The children, though shivering badly and almost unresponsive, could be carried out if necessary. Leaving the parents behind, however, was surely a death sentence for them.

They had no choice but to spend the night in the burned-out hulk of the Watson home. Jacob and Isaac cleared an area in front of the fieldstone fireplace. Isaac filled the fireplace with wood and used a burning coal from outside to start a fire. They located additional clothing as they moved piles of debris. Once the family was settled, Jacob again doled out food and water for everyone, saving a small amount for the next morning.

Isaac and Jacob took turns replenishing the wood supply during the frosty night to keep the fire burning as intensely as possible for heat. After a long, sleepless night, the first rays of sunrise shed light on their desperate circumstances. The woodlands around them were gray and foreboding, smoke curling upward from countless smoldering blazes. Jacob handed out what remained of the rations. They huddled near the fire to eat the last of their food and discuss their options. A glow to the north was proof that the fire was continuing on its destructive path. It seemed clear that Jacob or Isaac would have to go to the village to get help. A horse-drawn buggy could traverse the trail that connected the Watson homestead to the main road. That seemed the only option now available to evacuate the Smith family.

Jacob and Isaac were discussing which one would go when they heard shouts. Going outside, they saw men with lanterns approaching. Running toward them, Jacob saw that Robert and Jerome were part of the group. He embraced them both, saying he had never been happier to see them. They all gathered inside the shell of the home where the story of the Smiths' ordeal was told once again. Jerome explained that when they didn't return by dark the prior evening, a search party was organized. Jacob assured them that they were a wonderful surprise. The new team of rescuers brought fresh food and water, as well as cloths to use as bandages. Everything was put to beneficial use while plans were being finalized.

It was agreed that with as many helpers as were now available, they could build litters to carry the Smiths out. This option meant that the family could be taken to safety much quicker than if someone went back to the village to get a horse and buggy. Men volunteered to take turns carrying the children, whose condition from the cold, injuries, and exertion had seriously worsened overnight.

The group caused quite a reaction when they emerged from the woodlands at midday. The family was taken to the school building where Doctor Leepson treated their injuries. Timothy Fischer was assisting Dr. Leepson in the school building, taking an interest in treating injuries. Another team gathered to go to the Watson home to retrieve the body of Chuck Watson with a horse and wagon.

By late afternoon, the fire moved far enough north that it was no longer a direct threat to residents. There was no longer any ability to influence the intensity or direction of the fire. The heroic fire lane and bucket brigade efforts successfully kept the fire far enough away that it did not damage structures on the west side of the village. After ensuring that any scattered small fires that remained were extinguished, the men and women who fought the fire for the past two days put their tools down and made their ways to their homes and families.

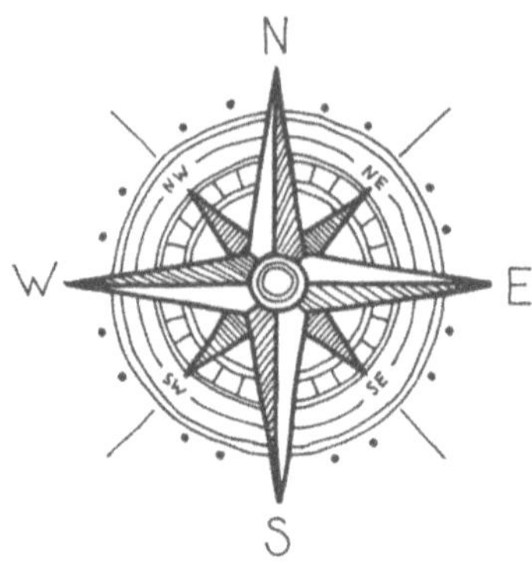

Chapter 22

FINALLY ALONE, JACOB WALKED WEST on the road a mile or more. He felt a need to be alone to absorb what happened over the past two days. Jacob knew that the terrifying menace had not ended, it only moved away from the people he knew. He was keenly aware that though the danger was over for them, settlers he knew nothing about, with stories so like his own, were going to face the wrath of the fire as it advanced according to the whims of the wind. It is possible, he thought, that it would keep burning until winter's snow finally smothered the flames.

Jacob could not help but think about the far-reaching impacts of the fire. Things were unmistakenly different now than two days earlier, even if a person did not suffer any harm. The fire would have immediate life-changing consequences for some. For others, unforeseen effects would be felt well into the future. Several affected families would no doubt be forced to leave because of deaths or injuries, to go back to their original homes in the east. Others would start anew, hoping for the best. Some would lose their homes and land due to the inability to pay back loans used to purchase the land, or the inability to pay taxes imposed by the territorial government. Some would not have the resources needed to start over. Forced to sell at a loss, their land would likely end up in the hands of speculators of the sort that Jacob encountered on his journey west.

Emotionally and physically drained, Jacob sat down along the road that he once spent so much time helping to build. The road carved a tunnel through the burnt hulks of the trees, stretching as far as he could see in both directions. In a sense, he viewed it as his road. He'd built it, and it served a major role in his life. Nothing, he concluded, no matter how bad it might be, was going to stop more people from seeking a better future here.

The quiet solitude brought a calmness and sense of normality to Jacob after too many hours of desperation, allowing him to think about all that transpired. *So many lives have been changed by this road*, he thought. *The fire isn't going to change that or stop people from moving here. It was a deadly reminder of our frailty, but we will move on. It won't stop people who are seeking better lives.* Feeling deep fatigue spread over his body, he laid back and closed his eyes for a few seconds. He awakened after an hour of badly needed sleep.

When Jacob awoke, he was glad that no one had witnessed him napping. It felt wrong to rest on such a momentous day, though it was needed. He walked east toward the village, away from the ravaged land that would bear scars from the fire for years.

As he passed by the Fischer house, Mary saw him and ran out to greet him with an unabashed warm embrace.

"I'm so happy to see you!" she exclaimed, wiping tears from her eyes. "I was so worried when you didn't return last night!"

Jacob, overwhelmed with emotions, simply held her tight. Finally able to speak, he said that since it looked like everything was under control, maybe they could go sit on her porch and rest. He said he had a lot to talk about.

Mary led Jacob to the porch and asked him to sit down while she got some refreshments. She assumed that he hadn't had much to eat or drink during the two days of extreme exertion. Jacob marveled at her caring attitude and understanding. *Not everyone would be so kind*, he thought to himself. *I need to do something. I can't lose someone as wonderful as her. Someone will marry her soon if I don't do something first. Though I don't know what the hell I can promise her that would make her want to marry a farm boy like me.*

Jacob was deep in thought when Mary came back outside. The sound of the door closing startled him, and Mary apologized for alarming him.

"You have nothing to apologize for, Mary. I was just deep in thought about the events of the last two days, and of how much everything will change as a result. It's just that ever since I left home, so many unbelievable things have happened. I used to think that life was basically predictable, and that if a person was smart and careful, they could avoid bad things happening. Now I know better. All of life is so uncertain, and nothing can be assumed or taken for granted. It sure is more complicated than I thought it would be!"

The look on his face told Mary that he was trying to make sense of the inexplicable. She shared his sorrow. *He once viewed life with the simple awe of a child. It's so unfortunate that life isn't as he thinks it should be. We would all be better for it. He is a good man. A man who sees the world in the same optimistic manner I do.*

Staring down at his hands, deep in thought, Jacob suddenly realized how he looked and smelled. He was filthy, his clothes badly torn. He had not yet had the opportunity to wash blood from his hands. Standing up suddenly, he looked at his hands and clothes and apologized profusely for his appearance.

"I'm so sorry. I need to go clean up. I should not have stopped here looking the way I do!"

"You are fine, Jacob. If I thought something was wrong, I would have said so; I'm not bashful, as you probably noticed! You have been out saving lives and helping people—why in the world should you ever apologize for doing that? You are fine the way you are, and I am proud to know you looking exactly as you do."

"Thank you, Mary. You are truly too kind. Do you think I could use the well in your backyard to wash up a bit before we eat? It's the least I can do."

"Certainly. I will bring some soap and a towel out for you."

After cleaning up as best he could, Jacob felt much better. No longer having blood from the Smith child on his hands was a huge improvement. As they shared the refreshments, Jacob talked about the tragedies he saw at the Watson and Smith homesteads. More than anything, he explained, he was horrified at the similarities between them and people like himself and Mary and many others like them who were venturing out to start their lives. Despite intellectually knowing that fate and myriad other factors were the overpowering forces at work, the fundamental injustice of youthful tragedies still clearly bothered him.

Mary could see that that was a basic part of who he was. *He and I are so alike! At the core he's a visionary who refuses to let the world stand in the way of his dreams. Me too! That's why I love this guy! But how do I make him understand how I feel?*

After eating, Jacob asked Mary if she would like to take a walk east to where the creek crossed the road. It was a peaceful place. The sound of water cascading over the sandstone and the maple trees in full autumn foliage made for a badly needed refuge. Mary readily agreed. Walking along the road, Jacob clumsily took her hand into his.

"I am so happy that you are here and that you take time to listen to my ramblings. Thank you. I've never met anyone like you before. You are an amazing person."

"Thank you for that. Coming from a man like you it means a lot. Praise from the praiseworthy. Because though I don't know if you are aware of it, you are also an extraordinary person, unlike anyone I've ever met before. I enjoyed the time we've been able to spend together and am so grateful that you are here. After all, what were the odds that we would meet?"

They talked about many things as they slowly walked down the road. Arriving at the creek, they sat under an ancient maple tree on the stream bank. Its crown was resplendent in orange and crimson leaves, some gently falling as they sat in silence enjoying the sound of the water. As dusk deepened, they began a slow walk back to the Fischer residence. Reluctantly, Jacob said that he should saddle up Molly and head back to his cabin to make sure everything was okay, and to clean up properly. Mary suggested he could spend the night in the village, but she knew he wanted to get back to his own home.

"By the way, Timothy took care of Molly while you were so busy on the fire. She is stabled in our barn."

"That was kind of him! I must remember to thank him the next time I see him. I feared that she was still wandering around where I left her to graze."

Once at the Fischer home, Jacob said goodbye to Mary and walked to the barn to get Molly. Jacob had wondered what happened to Molly while he was in the forest. Learning that Timothy took care of her came as a great relief. After saddling her and leading her out the barn door, he saw Mary walking to the barn with a package. It was food that she quickly threw together for his supper. Tying Molly's reins to the gate, Jacob's emotions overwhelmed him. Taking Mary into his arms, he gave her a long hug, followed by a passionate kiss. Mary welcomed it joyfully.

"I love you, Mary," Jacob said, holding her close and looking deeply into her captivating eyes. "More than I ever thought I could love anyone. I hope I don't sound like a foolish, lovestruck farm boy, but you are the most remarkable woman I have ever known. The first time I saw you nearly two years ago, I fell in love and hoped that someday you would be my wife. And my feelings for you have grown every day since, as I have had the privilege of getting to know you better."

The usually careful Jacob threw caution to the wind and took the step that would change his life as much as his departure from Vermont years earlier. He would not be able to live with himself if he lost the best thing in his life because he failed to act boldly when the opportunity was literally within his grasp.

"Mary, would you marry me? I promise to love you every bit as much as I do right now for the rest of my life. You're everything I could possibly dream of, and my life would be empty without you."

"And I love you, Jacob. You are a remarkable person, and I consider myself the luckiest woman in the world to know you. Yes, I would love to be your wife and friend for the rest of our lives."

Another long kiss followed. The affection of their prolonged passionate embrace kept them warm as the sun slipped fully beyond the horizon.

Darkness had settled across the land by the time Jacob finally left. Riding north toward the trail to his farm, he encountered Robert and Jerome, who were also returning to their homes. After bidding Jerome goodbye at his home, Robert and Jacob continued to Jacob's cabin, where Robert bid him adieu. Jacob asked if they could meet in a couple of days to dig up some coal for upcoming deliveries.

He added, "And just like three years ago, I once again have something important to talk to you about."

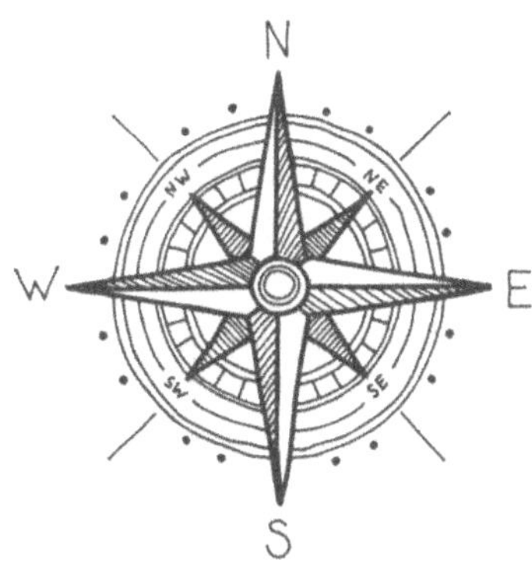

Chapter 23

THINGS CHANGED IN THE COMING months. Some developments were the result of the fire, while others would have happened regardless, an inevitable result of progress. Three funerals were held at the new church in October. Chuck Watson's young family left the area after his funeral, his widowed wife returning to her Philadelphia home with her young son, having lost any desire to remain. Teams entered the burned over land after the fire to search for victims. A young couple was found in the remains of their log cabin two miles west of the village; they were also buried in the new cemetery. A notice was mailed to their family in the East, and four weeks later, a representative arrived to put their land up for sale. A young lawyer who set up an office in the village just months prior to the fire was kept busy with its resultant legal issues.

Late autumn and winter were a dark and dreary phase, made worse as the cold weather and snow trapped the land in its frigid embrace. The only bright news was Jacob and Mary's wedding. Most residents ho-hummed the news. It seemed to be a case of an obvious event finally occurring. Everyone agreed that they made a wonderful pair, and the spring wedding loomed as a bright spot in a grim period.

Despite unusually cold, snowy weather, a Christmas Eve celebration was once again held at the Thompsons' home. With all the hardships—and triumphs—the community had gone through this year, everyone felt that the event was especially important this particular year. The event brought most residents together to discuss issues relevant to the growing community. Everyone was thrilled when the Smith family showed up, announcing that they had largely recovered from their injuries and were going to rebuild their house and barn. They received many offers of help.

A meal that neighborhood women spent the afternoon preparing was served to the enjoyment of all. As in the past, Mary sang while her mother and Jacob accompanied on the piano and violin. A new resident, Mr. Riley, played the flute, adding to the festive atmosphere. It was nearly midnight when the last of the Christmas carols were sung. At the end of the festivities, Edna Fischer, Pastor Thomas Jackson, and the Thompsons made an important announcement. The Thompsons said that since they no longer used it, they were going to donate their piano to the new church. The pastor and Mrs. Fischer agreed that she would not only play on Sundays, but that she would also use the piano in the church to provide free lessons for local children to enhance their cultural education.

1835 dawned with the promise of renewed good fortune. Everything was looking up for the Michigan Territory. Settlers were pouring in and the economy was booming. In January, Territorial Governor Mason declared that the territory was ready to become a state, further strengthening its place in the American economic and political realms.

Jacob and Mary had little time to spend together during the winter months. She taught most days, and evenings were spent preparing lessons and grading papers. To make it possible for the two of them to travel together, Jacob purchased a sleigh. He and Mary made several trips to visit friends and to his cabin during the winter months. The snowy forested backdrop made for marvelous Sunday afternoon sleigh rides. Time warming up in front of the cabin's fireplace was well spent making plans for their future lives together.

Coal was discovered in other nearby locations, including along the Grand River in Jacksonburg. As a result, Jacob lost the contract with MacDonald due to a lower cost proposal by a nearby landowner. The loss of that contract proved to be positive in the long run. It took a full day to dig and load the coal and make the round trip to Jacksonburg. That time could be better used by Jacob on his farm improvement tasks. He continued to deliver coal to the general store, Isaiah Woodbury, and the church and school. With occasional help from Robert, he felt that he could continue at that level for some time. Though it was time-consuming and difficult work, Jacob knew that income from those sales allowed both him and Robert to develop their farmsteads faster than otherwise would be the case. The extra money he was saving would be critical once he and Mary began a family. Despite the current prosperity, he had no doubt there would be hard times ahead that he must be prepared for.

The foursome of Robert, Jerome, Isaac, and Jacob spent much time together over the course of the winter. Many of the necessary tasks on the growing farms required more than one person to perform. With an eye to the future, they moved from farm to farm to improve barns, build fences, and clear land for crops. Log cabins expanded into comfortable multiroom homes. As envisioned from the beginning, they were progressing from the crude homesteader standard of living to that of successful farmers.

The men also spent an increasing amount of time hunting for food. The deer population dwindled dramatically because of the increasing number of people moving into the area and the clearing of their habitat. Venison was the staple meat on which many residents depended. They either shot the animals themselves or paid or bartered for venison killed by others. Other wildlife populations were also decreasing due to development and unrestricted shooting by landowners for food. Aggressive hunting by the early settlers had largely eliminated wolves and bears by this point, allowing livestock to range free. The reduction of wild animal populations resulted in more farmers bringing in cattle and pigs. Though pigs could scrounge for food in the forest, cattle had to be fed year-round, which resulted in more woodlands being cleared for fields and pastures.

A troublesome issue in Jacob's life concerned Mary's job as the school's only teacher. It was at least a mile from Jacob's farm to the school. Traveling the unimproved trail in the winter, or during wet periods, would be challenging at best once they were married. Mary and Jacob met with her parents with a proposal. Is it possible, they asked, that for the next year she stay at their home during the school week? It was an option that the Fischer family fully supported. Though the agreed solution was far from ideal, Jacob, Mary, and her family knew that the only other option was for her to quit the job she loved and performed so well. Quitting was not on the table for discussion. It was unthinkable for Mary, and the local children would have suffered the loss of an excellent teacher. On this issue, Mary enjoyed Jacob's full support.

THE MAY WEDDING WAS A grand affair. It occurred nearly three years to the day of Jacob boldly walking out of his Vermont home for the last time. Nature itself seemed to join the ceremony, with warm sunshine and a gentle breeze wafting the smell of blooming lilacs. It was the first wedding ceremony in the new church building and Pastor Jackson's first as presiding minister.

The church was filled with neighbors from far and near. The women dressed in their finest clothes, proudly displaying modest jewelry and accessories. The men wore clean work clothes, since most did not possess what would be considered dress clothes. Their hair and beards were neatly trimmed in honor of the special event. Jacob waited in the front pew with bated breath while Mary, and Helen as bridesmaid, were in an adjacent room finalizing preparations for their grand entrance. Robert sat next to Jacob, serving as the groomsman. Neither man ever served in a wedding party and were trying to remember everything that Pastor Jackson told them they must do and say. Jacob was also on edge because he suspected that Robert would revert to his old form and play some sort of prank during the event.

When the bridal party made its entrance, Jacob was spellbound by Mary's beauty. He had never seen her dressed as finely as she was at that moment, adorned with jewelry and sporting a lovely, extravagant, never-before-seen hair styling. Helen was similarly stunning in her appearance. No one would have known that their dresses were handmade, having been a secret project taking three months. Friends that filled the pews buzzed with amazement at how marvelous the two women looked.

Neighborhood children, used to seeing Mary in her practical teacher's clothing, were wide-eyed in awe. The actual wedding ceremony went splendidly, Jacob and Robert remembering everything they were supposed to say and do. When the pastor asked Mary if she would take Jacob for her husband, she looked him square in the eyes and in a firm, clear voice said, "I will." It was clear to everyone that she meant it. Jacob's voice wasn't quite as clear and firm. Not from a lack of conviction certainly, but from overwhelming emotions. In his mind, this was far and away the best day of his life.

Robert impressed everyone by being a refined gentleman. Jacob later wondered where he learned to act that way. Robert was a dear friend, but no one would have ever used the words "refined gentleman" to describe him in the past.

Mrs. Fischer filled the building with music, and the reception and dinner that followed would be remembered for years. The local children were especially thrilled when Mary told the families that there would be no school on the upcoming Monday and Tuesday. As the sun was setting through the emerging greenery of spring, Jacob and Mary departed in their buggy. Unknown kids had decorated it with a variety of banners and noisemakers. The wedding duo thought it was perfect. They rode the familiar trail to what was once Jacob's crude cabin in the forest. It was now their home, surrounded by fields of promise.

Life was good in the summer of 1835. The Michigan Fever burned hotly. Unlike the fever and chills that governmental surveyor Edward Tiffin warned about two decades earlier, this fever was the result of more settlers and investors purchasing land in Michigan than in any other state or territory. Michigan land became the most sought-after investment on the market. Government land offices in the territory were the busiest in the nation as speculators and homesteaders alike enthusiastically bought land.

Jacob and Mary's farm in Jackson County was at the center of it all. With more settlers came more development. Section line trails connecting primary thoroughfares with interior holdings were constantly being improved by township and county governments. Many, including the trail Jacob had first cleared two years earlier, were now roads that were passable in all but the worst conditions. These roads were often given the name of an original settler along the route. Thus was the road past Jacob's farm called Hart Road.

A rapidly growing population supported those willing to invest in the territory. Businesses and small factories set up shops, selling or making items needed for farming or daily life.

Being made locally resulted in significantly lower costs for many necessary items. Growing and selling produce was profitable because of the increased demand from more homesteaders into the region and the ability to ship products long distances on improved trails. Jacob and Mary spent the summer of '35 clearing more fields and improving their barn and fences. Cattle were in their future, and with livestock came the requirement of sturdy fences.

Jacob and Mary's wedding convinced Robert that it was time for him to take the big step as well. Though they communicated often by mail, he greatly missed Fiona during the year they were apart. After Jacob's wedding, he sent her a letter, proudly describing their new home and declaring that it was finally suitable for her. Arrangements were made for her to arrive in mid-July, with the wedding as soon after her arrival as feasible.

In the meantime, Robert did everything he could to make the house the sort of home that Fiona would be proud of and happy to live in. The rough trail that once existed between his farmstead and the section line road was now an all-season road. Robert's house and farm were no longer a crude cabin in the forest but things in which he could take immense pride. A new coal-burning stove provided heat as well as being a modern centerpiece in the kitchen. The new barn housed a pair of horses. After many days of work, and moving specially purchased furniture in, Robert, Jacob, and Jerome declared that it was now fit for a queen. The only thing missing was the queen herself, who was scheduled to arrive within a few days.

It took a relay of couriers to get the message to Robert that Fiona was waiting at the Thompson house. Hitching his horse and buggy, Robert responded as quickly as he could. Passing by Jacob's farm, he saw him in the yard.

"I just got word that Fiona is at the Thompsons' house. Do you want to go with me to pick her up? She would love to see you again—what's it been, four or five years?"

"I'd love to! Give me five minutes to clean up a bit."

It was a joyful reunion to say the least. Robert and Fiona were ecstatic to see one another again, and Jacob was delighted to see childhood friends all grown up and delightfully happy with their situation in life. After the exuberant joy of the reunion subsided, Robert said he had an idea.

"What do you say we go to see Pastor Jackson at the church as long as we're here. We can decide on a specific date for the wedding. And Jacob, this includes you, because after I did such a marvelous job as your groomsman, I want you to return the favor!"

They found Pastor Jackson in his small office. He was fully supportive and suggested making the date three weeks out so that folks could plan for it. Looking at a wall calendar he received from Mr. Johnson at the store, Pastor Jackson suggested Saturday, August 8th. The trio agreed that it was perfect.

Marriage plans quickly fell into place. Mary and Jacob happily agreed to be part of the wedding party. Neighbors met to arrange food for the event. Jacob, Mary, and Edna Fischer secretly met to plan the music to be played after dinner. When the big day arrived, everything was in place.

The weather was typical of the dog days of August—hot and humid. The conditions were what everyone was used to, however, and no one seemed to notice. A pleasant breeze flowed through the open windows and doors of the church. The pews were again filled for the second wedding of the year. Once again, Jacob and Robert nervously stood in front of everyone on their best behavior. They both felt strange dressed in their best clothes. When Fiona and Mary made their entrance, there were the same reactions of awe as three months earlier. Fiona was stunning in a lace dress her mother made for her, which she had carefully packed and brought from Vermont. Mary looked as gorgeous as she did on her own wedding day. After the vows were spoken, Robert turned to Fiona, also fluent in the Gaelic of her home country, and whispered, *"Bidh gaol agam ort a-chaoidh."*

The after-dinner entertainment was spectacular. The musicians had secretly practiced some traditional Scottish tunes and performed them flawlessly. Tears were in the eyes of many after hearing "The Bothy Ballads," "Loch Lomond," and "Auld Lang Syne." Mary topped off the evening by singing two Burns's poems: "A Red, Red Rose" (chosen as especially appropriate given the shade of Fiona's hair) and "My Heart's in the Highlands." It was after midnight by the time the last of the participants rode back to their homes scattered across the woods and fields of Jackson County. The brilliant glow of the Milky Way delivered an appropriate blessing as a marvelous day came to an end.

The remainder of the summer all too quickly faded away with the work of running a farm. Jacob and Robert excavated a significant supply of coal for delivery to customers after cool weather descended on the community. In the fall and winter, Mary spent much more time living with her parents to be near the school. On those days when school was not in session, she came back to their farmstead.

Several of the men in the township made a trip to Jackson in October. The event was one that Jacob and his friends would not miss for any reason: the chance to vote on a draft Constitution for Michigan and to elect the new state's first governor. If approved, the process for statehood would proceed. It was a once-in-a-lifetime opportunity to shape the future of the land they all considered home. Jacob was pleased when he later learned that the proposal passed, and Stevens T. Mason was elected governor of the new state, once formally approved by congress.

It was an exciting period, and it piqued Jacob's interest in broader public policy affairs. Until this point in time, Jacob was focused primarily on issues with his personal life. He played active roles in events, but often in the background. He possessed the talent and credibility to influence activities without having to be the public face.

Life fell into a comfortable routine. The annual Christmas Eve party, which everyone agreed was an important tradition, was larger than ever. It was held in the church for the first time. The building proved to be much more conducive for the event than the Thompsons' house, which could not have accommodated the crowd. There was music, food, and good cheer for all. The annual event was one of the few opportunities each year where all the residents in the township could meet and greet new folks and, more frequently every year, reminisce with fellow old-timers. Despite the many signs of progress, it was still a rural community. The day-to-day work of operating a profitable farm was never-ending, and there was little time for distractions such as social events.

The year ended and life went on. Late in 1836, Jerome and Helen Walker became the proud parents of Eileen, their second. Robert and Fiona MacIntosh welcomed a son named Angus, in memory of his grandfather. It was a year of growth and good tidings. There was much celebrating when Michigan was declared a state early in 1837. Things seemed on an unending course of growth and prosperity.

Homesteaders carving a new life out of the Jackson County forests cared little that their new state was given additional land in the northern portion of the state in return for former territorial land ceded to Ohio, including Port Lawrence and the mouth of the Maumee River. For Jacob's part, hearing of this development brought back strong memories of the brief period he had spent at the village of Port Lawrence, allowing him to share this heretofore undisclosed part of his life with Mary and a few friends.

Timothy announced his plans to leave Michigan to attend university in the East. He had developed a strong interest in medicine and hoped to become a doctor. Working part-time jobs in addition to helping his parents on their farm, he felt that he had set aside enough money to cover his expenses. There were no doubts about his future success, especially for those who remembered when he helped take care of injured people during the forest fire.

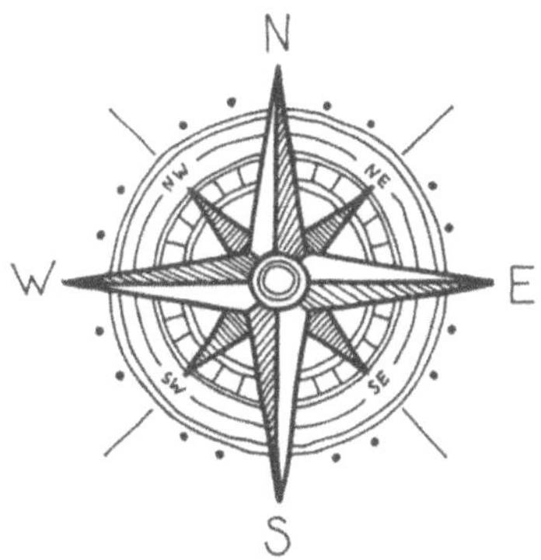

Chapter 24

DESPITE THE OPTIMISTIC OUTLOOKS OF Jacob and his neighbors, tendrils of doubt, even fear, began creeping into rural communities of Michigan because of circumstances far removed from the state. Unsettling and inexplicable developments began occurring. During the summer of '37, well-dressed strangers occasionally appeared at the offices of county officials. Lawyers and representatives of out-of-state businessmen or land holders brought legal documents that forever changed the lives of unsuspecting families. By the end of the year, there were rumors of families who lost their farm because the holders of their loans demanded payment. Others suddenly found themselves without money because notes issued by wildcat banks became worthless overnight. Inexplicably, circumstances had changed from positive to worrisome. There was word that the national economy was collapsing. Markets where produce was sold in the past shrank or disappeared. The word "panic" was used to describe the mysterious circumstances that silently changed everything.

Despite this, life in rural Michigan continued in its agricultural rhythm. The growing of crops and raising of food were controlled by seasonal and weather dictates, not the whims of politicians or businessmen, but adjustments were made in reaction to the national economic woes. Farmers focused on becoming self-sufficient to survive the economic storm. They grew enough food for themselves and raised cattle or pigs to meet their own needs. Bartering items or labor became a primary means of obtaining what was needed without spending precious money. Homesteaders became self-sufficient as much as possible, depending on one another rather than the outside world.

Most of the people Jacob and Mary knew took precautions to survive tough years. They were careful to have enough money on hand, issued by chartered banks and not wildcatters, to get them through rough periods. They paid off land purchase loans as quickly as possible to make sure they did not lose their homes to banks or by sheriff sales. The Walkers and MacIntoshes were in no immediate danger of losing their land, nor were the Harts. Nevertheless, belts were tightened as the outlook appeared poor for years, not just months. By the end of '37, everyone knew that the situation was going to be long-lasting.. Somehow, the world had suddenly changed.

The coal business that Jacob and Robert operated helped keep them above water. They adjusted the contracts downward as the economy shrank, but the extra income was still a godsend. Mary's small income also helped. Jacob purchased a strong draft horse, three cows, and some pigs from a neighbor who was leaving. He and Mary thought that it was a strategic time to grow their farm. While they did not plan on purchasing additional land, they were ready to expand beyond the basic cash crop approach of the past four years. Larger fields meant that a draft horse was necessary to till the land.

Life in their rural community went on despite rapidly evolving circumstances. The early promise of the village of Barry faded as years passed. It became a pleasant settlement, no longer striving for greatness. Elsewhere, progress was dramatic. Ann Arbor grew rapidly. It was under consideration as the state capital and became the home of a university. The town of Jacksonburg became known simply as Jackson, a change many residents had wanted years earlier. It was where government offices were established, including a state prison, and there was even talk of a railroad connecting Jackson and Detroit.

Jacob and Mary were blessed with a daughter in May of 1839. Named Emily, she mirrored her mother's lovely appearance right down to her charming dimples. A son, named Michael, was born the following year on an October morning when the garden produce was covered with heavy frost. As the years passed, the children of Jacob and Robert and other families of similar ages became close companions. History was repeating itself—mostly. But unlike his own father, Jacob did all he could to spend time with Michael. Farming and other duties did not take priority over raising his children.

Jacob communicated regularly with his family in Vermont. He was now an uncle several times over. He occasionally received letters written by one of his siblings instead of his mother. Letters from his mother focused primarily on babies and the goings-on of neighbors. Those written by his siblings were franker and more honest about the health conditions of their parents. In the most recent letter, from his sister Jasmine, she went into detail about the current situation. Their brother Joe was taking over responsibility for running the farm. He professed to be a lifelong bachelor, so his interest in taking over the farm and making necessary improvements made sense. The youngest brother, Daniel, openly expressed his desire to move to the big city to pursue an advanced education. His time on the farm was limited. Mr. Hart remained as active as possible, but it was clear that Joe was taking the lead in the operation.

Mary ended her full-time teaching position after the birth of Michael. Knowing that she would be leaving, the school board chose her successor a month earlier. Because of her mother's failing health, Mary took over Edna's work as a music and voice instructor. It allowed her to continue to tutor local children but eliminated the daily requirements of her former job.

Jacob and Jerome became active in local political affairs. Jacob took cues from his father-in-law, who had been active in local affairs for some time. As Max Fischer expanded his farm operation, he found it difficult to run the farm and perform the myriad other duties he had taken upon himself. Jacob and Mary discussed the matter, and they agreed that it was time for him to become involved more extensively.

Jacob and Jerome successfully ran for township level positions in 1840. As the township grew, the involvement of residents in public affairs became critical. It was no longer a wilderness with scattered homesteaders. With development and statehood, new issues arose, issues that had to be handled at the local level. Roads, schools, law enforcement, the establishment of a county farm to address the needs of the poor, taxes, and other realities of modern life needed to be resolved. These were just a few of the difficult issues that Jacob and his neighbors found themselves struggling with, often discussing them at the new tavern or at a meeting of officials in the township hall.

Construction of an additional school was a high priority for both men. After meeting and talking with residents over a two-month period, the pair's lobbying efforts for a second school were successful. This meant that some children would no longer have to walk or ride several miles to attend school. As a result, more of the township's children were able to attend school. Mrs. Murphy, a mother of two children of her own who recently moved from Boston with her family, was hired as the teacher in the new school. The school board of trustees, which now included Robert and Isaiah, played a personal role in ensuring that the new teacher met the ambitious standards that Mary had established during her tenure.

As the Panic of 1838 so clearly demonstrated, a variety of major national economic or political issues affected daily life. The complex issues that the growing country struggled with touched everyone but could not be resolved locally. Changes for both good and ill came at a dizzying pace to the once quiet villages across southern Michigan. Life had transformed in the decade since Jacob built his original cabin in the forest.

Completion of the Michigan Central Railroad connecting Jackson and Detroit in 1842 brought economic power to the region. Jackson County became a coal mining powerhouse, as mines were dug deep to access coal to power Detroit's burgeoning industry and run the many steam locomotives that now connected Michigan with the outside world. Jacob and other farmers likewise benefited from the ability to more easily ship their farm produce to eastern markets. Regular contact with the outside world was now possible thanks to the railroad, scheduled stagecoach services, and the relative ease of travel on the Territorial Road. This access not only brought in new residents, it also enabled the entry of varying beliefs and attitudes. No longer a backwater village, Barry now experienced firsthand the benefits and problems of a rapidly changing nation.

As the 1840s progressed, two of those difficult national issues, slavery and states' rights, were topics of discussion in every tavern and meeting room in the nation, including southern Michigan villages.

It was fair to say that Jacob and his friends were abolitionists. It was not a topic they publicly discussed at any length, however, prior to it increasingly becoming a national topic of conversation. They opposed slavery but had no influence or control over it and thus did not spend time debating the matter. This was about to change.

ON A WARM SPRING DAY in '48, Mary and Jacob took their children to see their grandparents. It was something they did as often as possible. Because of the many farm-related tasks that must be done in the spring, it was three weeks since their last visit. The visits were a welcome respite from daily routines. Everyone not only enjoyed the company of the others, but the kids found the many stories that Max and Edna told to be of great interest. On this particular day, Max asked Jacob, in private, to come out to the barn with him. Jacob assumed it had something to do with the farm or help on a particular task. In his formal, Old World Mennonite style of speech, Mr. Fischer brought up an issue that Jacob never would have expected.

"I apologize for what must seem like a somewhat devious means of having a conversation with you, but what I must speak to you about cannot be discussed openly in the house or among others. I asked you to come outside because I have something serious to discuss that I feel strongly about and am quietly seeking support from people whom I trust. But for the safety of many people, including our families, this must be kept secret."

"Of course, Max," Jacob said, his curiosity growing. "You know I would never betray your trust or our families' safety. What is it that is bothering you so much? And is Edna aware of this situation?"

"Yes, Edna knows about it and fully supports me. In fact, it was she who had the courage to get us involved in this issue in the first place. Mary and Timothy were also somewhat aware of our involvement while in New York, but they do not know about our current plans. You will be the third. It will be up to you as to when to talk to Mary, but it must not go beyond the two of you."

"I understand, and I will not tell a soul. Please, what is it that is weighing so heavily on you?"

"For some time, I have been in correspondence with Quaker abolitionist leaders in New York City who we knew when living there. Edna and I were active on the issue even then. They have given me names of some families in Michigan who are secretly helping escaped slaves get to Canada. They risk their lives and property to do this—it is not a light thing that we are discussing. The people and places involved in moving escaped slaves to freedom is being called the 'Underground Railroad.' It depends on people like us to work. I have agreed to help."

"Help? What can you do?"

"We can do much. Fugitive slaves require food. They need safe lodging until they can safely move on. They often depend on the help of local people to arrange their transport to the next safe house. They must have people like us, known by locals but unsuspected of assisting fugitive slaves. Edna and I can help them communicate with family members or key people in Detroit or Canada with whom they will finish their trip to freedom.

"We want to do all the things I just mentioned to the degree that we are able. But we wish to do more. A critical need for fugitive slaves is a place to hide for periods of time when slave hunters are chasing them. We wish to become a house of refuge. Safe houses that fugitive slaves can live in for several days or weeks are one of the most important parts of this entire plan."

"So, you're considering having fugitive slaves live with you here?" Jacob asked, his mind reeling. "How can you do that secretly? It seems that neighbors and travelers on the road will see the fugitives. After all, their race gives them away. Though Blacks are occasionally seen on the road, it's difficult for them to travel unnoticed."

"You are correct. Providing a short-term living space for runaways will take great effort. It will involve digging a secret room under our house. But equally important is to get them to the next house, which is in Jackson, and the next is in Ann Arbor. I am looking for help transporting runaway slaves to safe houses in Jackson or Ann Arbor. From there, other people will transport them to the next in a series of homes where they will be welcomed and protected."

Jacob was overwhelmed. Of all the topics Max might have discussed with him in the barn, this one was truly unexpected. Jacob assumed that Max was going to wax eloquently about his growing herd of milk cows.

"My God, Max. This is an incredible thing you are telling me! How will you dig this secret room, and who will transport runaway slaves? I assume this will happen at night for everyone's protection. What do you want me to do? Clearly you are telling me this for a reason."

"Yes, Jacob. I am asking you to become part of the network. People who are willing to risk themselves to help others are what America needs right now. Over the years, I have known you to be this sort of man. I believe the need for your leadership has arisen once again."

"What exactly is it that you think I can do?"

"First, I'd appreciate your help on making necessary alterations to our house. It must be done in a manner that doesn't cause curiosity. In the long term, I believe that your involvement can be most valuable in terms of transportation. This could involve bringing a fugitive from Albion or Marshall to my house. Or, perhaps taking them to the safe house in Jackson. Locals often see you on the road with your wagon, delivering coal to your customers, or grain to the mill in Jackson. Your being on the road with a covered wagon would not incite any interest. Passing along messages in person will also likely be required. That could be the most frequent involvement.

"Communications are person to person, sometimes to expedite matters, but also to avoid written documents that could be found and used against us. We are just getting this effort underway, so at the current time, there are few men or women who need our help. I can assure you that the number will increase in coming years."

Mrs. Fischer called out to let the men know that supper was ready. She made certain that the pair had had enough time to adequately discuss the matter before calling them in.

"I will talk to Mary about this the first chance we get to be alone, and you can be assured of my silence," Jacob assured Mr. Fischer as they walked to the house.

The conversation around the dinner table was largely about Emily and Michael, both of whom attended the new school. With her ability to read and write already well developed, Emily found school to be quite easy. It was a social affair for her, a chance to be with other girls from the area in a time when distances between farms made spending time with friends problematic. School satisfied the desire to spend time with friends as much as accomplishing educational goals.

Michael was an example of the fruit not falling far from the tree. He was a serious but open-minded student who was filled with curiosity and awe of the world around him. He spent much time observing and learning on his own.

Jacob was grateful for the presence of the Fischers. They were excellent grandparents in every regard. They mentored the children through hands-on activities and stories, as well as by the example they set through actions and words. They had long been admired and respected by all their neighbors.

The buggy ride back to their house at sunset reminded the family why they loved their home so much. The narrow road cut through woodlands and fields, putting the beauty of nature on full display. Trilliums, anemones, and marsh marigolds dazzled the countryside. Colorful songbirds busily carried food to their young, and far overhead, red-tailed hawks circled on the rising warm air. In a nearby vernal pond, a hen mallard led her brood to safety, away from the noisy buggy. Nature was a classroom that Jacob and Mary often used to teach Emily and Michael about the broader world.

After arriving home, Jacob took care of Molly, asking the children to help with her food and water. When chores were finished and Emily and Michael focused on their own interests, Jacob asked Mary if they could go for a walk to discuss some farm issues. When they were far enough away to be certain they could not be overheard, Jacob told Mary about his unusual conversation with her father. Mary listened intently, recalling faint memories of conversations between her parents that she overheard as a child. She was aware that her parents held strong feelings about slavery and abolition, but had no idea as to the depth of their commitment and of their current intention to take constructive actions toward assisting runaway slaves.

Jacob and Mary were both torn. They supported the concept and were willing to do what they could but admitted to having concerns about safety. Mr. Fischer's description of armed slave hunters kidnapping fugitives and attacking their helpers was worrisome. How would their involvement affect Emily and Michael, they wondered. On the other hand, they felt a moral obligation to do something meaningful. In the end, they agreed that at a minimum they would help construct the secret room at her parents' home, and that Jacob would function as a messenger in the network.

Because Jacob was busy with farm work for the next week, Mary went to see her parents following their conversation. She told them what they agreed to do. The Fischers were pleased that they would be involved, and assured Mary that with secrecy came safety. They promised that they would never do nor ask anything of them that could endanger the children.

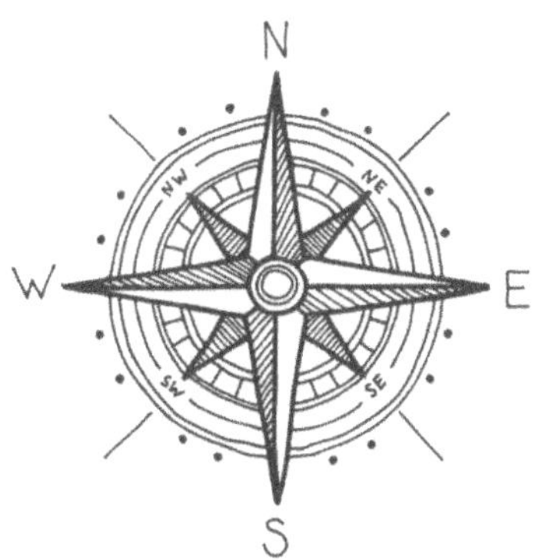

Chapter 25

WITH FIELDS PLANTED AND SEASONAL tasks completed, Jacob arranged to help construct the safe room at the Fischers'. There, he met two men from the town of Albion who had been so-called Underground Railroad conductors for two years. Max told him that they were completely trustworthy, introducing them only as James and Henry. For safety's sake, the last names of volunteers were not given, he explained. Jacob inquired about how often escaped slaves used the Underground Railroad.

"Far more often than anyone would imagine," James said. "For the past year, we have moved escaped slaves down this very road three or four times per month. And the frequency is increasing. More southern slaves are attempting to escape. The word has spread throughout the south about networks like ours that help runaway slaves find freedom. Many of the escapees go all the way to Canada to be certain they can't be captured and forcibly returned. Others stay in places like Michigan where they start new lives.

"But as the number of escapes increases, so does the aggressiveness of so-called slave catchers who are paid handsomely to capture and return escaped slaves, no matter how long they have been free. I have personally taken four people down this road in the last month. No one knows about it because of the secrecy involved and because we transport people only at night."

James's explanation was an eye-opener for Jacob. It brought home the emotions and importance of what Max tried to explain weeks earlier. Working covertly on the back side of the house, the men dug a partial basement, taking loads of dirt far into the woods so it would not be noticed. They built stairs into the lower level and constructed a concealed door into the space from the outside. They also built a trapdoor on the floor above the space, covering it with a carpet. The two men from Albion returned home when the project was completed. The Fischers then spent several days making the small basement as comfortable as possible with a bed and basic furnishings.

A month after the room had been finished, James appeared at the Fischers' door one evening. He said that a message from a safe house in Battle Creek suggested that three former slaves might need to arrive within a week. The family was being pursued by a posse from Kentucky. Though the runaways' refuge had yet to be discovered, it was feared that it was only a matter of time before aggressive posse members discovered it. Before departing, James instructed the Fischers as to the secretive process for communicating and the signals used to confirm the arrival of freedom seekers. He explained that the clandestine procedure was recently changed because of a suspected infiltrator. Max and Edna agreed to hide the family. They stocked the basement room with the necessary food and water in preparation for their arrival.

Only three days elapsed before the Fischers were awakened by a clandestine series of knocks on their door at dawn. Dressing quickly, they saw Henry at the back door. The family, he explained, was hiding in the brush about a hundred yards away. He briefly explained that, because of the imminent danger of discovery, they had to move sooner than planned. They had spent the prior day at a safe house in Albion and traveled through the night to the Fischers. Max opened the door to the hidden room and the three fugitives quickly made their way into the basement. It was a couple with a young child. From the look on their faces, it was clear that they had just experienced a harrowing event.

Henry explained that he must return directly to his own family in Albion, asking if there was a way to get a coded message to the Jackson safe house within two or three days. Max told him that he would talk to Jacob later that day to see if he could carry the message. Since it could be done during daylight hours, it required no special precautions. Henry said that he or James would be back in about a week.

After ensuring that everything was okay with the family hiding in the basement, Max hitched their horse to the buggy and rode out to Jacob and Mary's farm. Mary and the kids were outside digging vegetables in the garden. They were delighted to see him and went inside to clean up and enjoy some cool water from the well. Mary told Max that Jacob was at Robert's farm, helping him build a fence. Mary could tell that her father was anxious about something. She suggested that they go out to look at their crop of tomatoes. Alone in the yard, Mary's father told her about the escaped slaves hiding in his basement, explaining the need for a message to be carried to Jackson as soon as possible. Mary was dumbfounded. Aware of her parents' renewed involvement in helping runaway slaves, the reality of a family that escaped slavery from hundreds of miles away making it all the way to her old home was hard to comprehend. She immediately understood the significance of the situation.

"When Jacob returns this evening, I will give him your message. I don't know for certain, but it is likely he can get to your house tomorrow morning. The kids and I will help get the morning chores done so that he can leave early."

Jacob arrived early at the Fischers'. The request for help was not a surprise, but it came sooner than he expected. Already taking precautions, he looked around carefully before entering the house. Nothing seemed out of place. The Fischers introduced him to the family. Just that morning, they learned that the family's names were Virgil and Daphne Johnson, and their son, James. Edna was horrified to discover that the family had fled after learning that their son was going to be auctioned off to another farmer.

Jacob confirmed that he would indeed ride to Jackson to deliver the message. After Max recited it multiple times, Jacob felt confident he could remember it. He also gave Jacob the location of the safe house and the signal to confirm his identity.

Jacob took the lunch that Edna prepared for him and departed. Everything about the visit and his riding toward Jackson would have looked normal to an observer. The trip and encounter in Jackson went smoothly. The safe house expected the Johnson family to arrive on the following Tuesday night. Jacob returned briefly to the Fischers' and was home for supper. When he and Mary eventually found some privacy, he filled her in on the day's events. The story of the Johnson family's escape brought tears to Mary's eye, imagining such a horrible situation. The tremendous impact they could have on the Johnson family's lives made them appreciate the value of what they were about to do.

THE FISCHERS WERE IN THEIR garden near the barn when they noticed an unusual group of three men on the road moving in their direction. One was driving a horse-drawn wagon and two were on horseback. These strangers, dressed distinctively from the locals, were clearly searching for something. They saw the group stop at a house west of them. They walked around the yard first, and then knocked on the door. After talking to the homeowner, the strangers departed, proceeding east toward the Fischers.

"Act calm and friendly, Edna. These men are after the Johnsons. We must not give them any reason to be suspicious of us," Max said, staying calm. "But the fact they know the Johnsons are in the area is worrying. Perhaps they even know that they are supposed to be moved in two days."

"And remember," the driver of the buggy called to the neighbors as they left. "You'd better be careful old man. There are some dangerous escaped black criminals in the area. They would steal everything you got if they could."

The men rode across the yard to the Fischers.

"Good morning, sir. My name is Tom. This is my wife, Esther. What is this about escaped criminals? We spend much time in the yard and barn but have seen nothing unusual."

"Well, they're a sneaky bunch of bastards, so you wouldn't see them if they didn't want to be seen. The trouble is, it's our own kind that are hiding them! White people hiding runaway slave criminals in their own houses! Can you imagine such an abomination? It's our job to catch them, and it's only a matter of time before we do. Then, we'll haul them back to Kentucky to face justice the old-fashioned way. By a rope around the neck!"

"No, I can't imagine hiding dangerous criminals," said Max. "It's because of all the garbage they're teaching kids in school nowadays. Talking about everyone being equal and the like. Such ridiculous bullshit!"

"Maybe we'll just look around a bit, as long as we're here."

"Certainly. In fact, you might want to give your horses some hay and water and let them rest a bit."

Looking around the barn and the yard, the posse saw nothing suspicious. Max was concerned that they might insist on looking inside the house but felt comforted knowing that they had not forced their way into their neighbor's home. He was desperately hoping that his playacting fooled them.

It apparently had, as the men departed after a cursory search of the yard and barn. Max bid them farewell, he and Edna remaining in the garden until the men were out of sight to the east. From a concealed location, they watched the posse stop at more houses. They also stopped at the church for a lengthy period, and then the general store.

"This is serious," Edna noted after watching the group's activities. "They clearly suspect something. Somehow, the movement of the Johnsons to this area has become known to the bounty hunters. Getting them to Jackson is going to be more perilous than expected."

When the gang finally moved out of sight to the east, the Fischers went to the church to talk with Pastor Jackson. He said that the posse members had refused to believe him. It was only after he let them search every part of the building and his adjacent rectory that they finally left.

"For the first time ever, I feared for my life! These are cruel men who will not rest until they can claim their reward for capturing the people they're after. I don't know why they think the people they seek are here in Sandstone Township, though."

"They are obviously mistaken," Max offered.

Max made another trip to Jacob's farm the next day. Once again, finding a place to talk away from the children, he told of the nerve-wracking encounter with the posse. He explained that he felt certain that the gang was going to remain in the Sandstone Township area until they were satisfied that their prey was not there. This created the need to get a new message to the Jackson safe house as soon as possible. They both agreed that the transfer should be put off for a week.

Jacob agreed to deliver the message. He said that he could take a load of wheat to the mill in Jackson the next day to cover his trip. While on the road, he would also carefully look for any signs of the posse so that the information could be shared with other conductors.

Jacob's trip began well enough. Leaving home at a normal time, he made the trip to the mill in Jackson without incident. His business at the mill took some time, after which he rode to the general store, which was near the safe house. Having become constantly aware of what was going on around him, he secured Molly as if he were going to the store. He instead stayed in the wagon until he was confident that he was not being watched. Only when he was certain no one was watching him did he walk to the safe house to deliver the information about the posse and the need to delay the transfer of the Johnsons for a week.

Leaving for home, he passed a tavern in Jackson. It had been a long, warm day, so he decided to stop for a beer. He took a seat at a quiet table to enjoy a drink without being bothered by loud patrons. He was almost finished when three men walked in. They were boisterous, and when they were close enough for Jacob to overhear their loud conversation, it was clear that they spoke with a southern accent. They took a table near Jacob's and motioned for the woman tending tables to come over.

"Hey, sweetheart, you got a couple friends and a place where we can spend the night? We're far from home and mighty lonesome!"

Keeping well out of their reach, the waitress glared while the men laughed and made insulting comments about cold northern women. After she brought the bottle of whiskey and glasses they demanded, the men settled down.

"I know damn well that those coloreds are around this area

somewhere. Joseph said that they had been moved from Battle Creek and Albion over to Sandstone Township somewhere."

"Well, we searched that area two days ago and saw nothing suspicious," countered another of the trio.

"Look, Joseph has never done us wrong. He is trusted by everyone involved in the so-called 'Underground Railroad.' His information has always been good."

"Then we stick around until we find them. We know they're going to be taken somewhere here in Jackson soon. So, we wait until they try to make the trip. We also know that they'll try moving them at night—that's what they always do. They're not stupid enough to move them in the daytime. This time we'll have a little surprise for them. It's time we taught these hicks and their goddamned Underground Railroad a lesson!" the third member declared, pounding the table with his well-used Henry flintlock pistol.

Jacob did his best to pretend that he cared nothing about the trio or what they were saying. He slowly drank his beer, looking in other directions but still focusing on their conversation. Occasional glances in their direction allowed him to compile a physical description for each man. When he finished his drink, he paid the bartender and left without giving them a glance. They likewise paid him no attention. He was obviously just a poor local farmer who was not worthy of their time. On his way out, Jacob took a close look at the horses used by the posse so he could also describe their appearance to other conductors.

On his way home, Jacob thought deeply about what he saw and heard at the tavern. The enormity of the situation fully sank in. He had heard about the depravity of slavery before, but witnessing the attitude of the slave hunters and their relentless pursuit of escaped human beings made the urgency of what he participated in even clearer.

Jacob occasionally felt guilty about not telling any of his friends about his activities. He knew, however, that it was not a matter of simple trust. He trusted Robert, Jerome, and Isaac. He knew they would never deliberately reveal sensitive information. It was the accidental unintended slip of the tongue that he had to be concerned about. He did not want to put his friends in a position where they might unintentionally cause harm to a conductor or a fugitive family—or themselves.

It was dark by the time Jacob arrived. When he found a chance to speak privately with Mary, he told her about what he observed. They agreed that since nothing was planned for tomorrow, he should wait at least one more day before going to see the Fischers to avoid doing anything that appeared out of the ordinary.

"Henry or James will be at your parents' house in three or four days, so I have some time. I will deliver the message the day after tomorrow. That way everything will look normal, and when the conductor shows up, they can plan accordingly."

Jacob and his family went to the Fischers' two days later, as planned. In every respect it looked like a typical family visit. They prepared a picnic to eat outside in plain sight, under the large oak tree that graced the Fischers' front yard. As the meal was being set up, Max and Jacob went to the barn to check on a sick cow. Jacob relayed all that he had seen and heard two days earlier in Jackson. The news confirming a spy among the conductors was especially disturbing. Max said that he would relay the name of Joseph to others in the network. It likely wasn't his real name, but it might help locate and eliminate the informer from the network.

Max was concerned about the planned relay within the week.

"They will be waiting for any wagon or buggy traveling toward Jackson after dark. Anyone on the road at night will be stopped and searched by the posse."

"But what if we fool them?" proposed Jacob. "Their conversation made it clear that they are expecting only nighttime relays. They likely won't be looking for them during the daytime. When you talk to James or Henry, tell them that I am willing to pretend that I'm delivering a load of coal to Jackson. Everything will look normal, covered wagon and all. I will even dirty my hands and clothes with coal dust to look authentic."

After pondering the suggestion for a minute, Max reluctantly agreed, but with one alteration.

"Edna and I will proceed east on the road about ten minutes ahead of you. We will pretend we are taking our plow to a blacksmith for repairs, covering it so that a person might think there are people under the canvas. If the posse is out, they will stop us to search our wagon. I will put my white hat on if they stop us. You should have plenty of time to see what's going on and turn around.

"Your help is greatly appreciated, Jacob. It was never my intention to get you so deeply involved in this undertaking. The safety of your young family is of utmost importance."

"I agree. Mary and I have talked about it, and she agrees that a daytime trip would be much safer for everyone."

"Then it's agreed. After I talk with the Albion contact, I shall come visit you with a plan for the relay. The Johnsons will be eternally grateful for your help."

As planned, Max met Henry to discuss the upcoming transfer. After being informed of the valuable information Jacob discovered on his Jackson trip, the agent agreed to the unusual daytime transfer. Max then went to Jacob's home three days later to coordinate the plan. Jacob was to meet at the Fischer house at midmorning in two days' time.

When the appointed day arrived, Jacob put some coal in the wagon, making it a point to get his hands and clothes dirty. He covered it with the tarp and bid his family goodbye. On his way to the Fischers', he carefully looked around but saw nothing unusual. He felt a bit silly being so cautious, expecting spies and danger at every turn. And yet, he knew that he participated in something for which the consequences were great, especially for the freedom seekers they were trying to help. He imagined what it would be like for him and his family to be captives seeking freedom; that thought drove him forward.

At the Fischers', he pulled around to the back of the house, as if he were going to the barn. After they deemed it safe, he pulled the wagon close to the basement's concealed door. The Johnson family quickly climbed onto the wagon and Jacob and Max securely covered them with the canvas. The overhead sun soon made the concealed space under the tarp unpleasantly hot. Having to lie down on the hard wagon under such circumstances was going to result in a difficult trip for the family, but they knew better than anyone that concealment was paramount. Max and Edna's team was already hitched, and their wagon loaded with the covered plow. It had the desired appearance. Confirming their plan, signals, and meeting location in Jackson, the Fischers departed. Jacob remained behind the house, out of sight, for about ten minutes and then proceeded east.

Jacob had gone about a half mile when a very unexpected development occurred. He encountered Robert on the road. He was in his wagon on his way to the equipment dealer near Jackson. Jacob had no choice but to pull to the side of the road, with Robert pulling behind him. Jacob hoped that he could come up with an explanation that would enable him to get underway again quickly.

"Hey, I thought you were done selling coal in Jackson. What's up?"

"I got a request for one small load, and I thought I'd take care of it today, to get it out of the way. It's a one-time thing so we won't have to worry about it anymore."

"Oh. I wish you had mentioned it, we could have ridden over together. I'm heading that way too."

"Yeah, I didn't even think about it."

At that moment, a slight movement under the canvas caught Robert's attention.

"What the…? What's under your canvas? Something moved."

Robert started to lift the canvas, but Jacob quickly stopped him.

"What's going on, Jacob? Someone is under there!"

Jacob led Robert away from the wagons to the side of the road.

"Robert, you've been my most valued friend for a long time. I have something very important to tell you, but first I must ask for your absolute secrecy. No questions asked. If you do not confirm that you will never speak a word about this matter, I cannot tell you anything more. I will get on my wagon and leave."

"And I've known you for a lifetime and trust you completely, my friend. Of course you have my promise of silence. You are apparently doing something of great importance."

Jacob quickly told Robert about the Underground Railroad and of his involvement. He informed him of the critically important relay that he and the Fischers were conducting at that moment. He also informed Robert that he must resume his trip to Jackson as quickly as possible.

"Then it seems to me that you might need help. You have my vow of silence. I will follow behind you in case something goes wrong."

Jacob proceeded east, maintaining a speed that would minimize bumps felt by the Johnsons on the hard wagon floor. Robert followed behind. An observer would have no reason to suspect anything unusual. The late summer day was hot and the road dusty. Jacob could not help but imagine how stifling it must be under the concealing canvas.

When they were about a mile from Jackson, Jacob pulled the reins hard. He could just make out the Fischer wagon ahead, stopped, with Max wearing a white hat. The posse had stopped them. He yelled to the Johnsons and Robert that they must turn around and head back west because the slave hunters were up ahead.

He and Robert turned their rigs and started westward. Because of the presence of the Johnsons in his wagon, Jacob could not go beyond walking speed. They were underway for only a minute when Robert called out that two people on horseback were coming their way at a gallop. Jacob knew there was no option but to continue. Perhaps the riders were not after them.

As the vigilantes approached, they made it clear that it was Jacob and Robert that they were after, ordering them to stop. Seeing them turn around did indeed arouse suspicion on part of the slave hunters. Jacob and Robert stopped, standing behind their wagons. Jacob recognized both men as having been in the tavern. There was no question about what their intention was as they walked toward them, one holding a pistol in his hand.

"What's your hurry, boys? Why did you turn around and try to run away when you saw us up ahead? Something to hide maybe? What the hell you got under that canvas, plowboy?"

"I don't see that that's any of your goddamned business. Who the hell are you and what the hell do you think you're doing, waving a gun at us for no reason? You must be a mighty damned hard-up pair of thieves if you're trying to steal a load of coal."

"We'll see who the outlaws are. Like I said, what the hell are you hiding under that canvas? Since you don't want to tell us, we'll just see for ourselves."

Robert slowly walked to Jacob's side. When one of the posse members began to pull the tarp off the wagon, he and Jacob reacted immediately, tackling both men. A desperate fight ensued in the dusty road. Jacob grabbed the hand of the man with the pistol, trying to wrench it away, or at least keep it pointed toward the ground. After a brief intense struggle, the gunman broke free momentarily, pointing the pistol in Jacob's direction. Jacob made a desperate swing at the assailant's arm, knocking it away and causing the outlaw to pull the trigger. Fortunately, the result was a ball harmlessly shot into the ground. The single-shot handgun was no longer a threat. The two continued rolling in the dirt, taking ineffective punches at the other. Jacob was finally able to grab his assailant by the collar and partially lift him up. With enough room to maneuver, Jacob made a final swing as hard as he could to the man's gut, and then as he was doubled over, a powerful swing to his jaw. The vigilante hit the ground hard, gasping for breath. Jacob quickly suppressed any further struggles.

Robert was involved in a more traditional fist fight, a skill that had brought him considerable notoriety in the Vermont hills. Two quick swings from his muscular arms resulted in howls of pain and blood flowing from his opponent's nose. Both attackers were unceremoniously restrained by tying their hands and feet and placing a gag in their mouths. To get them out of sight should other travelers pass by, they dragged the two men far into the woods on the south side of the road.

Going back to Jacob's wagon, the duo wiped blood off their hands and raised the canvas to speak with the Johnsons. It was the first time Robert had seen the family. He was moved with sympathy by the pitiful scene before him. As much as Virgil Johnson wanted to get out and fight for himself, they were able to convince him that the family must remain hidden at all costs. No one could see them for fear of news of their location spreading to unwanted ears.

After ensuring that the road was clear of travelers, the family was helped into the nearby woods on the opposite side of the road. Jacob took a minute to brush away the footprints they left in the dust.

Robert and Jacob were discussing their options when they

spotted a team and wagon approaching quickly from the east. *What now?* thought Jacob.

Pretending to simply be friends who encountered each other on the road, the pair stayed in place, hoping that the stranger would continue past without stopping. But they did not pass by. The teamster approached them with a partner, pointing pistols toward the pair.

"I'm Sheriff John Flynn. I was just notified by an elderly man and his wife that there was a gang of robbers on the road. He said that they were accosted and that he saw two of the robbers jump on their horses and chase after another traveler behind them. I see two riderless horses over there and the two of you stopped for some reason. How about you tell me what the hell is going on here."

Sheriff Flynn was a thin, bespectacled man that Jacob would have guessed to be a schoolmaster or bank clerk, rather than a lawman. His commanding voice and no-nonsense manner, however, made it clear that he was not to be underestimated.

"As a matter of fact, Sheriff, we'd be happy to," Jacob said. "We were attacked by the two men who were on those horses. They tried to rob us, even though all they would have gotten is a small load of coal. We fought them off and were just pondering what we should do about them. That pistol on the ground over there is what they used when they attacked us."

"Well, we just arrested the ringleader a few minutes ago. He was stupid enough to stay in the same spot where they tried to rob the other travelers. A deputy is taking him to jail right now."

"And we have a gift for you, Sheriff. We weren't going to leave them there, but as I said, we didn't know what to do. We overpowered and tied up the two men who accosted us. They will be glad to see you. I imagine the mosquitoes must be biting them quite badly."

The friends led the sheriff and his deputy into the woods where the two men lay. Helping them get on their feet, the two vigilantes stared sullenly as Sheriff Flynn and his deputy removed their gags and identified themselves. It was only after they learned that the two new men on the scene were lawmen that the older of the two became agitated and vociferous.

"Sheriff, you got to arrest these two men! Don't let them fool you. I know damn well that they are transporting runaway slaves that we have a legal court order to capture!"

"What in Sam Hill are you talking about, boy?" the sheriff said. I just saw their wagons; they don't have no runaway slaves or anything else that might be questionable. There is coal in one wagon and the other is empty. No sign of any people anywhere. You might have a legal contract of some sort, but there sure as hell aren't any slaves around here, escaped or otherwise."

"But you gotta believe us, sir. We're certain they were going to take escaped slaves, name of the Johnsons, to Jackson today. We got it from a reliable source. They are involved in this here Underground Railroad and are hiding fugitives from the law."

"The only fugitives are the two of you. Since you're already tied up we don't have to waste time doing that. Get going, we're taking a trip into town. You'll be happy to see your friend who is already there."

The sheriff departed with the two riderless horses tied to their wagon. Jacob and Robert waited by their rigs until the road was clear. After Jacob took what little food and water he had to the

Johnsons, they discussed their options. Robert said that he was familiar with a small road south of Territorial Road that went into Jackson. It was lightly used with minimal likelihood of additional posse members watching it. They decided that Robert would continue alone, and Jacob would turn onto the trail, taking it into town. Jacob informed his friend of the designated meeting location if everything was successfully accomplished. After waiting long enough to be certain that they were safe, the Johnsons climbed onto Jacob's wagon. They were once again carefully covered for concealment.

Jackson was small enough that Jacob had no problem finding the safe house from the new direction. Expecting their arrival, the homeowner quickly opened the door upon hearing the coded knock. It took extra effort to ensure that the Johnsons were not seen as they quickly moved from the wagon into the safe house in broad daylight. To not draw attention to their activities, Jacob left immediately.

He arrived at the city hall, the designated location, soon after. The Fischers and Robert were already there. They were still in conversation, the Fischers having been shocked to see Robert arrive and hear of his involvement. Max explained that once the posse was satisfied that they were clean and let them go, and two mounted men raced toward Jacob's location, he and Edna hurried to the sheriff's office to report thieves on the road. His quick action saved the day. Jacob said that it was certainly the act of turning the wagons around that aroused the suspicion of the kidnappers. Everyone agreed that Jacob had had no choice. If he continued eastward toward the posse, the Johnsons would be their captives right now.

To minimize the possibility of being observed by unfriendly parties, the trio returned to Sandstone Township separately. Robert was the last to leave. Jacob asked him to stop at his house when he got back. The trip west was uneventful, as expected. Jacob had just finished filling Mary in on the events of the day. When Robert arrived, Mary gave him a warm hug for his role in protecting Jacob and the Johnsons. Robert's chance involvement was a godsend, she said, and she agreed that he was one of the most trustworthy men in the county. Jacob apologized for not telling him about everything sooner, but Robert dismissed his apology.

"You did exactly the right thing. You could not jeopardize the network. And I appreciate your concern about exposing my family to the dangers that come with the job."

As Robert was leaving, he added, "I don't know how I'm going to explain to Fiona that I was gone all day and yet didn't accomplish what I set out to do this morning."

Mary and Jacob both agreed that their quick-witted friend would think of something before he arrived home.

The exposure of the Fischers, Jacob, and Robert to posse members reduced their ability to serve in the network. It was only three days after the incident in Jackson that the trio of vigilantes was seen in Barry again. Riding westward, they stopped briefly in front of the Fischer residence, having remembered their initial encounter here days earlier. They knew that it was Max who alerted the sheriff. There was no doubt that Jacob and Robert would also be recognized by two of the gang members, who would be eager for revenge. Their active involvement would have to be curtailed for some time.

Allowing ten days to pass, Max met Jacob, Mary, and Robert at Jacob's house, a safe place to gather due to its distance from the main road. Max explained that James had contacted him two days earlier. Word of the narrow escape that he and Jacob had with the posse made its way through the underground network, raising concerns as to why the bounty hunters were in place during the daylight hours. Was there another informant in the network? Max explained that the other volunteers felt it best that he and Jacob refrain from continued involvement for at least six months. Given the risk of recognition and the posse's suspicions about the Fischer house, it was deemed best for them to not be involved for a while. Their hiatus from the network could end sooner if it was certain that the hunters they had the run-in with left the state. That they would leave was a safe assumption, as vigilantes like them were on someone's payroll, and their presence in Michigan generally limited to the capture of a specific family or person. Regretfully, the three agreed to refrain from Underground Railroad activities for the time being. Doing nothing about an unacceptable situation did not sit well with them.

As the discussion ended, Mary offered a suggestion.

"I refuse to accept that we can do nothing. Just because we cannot participate as messengers or in the transfer of escapees doesn't mean that there is nothing for us to do. We can help in other ways."

"What do you have in mind, Mary?" asked her father.

"Now that we know that freedom seekers are secretly moving through our village, there must be other ways to help them. They need clothes, their children should have textbooks, and they need money to use once they arrive in Detroit. There are many things that they need but do not have. They travel with only the clothes on their backs. We can help change that."

"What do you propose?"

"Local people can put together packages. I can get friends and church women to help. I will tell them that they're for poor children in Jackson County. I can get books from Detroit, and I still know the people there who print them. They offer textbooks at low prices for teachers. Helen and I and others can make clothes, especially for children. We can get salves and other medicines, and donations of money. We can talk to Pastor Jackson about using a closet in the church to store these packages. When we learn through messengers that a family is coming through, we can hide packages along the road at designated locations where they can be picked up or get them to the people in some other way. And if some poor local children end up with a parcel, that's fine too."

"That's a wonderful idea, Mary. I agree that it's needed and that we can make it work. I will meet with Pastor Jackson; I trust him completely and think it's time he was informed and involved. Let's all work together and make your idea happen."

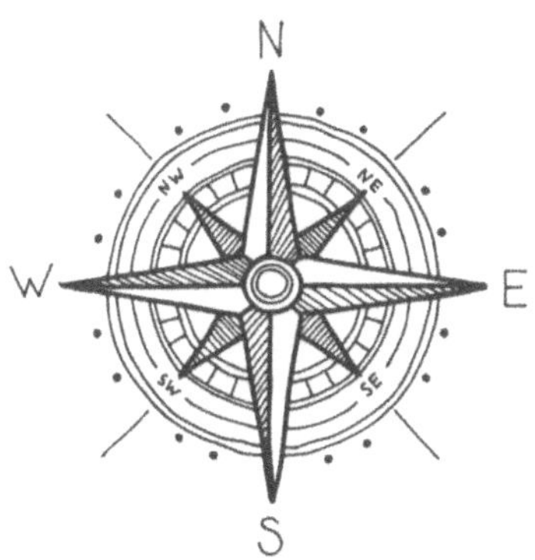

Chapter 26

ASPIRATIONS EVOLVED INTO AN ANNUAL reality. As the end of another successful growing season arrived, focus was once again on the harvest. It was a time of relentless hard work and constant worry, when all other activities were put on hold. Harvest time was a precarious few days when bad weather could undo an entire season's work. As blacksmiths were wont to say, one must strike while the iron is hot. A farmer must reap on the few days each year that crop maturity and weather conditions dictate. Everyone hoped for a bountiful harvest this year. The national economy improved to the point that the sale of farm produce was once again profitable.

At harvest time, entire families worked in the fields and granaries. Michael was strong enough to help Jacob with the scything this year. Mary and Emily then gathered the stalks for threshing. They were taken into a shed where wheat and oats were separated from the hulls. The winnowing process then separated the grain from the chaff. Working in the threshing shed was a decidedly unpleasant task. Dust made breathing difficult, while irritating particles that got under one's clothing caused unbearable itching on hot, sweaty days.

Grain must be kept dry to avoid mold. Mice and other pests also had to be controlled; mice droppings in wheat or oats disqualified it from sale as surely as the presence of mold. Selling grains meant transporting it, another precarious part of the process. Virtually all local farmers were forced to sell or grind their wheat or oats as soon as the crops were harvested. This meant selling at the lowest price, when the market was being flooded with produce. Few farmers had the ability to safely store grains for later sale when the value was higher.

Mill-ready grain was loaded onto wagons and covered with tarps for the trip to Jackson. During the brief harvest periods, local farmers made many trips to the mill. It was there that produce was either further transported to the port of Detroit for shipment to eastern markets or processed locally for flour or grain for cattle.

The Harts were pleased with the yield. It was enough to stay out of debt and have some money to improve their farmstead. Some of their profit went toward a new horse. Molly had died of old age one night, found the next morning when Jacob did his usual morning chores. Since a horse was so critical, a replacement was soon purchased. Emily suggested naming her Molly 2.

Proceeds from the sale of grain also allowed for some extras. One day, while in the village, Jacob paid Mr. Johnson a visit at the store. He needed new violin strings again, but the primary reason was to order a special gift for Emily's upcoming tenth birthday—a flute. It would be several months before it arrived, making a timely purchase important. Emily loved the haunting sound of a flute from the first time she heard one at a village concert. She spoke of someday learning how to play. Had she known that "someday" was only six months away, it would have been impossible for her to bear the anticipation.

Jacob's other reason to be in town was to take a dozen packages to the church for use by escaped slaves on their way to freedom. Mr. Fischer, still active in the informational network, agreed to inform Pastor Jackson whenever a need for the distribution of packages arose.

Winter found the two local schools filled with children. Local officials engaged in heated debates regarding the need to replace the original building with a larger facility capable of handling the needs of a growing population. Some of the families with no children opposed the significant expenditure, but in the end, the proposal was broadly supported and approved. Construction was to begin in the spring of 1849 to be ready for use at the end of summer. The thought of tearing down the old school building, which meant so much to Mary and the early settlers, weighed heavily in their hearts.

Christmas Eve saw the traditional gathering in the church. The number of unfamiliar faces was startling. After a chance to meet one another and share a large potluck dinner, the music began. This time, it was two local youths that played the piano while Mary and a choir of children sang. Edna was not feeling well. Jacob joined in with his violin on traditional carols, but the show belonged to the youth of the community.

Spring arrived with the usual confident anticipation. It was at a special dinner at the Fischers' that Emily received her birthday flute. She was ecstatic. Mary told her that if she learned to play it well enough she could be part of the annual July 4th musical event. She further surprised Emily by letting her know that Mr. Riley, who played the flute at prior events, promised to give her lessons. Emily responded with hugs for everyone, even Michael.

The Fischers showed them a letter they had recently received from Timothy informing them of his acceptance into Princeton's Medical College. He extended his greetings to everyone.

It was also in the spring of that year that a letter arrived informing Jacob of his father's death. He died working in the fields, which Jacob felt was exactly how his father would have wanted it. He was grateful that his mother had the security of the family. The farm was prospering under Joe's oversight. He was also pleased to read that his siblings, and various nieces and nephews, were doing well. In recent years, Jacob often thought about making a trip to Vermont to see his family. He wanted to see them all again, but even though it had been seventeen years, the difficulties he experienced on his original trip still left powerful emotions. He also did not ever want to be away from Mary and his kids for the lengthy duration of the trip. Jacob put the letter with all the others and convinced himself that he would consider a trip later.

As with every aspect of life along the Second Tier Road, work on the Underground Railroad went on ceaselessly. As the effort to help escaped slaves increased, so did the repercussions. For those involved, whether as escaping slaves or network conductors, times were becoming more difficult. Fugitive slave hunters were more numerous and aggressive. They also operated in the open more than ever, trying to instill fear to discourage aiding escaped slaves. Hired thugs and lawyers for slave owners were using every power available to them to discourage northerners from helping escapees. Legal threats, possible arrest, financial consequences, and threats of violence were used to frighten conductors.

They were also now enticing cooperation by posting bills declaring a reward for information on escaped slaves. Most people tore down the advertisements when seen, but there was concern that another informer would be influenced by the reward money. It had recently happened, resulting in the location of the two escaped slaves in question being made known. As the consequence of increased pressures, it was becoming more important to move people across the state quickly rather than having them remain in one place. Though traffic on the Territorial Road was routine, travelers who did not fit the norm were spotted with increasing frequency. They clearly were not local farmers or settlers. Often, their accent provided additional proof of their identity and intentions. Their increased presence was spreading more fear and concern within the escape network.

Their efforts largely proved ineffective. The Underground Railroad continued because of efforts of impassioned volunteers like the Fischers, the Harts, and the courageous men and women who refused to be kept in chains.

Though Jacob's and the Fischers' involvement was minimized, they occasionally were asked to conduct missions, usually involving carrying messages.

MAX UNEXPECTEDLY ARRIVED AT JACOB'S house one day in June. Because of his age and his own farm duties, Max did not travel much, so his presence always presaged something important. He found the rough wagon rides to be painful in his arthritic joints, but this was so important that it couldn't wait. He informed Jacob and Mary that two escapees needed to be moved as soon as possible. Their presence in the western part of the state was known, and agents were en route to arrest them. They would be at Max's house within the next four days.

Max informed Jacob that there was a need for him to carry messages again. The first was in two days. Jacob was to inform a safe house that two escapees would arrive three nights later. The transfer was going to involve a new safe house located east of Jackson. It would be the first time the house was used, and there was concern about it being a trap. The freedom seekers would spend two nights at the Fischers' before being moved to the next sanctuary.

Despite Jacob and Mary's efforts to insulate Emily and Michael from their Underground Railroad activities for safety's sake, the children had noticed and were aware. Michael, in particular, made it clear that he wanted to help, insisting that he was old enough to be useful. Learning of his father's latest messenger duty, Michael asked to go along, arguing that a father and son traveling together raised less suspicion than a man traveling alone. After considerable discussion, Jacob and Mary reluctantly agreed to Michael's request.

It was with much trepidation that Mary watched Jacob and Michael leave the following morning, having heard reports that bounty hunters had been seen on the road recently. They hitched Molly 2 to the wagon and loaded coal on it to provide a reason for being on the road. The movement of coal from Jackson area mines to Detroit was now a steady business, as the demand for coal had increased in the bustling port city. Proceeding east, the pair saw nothing unusual. As they got close to the sanctuary home in question, Jacob stopped at a roadside stream. This allowed Molly 2 to drink, giving Jacob cover to stop and watch for suspicious persons. They waited in the shady location for several minutes.

As they were getting ready to continue on their way, two men on horseback approached from the east. The men stopped and inquired if Jacob and Michael needed help. Their accents, and the fact that they were armed, made their true purpose obvious. A nonchalant look under the canvas by one of the men convinced them that the father and son team were indeed just delivering a load of coal.

Jacob thanked them for stopping to see if they needed assistance but said all was well and that they were making the last coal delivery of the day. Satisfied that Jacob and Michael had nothing to do with the Underground Railroad, the men continued west, but not before Jacob observed their appearances to report their presence and to recognize them if needed. When the riders were nearly out of sight and everything appeared safe, they made their way to the house to leave the message. While Michael waited at the wagon, Jacob cautiously approached the house and used the coded knock. An older man opened the door, nervously glancing both ways before greeting Jacob. Jacob gave his message and immediately left.

The next day at the Fischer residence, Jacob met a new messenger from Albion. Going only by the name Jason, he said that two men matching the descriptions Jacob had given were seen on the road nearby, heading west. On the assumption they were no longer a threat, Jason deemed it safe to make the planned transfer to Jackson the following night. The relocation took place with no trouble. Both escapees carried a package of basic supplies with them when they left the Fischers'.

With the uptick in vigilante pressures, Jacob thought that it was time to discuss an idea that had long laid dormant in his mind. Ever since his initial contact with Sheriff Flynn, Jacob pondered the possibility of meeting confidentially with him to bring the fugitive slave issue to the fore. Jacob wondered if the sheriff could be a critical ally in the fight. His impression of the sheriff on that long-ago day had been positive. He appeared to be a forthright man with no apparent sympathies for out-of-state fugitive slave hunters. It seemed clear that the citizenry of Jackson County supported efforts to help escaped slaves elude their captors. It was logical, then, that their sheriff likely shared similar feelings. His support would be a major boost to the Underground Railroad's efforts.

Jacob first discussed the idea with Mary. She supported it because of her confidence in Jacob's judgment. Max Fischer likewise ultimately agreed to a meeting with the sheriff, fully aware of the chances they were taking. If the lawman was sympathetic to the southern cause, the meeting would have dire consequences. If he wasn't, the benefits could be considerable.

Jacob and Max arranged a meeting in the sheriff's Jackson office. After a few minutes of light conversation, Jacob came right to the point, stating that he and Mr. Fischer were somewhat involved in the network helping escaped slaves get to Detroit and Canada.

"Wait a minute. I remember the two of you now. There was that matter of an attempted robbery on the road. I hauled three southerners into jail but had to release them a few days later because I had no evidence."

"Yes, sheriff, that was my father-in-law and me. Those men were hunting a family that we were helping escape. The man, his wife, and a child, were hiding nearby in the woods."

The sheriff was astonished. "Well, I'll be damned! I thought something funny was going on that day. But I certainly didn't like the looks of those three rascals that ended up in my hotel for a spell. As for the whole issue of slavery and the hunting down of so-called fugitive slaves, I am no friend. I am not unaware of the situation of which you speak. What is it that you ask of me?"

"We ask very little, Sheriff Flynn. We want you to know that this is a main thoroughfare for the movement of escaped men and women seeking freedom. You should know that people like Mr. Fischer and myself, and many others across the state, assist in this mission. We ask that you not support the men from out-of-state that stop at nothing to capture and return these people back to a life of slavery. We wish to know that you are not an opponent to our cause of freedom. There perhaps will be circumstances in which your assistance might be sought. We come to you as allies in the fight for what is right."

"Well, Mr. Hart and Mr. Fischer, you can depend on me doing what my duties demand. I will protect the public—all portions of the public in this county. I will not support depriving human beings of their freedoms. I am not a part of your network, but as long as you are not breaking the law, you will have my support."

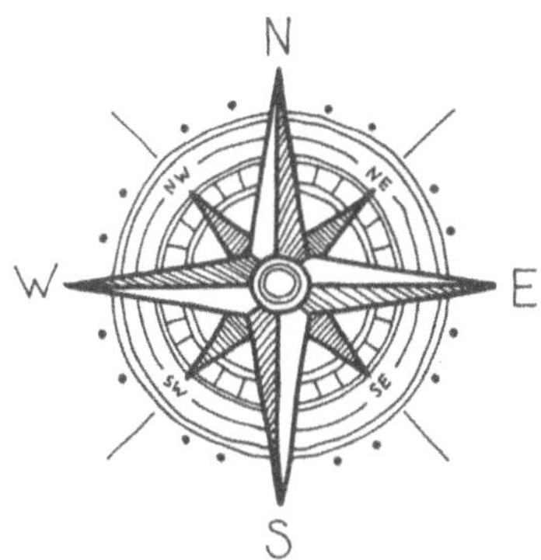

Chapter 27

LIFE WENT ON. THE ANNUAL Independence Day party was once again exactly what the community needed. It was a banquet worthy of the highest accolades followed by card games, and for some, naps in the shade. Recent young immigrants played a game in a large vacant field behind the church that was new to many people; participants called the game baseball. Local youth looked on in awe, and when the players finally left the field, these kids eagerly took their place. They were enchanted with the game, playing until it was so dark they could barely see the ball. Fireflies cast an enchanting backdrop with the rising moon before they finally stopped playing. The game was all Michael talked about for days. He and Angus and other boys announced that they were going to put teams together and play every chance they could.

Times were changing, and the generational music baton was likewise being passed. While Jacob, Mary, Edna, and Mr. Riley played as usual, it was the young musicians, including Emily, who got the applause. When the youth were done performing, Mrs. Murphy announced that with Mary's help, a choir had been formed. She informed the gathered families that a musical concert, comprised totally of local youth, would take place in the new school in September.

Jacob celebrated his fortieth birthday in May of 1852. The landmark occasion caused him to ponder how the pages had turned. He often thought about his seemingly reckless actions as a youth. Looking back, the idea of leaving an established home to strike into the unknown seemed rash indeed. But he knew that his decision to leave Vermont was one of the wisest he had ever made. He thanked fate and the stars on a regular basis for having had the courage to pull it off. But he more fully understood both sides now. Like his father before him, it was now himself carrying the responsibility of taking care of his farm and family. Facing the day-to-day issues that confronted Mary and him, Jacob understood better why his father did and said certain things all those many years ago. He knew he would someday face the reality of his children leaving, facing trouble and disappointment of their own without his being there to help.

His relationship with Michael was of special importance. He and his own father had never been close and were of a different mindset on many things. He wanted to have a warmer relationship with Michael, one based on love and respect. They spent a lot of time together. Often it involved work that needed to be done on the farm, but he was available for Michael's interests as well. Though Michael had no interest in music, he was blessed with mechanical skills and had a passion for making things.

Jacob met with Isaiah Woodbury, who agreed to take Michael on as a second apprentice, working one day a week on Saturdays so he did not miss school. As he got older, the time spent with Isaiah would increase.

Jacob became quite fascinated with the game of baseball. He especially enjoyed occasionally watching games played by local boys in the field behind the church. He believed that the field, along with the fascinating new sport, had become important to the community and that the game itself had the ability to bring the community together. It was a positive addition in the life of the rural residents. The vacant church property where they played was unused and unsightly. Jacob felt that improving the field was necessary to accomplish his goal of making the sport an integral part of life in the rural township. He met with Pastor Jackson, who agreed with his proposal to improve the vacant land. Jacob gathered a group of interested parents and youth and spent a day cutting weeds and brush. At the end of the day, an authentic baseball field graced what was formerly an eyesore.

The field was not just for the youth. Considering themselves naturally athletic and fit, Jacob and his friends took to the game with passion and played every chance they could, though they silently regretted it the following morning. Much to the delight of local youth, Jacob and Robert volunteered to manage a Sandstone Township team. Aware that east coast teams were beginning to be given team names reflecting their city or other unique qualities, they followed suit. Recognizing the history of the community, they named the team the Barry Batsmen. Competition was fierce among team members as to who could make the best homemade mitt and bat. Other teams in the greater Jackson area provided keen competition. Sunday afternoon games became a celebratory pastime, eagerly anticipated by many residents of the county.

LIFE FOR THE COMMUNITY OF neighbors settled into a comfortable routine as years passed. Besides running their farms, the families' days were filled with the miscellany of life. Much of it had to do with the next generation, which was rapidly growing up. Though they tried to be discreet, it was clear that Emily Hart and Angus MacIntosh were close friends, leaning toward the far side of friendship that often led to marriage. Jacob and Max continued occasional involvement in Underground Railroad issues. In '54, they were part of a delegation that traveled to Lansing to talk to legislators about passage of the Personal Liberty Law. The legislation was an attempt to counter the dire consequences of the 1850 Federal Fugitive Slave Act. The passage of the Michigan law the following year came as a moral victory to those involved in helping escapees find freedom.

As the decade went on, a new undercurrent of worry emerged. Passionate debates over slavery and states' rights issues were unfolding everywhere, from the dining room table to Capitol Hill. The country itself seemed at risk of tearing itself apart. Widely read newspapers from Detroit, Ann Arbor, and Jackson reported on the inflammatory situation. Jacob and Mary felt that the issues were so important that their entire family made a trip to Kalamazoo in 1856, where they listened intently to a speech by an ascending legislator from Illinois named Abraham Lincoln. He spoke in opposition to the expansion of slavery into new territories. The speech struck a chord with Michael. He became vociferously opposed to slavery and the threat the issue represented to the nation's future.

The following summer hosted Emily and Angus's wedding. It was held in the same building as their parents' weddings many years earlier. A new generation attended the memorable affair, along with many older people who had witnessed the pair grow up. The youth choir sang, and Emily and others played the piano and other instruments. Robert and Fiona surprised everyone later that evening when they told their friends that they were signing their farm over to the newlyweds, and that they were going to live in a small house they were building nearby.

Edna Fischer's health had been deteriorating for several years—slowly at first, but more aggressively as the years passed. It was early in the winter of 1858 that she succumbed to the illness that she fought so long and hard against. Even though her mother had been ill for some time, her death came as a crushing blow to Mary. She knew that everything she was she owed to her mother.

For Mr. Fischer, Edna's death was the single most difficult moment in his life. Rarely had a couple lived as one as Max and Edna Fischer had. Max could not imagine life without her. Loved and respected by everyone who knew them, her death was a blow to the entire community, to which she had given so much. The church could not hold all the people who appeared for her funeral service. Many willingly stood outside in the snow to show their respect.

On a spring day several months after Edna's death Jacob and Mary were surprised to see Max arrive at their home. It was a trip he seldom made anymore. Upon greeting him, it was clear that he had something serious on his mind. Seated at the table with the family, he spoke of the pain of Edna's death and other matters that weighed heavily on his heart.

"My dear Edna's death has nearly taken away my will to live. My life will be very different now, without her presence. I will no longer be involved in Underground Railroad matters; I cannot do it alone. I have also decided to sell the farm. It was *our* dream, and I alone cannot do all that must be done. I am an old man now. I will buy a small home in the village where I can live out my days. I will treasure my remaining time with you and the MacIntosh family and my door will always be open.

"I cannot tell you how proud and happy Edna and I were to see the life that the two of you have made for yourself and the family you have raised. You are a bedrock of this community."

Mr. Fischer never made the move into the village. He died less than three months later, on the farm that he and Edna had carved out of the wilderness.

AT EIGHTEEN YEARS OF AGE, Michael Hart was a man who knew who he was and what he wanted out of life. Years of exposure to the men he had grown up around gave him a strong concept of duty. He was ready to do his part. The issues he felt strongest about were abolition and helping escaped slaves find freedom.

As his nineteenth birthday approached, Michael told his parents that he needed to talk to them about something important. At the dinner table, he explained that he wanted to join the army. In response to his parents' looks of surprise, he explained his intentions.

"I believe our country is in jeopardy. A war between the south and the north over slavery is going to happen, probably within the next year or two. If that happens, the only way to save the union is through victory. If not, the country will never achieve what it set out to be in the Bill of Rights. I have given this great thought. I want to attend West Point to become an officer. In that capacity I can have greater influence should war break out. I am requesting that you support me. A letter must be sent by local officials to Senator Chandler recommending me for appointment to the academy."

Mary and Jacob were shocked at Michael's proposal and his fervor. It was clear that he had given it much consideration. Jacob thought back to his own struggle when he was nineteen, planning to leave home to strike out on his own into an unknown future. Though he had reservations about him being an army officer during such a perilous period, he admired Michael's idealism and knew he could not stand in his way. After an hour of emotional debate, Jacob and Mary fought back their deeply felt parental concerns and agreed that they would help arrange a letter on his behalf to the senator.

Township supervisor Jerome Walker and county Sheriff Flynn were only too happy to sign the letter.

The following year, Jacob and Mary became grandparents of a beautiful baby girl named Mary. Jerome and Helen agreed to be her godparents. When the baby was able to travel, the baptism was held at church. Pastor Jackson, who witnessed the comings and goings of two generations, officiated. After the ceremony, a dinner was held in the new church hall. A large and boisterous crowd attended the special event. The MacIntoshes and Harts were two of the oldest and best-known families in the area, after all.

In a sign of the times, instead of conversations about children and crops, the tenor of discussions at the church dinner was bleaker. A malaise had descended on America, whether in large cities or rural villages. Concern for the future replaced unbridled optimism for the nation's triumph. News of states threatening to secede and talk of civil war breaking out took cheerfulness out of social gathering conversations and at the family dinner table. Families were split along philosophic and political lines, and the mere mention of certain names, such as Abraham Lincoln or John Brown, guaranteed arguments and even bloody fist fights.

It was under these clouds of anxiety that a letter arrived at the post office for the Harts. It was enclosed in an impressive official-appearing envelope from Senator Zachariah Chandler's Washington office. Jacob brought it home where Michael nervously opened it.

The letter, on parchment, was addressed to Michael. It read: "Congratulations Mr. Hart! The Admissions Office has recommended you for an appointment to the United States Military Academy at West Point."

More pertinent information followed, but Michael had seen all that he needed. He handed the letter to his parents, who read it with that mixture of pride and concern that all parents feel when their offspring is about to depart on their own life journey. Jacob and Mary concealed their concern, expressing only the immense pride they felt. Long, emotionally charged hugs followed.

The day of departure arrived all too quickly. Almost the entire village was present when Michael got in the stagecoach to Detroit. There were countless tears, hugs, and handshakes. Remembering his own father's parting words to him, Jacob took Michael aside just prior to his departure, telling him with damp eyes: "You are a man now. Remember all that you have learned and live your life in a manner that will make people proud to know you. You will face many troubles. Face them head on and do what you know is right. I pray that your dreams all come true."

Taking a deep breath, he added, "You should know that, though you never knew him, the man whose name you honor would be as proud of you as I am."

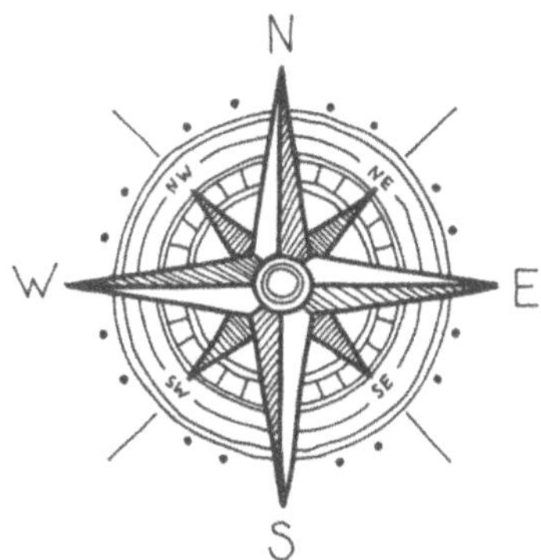

Acknowledgments

IN THE END, TO WRITE a book takes a village. The team at Mission Point Press provided much critical expertise to take an imperfect manuscript to a polished finished product. Special thanks to Sarah, Hart, Ed, Darlene, and Terese for their extensive roles, and to Misha for her expert leadership in the overall process.

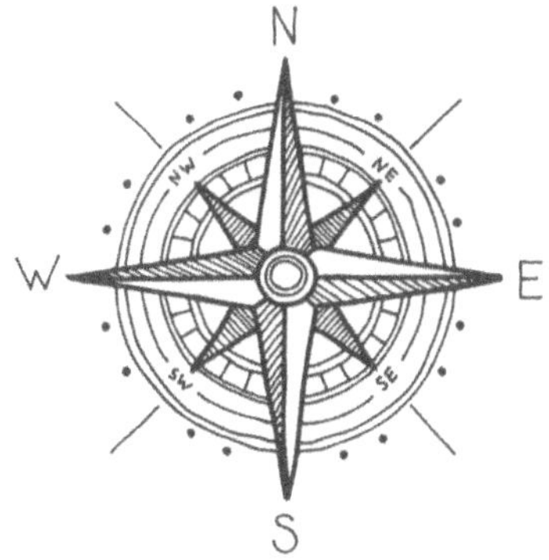

About the Author

WILLIAM MURPHY IS THE AUTHOR of ten books. He has also written numerous articles published by a variety of journals and magazines including the FBI Bulletin, Michigan history journals, travel magazines, and environmental journals. He is a former Marine and combat veteran of the Vietnam War. His recent award-winning book, *Not For God and Country*, detailed the history and reality of that war. After retirement from the Michigan Department of Natural Resources, Murphy took his talents to book writing. He has sold more than 25,000 books on various topics, mainly travel and history. Murphy was inducted into the Michigan Environmental Hall of Fame in 2018 following his career and volunteerism in the enforcement of environmental protection law. He lives in his native state of Michigan and his travels have taken him through all fifty states, much of Canada, his ancestral home of Ireland, and several other countries.